Indifferent

Branko Jovanovski

DEDICATION

To my amazing parents Vita and Borko Jovanovski,
to whom I owe everything.

CONTENTS

ACKNOWLEDGMENTS

To those that never understand: Thank you for
making this book possible.

PREFACE

After more than four obnoxious, and at the same time, irresistible years, my consciousness has finally been relieved of my conscious. That is the only way how I could view the publishing of what is my book. It took that long for the ascent to take place. I don't deem it a success; I don't dwell on it as failure. It is here, the same way I am, that same way I have always been – honest, in front of the world and many times against it, by myself but never alone. And I guess the Creator of the natural selection never meant to give me a face that is easy to read, but the heart has never been even remotely cold, and it has never turned against me. And the eyes could never give away a deceitful spark no matter how hard I have tried. In spite of all I have willingly made them go through. I would apologize to the way I have been treating them straight away, but there are no guarantees I have up my sleeve that would not make me continue my way. Maybe love would do that. One day. Today.

This piece of now, nicely wrapped paper has not always looked as gloomy. It took me more than a year to realize that such a development has to come out of me. Different events triggered its creation; one in particular cemented its initiation. And as much as that moment didn't sleep well with me, I praise the day for having it happened. It unleashed something in me that I had never thought existed – it unleashed my own consciousness. That moment of my own revelation is irrelevant to satisfy your unjustified curiosity. And that is the reason why I will not share it with you. Or with anyone else. I will keep it written in the mental film of the people that have remembered it, including myself.

One day, shortly after *the* moment, in a boring class of my graduate studies, the outline of this heart-full piece of paper started taking its confident shape. I can still remember the insecure professor's face with his ridiculous glasses while my eyes pierced through him, and at the same time not even considering that I was projecting my own beliefs. All I remember was when the class ended, I knew who the bells tolled for. I had in front of me a scheme of what I thought I could never bring together. But I guess something made me do it. I went home after the class. I was still unsure of the impact my little unexpected escapade had. I slept over it. I woke up. And I started. There was no going back. It took me more than a year to finish. When I would ask myself what made me keep on writing, I had only one thought in mind. To write it off me, to close it, and to literally burn it – it never failed on me. I saw the book burning as the only way I could award it some decency. Because of my promise. Because of my passion for it. Now it is here, to be shared with that small big part of my world that would perhaps want it read. I have betrayed my initial promise, and I have no defense against it. Despite that, I don't feel guilty about it. Because burning it would have been a flamboyant exercise that would mean the moment to me, but nothing more. The concept would have been discarded.

I have realized that this way only I could achieve what I had subconsciously intended to do in the first place – to have it challenged. Bring it on.

To all those who might have mistakenly interpreted the book's pages, and to all those that might seem obliged to do so: this book is not an autobiography like some would be tempted to accuse it of. In fact, it has nothing to do with me. It has only to do with the concept of all of us; the concept that none of us is shamelessly willing to accept. Why? Because it's real.

This book is devoted to my parents. And at the same time, this book reflects all my family and friends, along with the invaluable perfect strangers and all the love and safeness they have never deprived me of, those same feelings that ever kept me going. They know who they are. Thank you. And you will stay that way as long as I do. And as long as the Indifferent Concept lives on.

Sincerely indifferent,
Branko Jovanovski

25 May 2012

A great man, taxi driver from the Glorious Land

of the Sugar Cane, once told me: *"Life is something*

that is happening to us, while we are occupied with other

things"

Cuba, 2006

1 WALKING WITH THE GHOSTS OF THE PAST

It was over. The short, sweet excursion to the place where he always used to find most of his prayers answered was coming to an end, as any other illusion in life. He could see his breath freezing as he painfully paced through the white cover of the street that once symbolized his innocence, before selling himself to the world beyond his childish imaginations. The purifying, mystical odor that was spreading in the cold air surrounding him made living memories flash between his eyes; memories of a seemingly forgotten, yet beautiful past. Every footprint in the fresh snow beneath him invoked memories of friendships lost and dear people he would have gotten to know, as if he was looking for someone to share his tears with, someone he could trust, looking to relief the sickening burden that was pressing his chest more as every other second passed by.

Every now and then, he followed the prints as if trying to find a connection between what was left of him and his past. The hope of finding another footstep kept him going. But it seemed as if he was trying to avoid the certainty that none of them led to the memories and people he was longing for. Simply, the metaphysical gap was increasingly enormous.

Those seventy meters appeared like a pictorial illusion of his life, seemingly lasting for eternity. There was no time to reflect whether those illusions had actually been parts of his life, parts of himself, or only ghosts of the memorable, intimate street that were teasing his mind and affecting his body control. He instinctively opened the small gate of a nearby yard, almost at the end of the street. A strange mixture of a cold and hot breeze sprung through his body like a mighty lightning storming through the sea. There were many special things about the place he had just entered. He didn't even realize that it was that very same place that he had once called *home*, his safe place, in which he always found his inner strength. He had been there the night before, but in this cumbersome night, it all looked so different, and to him, so fucking, painfully distant. The agonizing feeling in his stomach was making it even harder for him to climb up the marble stairs. The surrounding vines and the old apricot tree were playing with him, as if reflecting the huge shadow living in his chest, in his thoughtful mind, in his soul. He sat at that very end of the staircases, that same place where he used to listen to *"Indexi"* when he would contemplate his further steps in life. He was aware he could not fight the natural chemicals, and especially not the emotional sensations that marked the life he had chosen, the life of a *wanderer*. And he knew it best because he had lost many previous battles with himself, battles whose outcomes had always intoxicated every single bit of his mind. Now, his intention was to accept his condition, be at peace with it, and gather the necessary strength to stand up firmly against his own self, not to fight anymore, but to preserve his identity, his birthplace, his memories...

He managed to arrive at the top of the stairs and as he was entering the house, he immediately felt the warmest embrace of the interior of the house. He felt safe, cherishing even the stale dust since he knew that once again he had to part from that warmth that never gave up on him. Every inch was priceless. He had to move on.

The first encounter he had as he was entering that sacred place of his was with a scared and indecisive person; mentally tired and visibly broken, yet still having that fierce look in his eyes. The two looked at each other as if trying to guess each other's thoughts. The sound of silence was interrupted by the words of the guest that had just entered the house, words he hardly uttered:

"No, it cannot be. I remember what I look like. This isn't me! I am a young boy with a vision, not this man with a worn out face full of pain and uncertainty!"

In fact, it was nothing he didn't already know, but he was always hoping that with every further glance in the mirror, he would be able to view himself as ordinary as before. He walked into the biggest room of the house. For five moments, he was just looking around as if he wanted to carve the interior deep into his memory. Once again, as if being a ritual to sadistically enjoy the night before he was leaving his home, he sat on the balcony and stared at the 65 meter cross that was coming out of the mountain to his right. He was looking for answers to many questions he didn't know. He felt abandoned, even though there were many people fighting in his head.

The amount of nicotine and alcohol in his blood that night didn't prevent him from lighting yet another cigarette; it simply made him feel as if he had a companion. Not even the freezing degrees on the outside had any effect on his inside; as if they both balanced one another.

"There used to be a huge linden tree down there", he mumbled as he was looking at the neighboring yard. "Now all there is left is a big hole in the ground."

He went back to the corridor where he had met himself a few moments ago, and walked into *his own room*.

His room looked like a fucking storage space with a very limited physical capacity but full of spirit and invaluable collections of his adolescent life. He glanced through the narrow window above the bed. It all seemed the same as every other time before, except that it went further in the dimension of time, time that he had missed. He praised the bed, full of conscious and subconscious experiences, but his exhaustion wasn't any helpful in finding sleep. He was turning uneasy in every direction as if feeling guilty of something he had done, like that teenage time he got drunk to the point where he thought his parents were quitting on him.

But that was educational; the current experience was painful. And dawn was nowhere to be seen, as if it was purposely detained in the Far East for couple of more hours. Not even the snow was white as he had remembered it. He thought he finally understood what people felt the last hours they were waiting for the final call to the guillotine. He just wanted to get over with it as soon as possible.

The squeaky footsteps in the hallway ignited the already organized butterflies in his stomach. The door of his room slowly started opening. He knew the following line by heart.

"Mojag[1], it's time", his father said with that deep, spooky morning voice as he switched on the lights in the room, his figure still a blurry silhouette.

"The rest is pure protocol, and I am the big star, I am the one leaving", the son added to himself.

He always admired the punctuality of his father and the sense of time he possessed, as if he was in command of it. On the contrary, Mojag was obsessed by time, and he was ultimately getting lost in it. But at that point it was all reflexive. He stood up, and spent the next twenty minutes in a state of uncomfortable numbness. It seemed like the road to the electric chair. He didn't feel a thing.

His mother, Rozene[2], was already awake as she was always the one making sure that Mojag had everything neatly packed, trying to make his departure as pleasant as his emotional burden would allow. Mojag sat on the sofa opposite his mother as he lit yet another cigarette so they could smoke together one more time before he left. The reality was that he wanted to vomit because of the disgusting taste of the cigarette following up two packs that day, but he could never give up a moment of smoking with his mother. It was always his best valued cigarette, toxics included.

His father's uneasiness and maybe too extreme awareness of time, depicted in his constant anxious movements, once again signaled the departure point.

---

[1] Native American male name of unknown origin. Its meaning is *NEVER SILENT (NEVER STILL)*.

[2] Native American female name of unknown origin. Its meaning is *ROSE*.

Mojag went on to the kitchen, crossed three times and briefly prayed to God.

"I hope I will come back again. I hope my family will be healthy and alive, and I hope I will not be forgotten."

He kissed his sleepy sister goodbye and moved on. He took the heavy bags and went down to his father's car. Everything was in place. Most importantly, his puny passport and travel visa were there. The stage was set. He wasn't feeling indifferent anymore; he had to say goodbye to his mother. He was never a mommy's boy, but these moments were always a heavy burden for his stomach. The hug was that warmest mother's hug. Her eyes got filled with tears; he seemed unmoved, but he was crying out so loud on the inside. At least that was what made him happy because she couldn't see his pain to the reality of its extreme.

"Bye, mother", he said and entered the car.

Whenever a person's emotions are overshadowed to extremes, even the stars and the whole universe plot against him.

The heavy snow underneath the moving car only extended Mojag's sufferings, as if it was deliberately slowing down the entire motion. He was destined to look at all the beautiful places he was emotionally bound to, and felt frightened as if they were to fade away from his memory forever. He dared not to look back, being afraid that he might experience all those ghosts from the past pointing at him.

"Why is there not a less painful way to leave home?! Will it ever stop!!!!!?" he shouted within but remained calm.

The silence in the car was far from relaxing. Even the normally noisy diesel engine was nowhere to be sensed. The contact with the outer world was completely blurred. Mojag was falling into an endless void, and he could not sense the bottom. He could not distinguish what reality was anymore.

"I better light a cigarette, and then I'd know that I'm still breathing at least. It was never this difficult before to kill the past."

The now beautiful city, Mojag's *hometown*, was almost left behind. Almost. There was one more, rather too emotional checkpoint left. As the green light flashed, he could see the building where his girl, his love, lived. He said goodbye to her earlier that day, but he could still imagine her tormenting tears as the car was just passing by the building where she was sleeping. He needed her so badly and yet, he was leaving her. They were still together, but he was leaving. He did not even feel better knowing what the song had told him that it was at least easier to leave than to be left behind. She was his link, his spokesperson to his twisted reality. How was he intending to cope without her in a different world with different life arrangements, when she was the only security he relied upon? He was left alone, and he was the one directing his own destiny, almost unconsciously. His motivation to go further derived not only from rational thinking, but he felt that the past four years abroad "entitled" him to seek satisfaction, challenge, and ultimately freedom so he could apply it to his own people when he would return. His determination was firm; his big heart ravaged. What he had experienced on previous journeys all those nights before leaving home was not even close to the never-ending pain that commenced that awkward night.

"Dad, yet another time I'm going into the unknown. I always wanted to explore, but it had never scared me this much, ever before."

His dad started talking to comfort him and to raise his son's self-confidence but Mojag didn't even bother listening for he did not have the will; he only focused on his father's eyes out of respect. His father always had all the answers to his questions, but not this time. This time it was up to Mojag to find a solution.

It was six in the morning, and daylight was still nowhere to be seen. Only the airport was approaching with fearful certainty. He had forgotten that he was holding his cell phone all this time while being stuck to the car's seat. It was all sweaty when it suddenly gave out its presence with its well-known ring tone.

"Ah, who the fuck could this be? Didn't I endure enough by saying thousands of goodbyes during the night? ", instinctively burst out of him.

One of his friends was apparently enjoying his university's winter break and was having difficulties to fall asleep. It is always encouraging to hear from a friend when you are forgetting that you ever had one.

"Dude, I'm on my way", Mojag started.

"I know idiot, and that is why I'm calling. I couldn't fall asleep so I just called to wish you a safe flight and I have no doubts that you are going to do well in your first job. Oh, and I don't need to remind you that women are a cornerstone to your existence…make sure you preserve your family's tradition", his friend said followed by a warm laughter.

"Thanks a lot, and don't worry, I have always been taught not to disappoint others, but I have never learned how not to disappoint myself."

"Hey! I don't want to hear any negative thoughts again!"

"The feeling is mutual. I wish I could get rid of them and have a stable life as others seem to have", Mojag replied with a reflexive indifference.

"Listen, think that you are coming back soon for a while and we will have many drinks together in *Bravos,* your most favorite place, along with the rest of our bunch and your favorite musicians that never fail to cherish your comeback."

"Believe me, that is what keeps me alive, but it burns me out when I think that the dates are going to be different and so many things I will miss… and many other things are not going to be as they are now or as they used to be. Even now you could feel that the gap has vastly increased. And it is not difficult to recognize the circumstances…I mean, who needs a friend, a person, a lover, with a worn out expression on his face and one who is already gone? You could not even imagine what I am mentally going through at the moment. I wonder if it will ever stop."

And then, with the tone of voice of a mother who always "senses" what is the best for her child, and even though with the best of intentions, his friend uttered the words of an inexperienced, materialistic ignorance, though motivating, that got deeply carved into Mojag's already defeated heart:

"You ungrateful idiot, you have everything there. Start appreciating and enjoying life! Do you know how many people envy you and would sell their soul to be in the same position you are in…"

2 MEMORIES

Two months earlier. May 2005.

A student life is perhaps the best period of a person's cycle in this world and it would be a sincere pity if one does not share the same judgment. Whoever disagrees has perhaps missed out on an opportunity to learn directing his/her own life. Most of the things you learn as a student clashes with your predefined set of a brain framework and dogmas, the ones that you have acquired and unquestionably accepted from your mother and father. As a student, you learn how to oppose those inflicted inner thoughts that you many times do not understand. Especially, living alone away from home and being a student at the same time, opens up a way for you to become a human, aware of your own self and your own existence.

* * * * * * * * * * *

It was a beautiful spring day in the city of Mojag's childhood dreams. After a hard work of two hours of snoozing, the disturbed alarm clock finally managed to wake him up around noon. The day was about to get started with the same ritual that had shaped his life for the past four years, yet with a special tone in the air. It seemed as if now, even the filthy trap of cigarette stench in the air tasted special, typically embedded in all exposed objects of Mojag's room.

"Ajde, *mrcino*[3] get up, the day has already passed", his roommate shouted as he was leaving the apartment while Mojag was trying to leave his own bed.

"Don't worry, everything is under control", exclaimed Mojag with that morning tone, recognizably ironic, and difficult to understand. He finally got up and turned on his computer while headed to the toilet for the morning cosmetics. After devoting those 30 minutes to physically satisfy himself, it was time for the everyday mental rehabilitation. That included very loud music and his usual breakfast – an extremely strong Oriental coffee and lots of nicotine contained in that irresistible tobacco paper. Not a single day had Mojag missed his breakfast for the past four years.

The music coming out of the powerful speakers of his computer announced the beginning of the new day, and only increased his euphoria that the beautiful day had inspired. The sometimes annoying people in the neighboring apartments knew that Mojag's day had started.

The music he was living with reflected his thoughts and his perception of life. And if that was not always the case, he was interpreting the songs in his own *revolutionary* style to mentally upgrade, and add up to his self-confidence. In all the songs varying from *Mozart* to *Metallica*, he was able to find and heal himself. The lyrics were his thoughts, and they usually agreed with his ideas. Many times he felt happy and

---

[3] Lazy bastard (expressed friendly)

many times he felt sad. And the songs in his common but extensive playlist had always offered him the necessary support. They always took good care of him. They knew his feelings, making him stronger when he was happy, and destroying him when he felt weak. It was a special metaphysical bond between Mojag and music. It meant a whole ritual to him. It was a whole science that not many people were eager to understand. It was that imminent dose of achieving his day, similar to the 7000 calories Sumo wrestlers are obliged to take in every day in order to reaffirm their strength.

Additionally, the life of a student narrowed his sense of time. For him, it was either a cold or a warm month. The only indicators he relied upon were that if the overall mood was depressing, and all of Murphy's laws applied, then it was winter, and summer followed when most of the average girls were turning extremely pretty, subsequently sensed through the boiling blood in his veins. His university exams gave him a better orientation of more specific dates. His life was beautiful, being even more fulfilling not to be dependent upon the biggest evil of mankind – *time*. That same day he knew exactly what the date was. Yes, he did have an exam, and its significance was much higher than his first university exam. This one was to be his last of the overall studies. This one was special, not because of the anticipated positive outcome, but because of a chapter's anticipated ending. And after all, who would then help him with the calendar?

The lock in the door turned only once. His roommate just entered the apartment.

"*Cimer*[4]!!!!!" shouted Mojag in that recognizable tone that signified their friendship.

"What is it, *virus*, getting forward to your last exam?" replied Wematin[5] in that sarcastic fashion that Mojag was already long used to.

"Ah, *cimer*, it is a really funny, mixed feeling. It brings me a sense of accomplishment, but it also brings about a strange sentiment in me that I cannot identify yet. In any case, it is not a good hunch."

"Ma, I think I do understand. And I think *you* understand it as well, and I guess it is quite a normal flow of a feeling. I have already seen couple of our friends finishing their last exams and not wasting another second to pack and get away from this city. The old group is splitting, and you know it, but you are still not fully aware of it, and neither am I. So, I guess it kind of shakes your faith."

"You are probably right…" Mojag stopped his gaze for a moment, as if he had gotten a confirmation of what his inner thoughts had in mind.

"But what about you," he continued, "have you decided yet whether you are staying along?", Mojag asked for perhaps the millionth time, still hoping with all his heart that Wematin would stay along. They knew more about each other than anybody else did. And regardless of the biological fact that they did not share the technical responsibility of a blood relation, they were reminiscent of brothers.

"I don't know, I'm still thinking a lot about it…" Wematin carefully sat on the couch, his face portraying

---

[4] Roommate
[5] Native American male name of Algonquin origin. Its meaning is *BROTHER.*

contemplations of an indecisive character. Shortly after, the vacant expression in his eyes facing Mojag's, depicted helplessness as he continued with the recognizable and rhetorical question.

"I don't know *cimer*, what do you think I should do?"

"Please, don't ask me this stupid question for a millionth time. I told you already everything I have on that matter before. Wematin, you are aware of the benefits of staying, and besides, I would be here, so I don't see a reason why we shouldn't continue our journey together. And your girlfriend, which is the love of your life, can join you here at any time. It's time to move on a step further, not get back."

Mojag knew that his *brother's* ambiguity of staying actually meant leaving. He also knew that his whole generation of extremely good friends were about to abandon him. Mojag was indeed a realist, and he knew that everyone righteously acted in their own interest. The only issue was that he didn't want to believe that. And that was frequently his main source of blunder and emotional terror.

"Ok, Wematin, I need to go, time is approaching for the final exam. I better go a bit earlier, smoke a cigarette and inspect the girls at the university."

Wematin felt the uneasiness in Mojag's voice, kept silent for a while and started talking in a voice full of unclear nostalgia.

"*Cimer*, I do understand how you feel. No need to keep your emotions sacked. As for me, I think I would never be able to decide what further steps to take, only if it weren't for the eternal pressures of time. And I am confusingly aware that postponing my decision will make it difficult for me to stay along... But don't get bothered now with extremes. Focus on your exam and good luck; no one has any doubts in you."

"Thanks", said Mojag, having saved the bitter smile for the privacy of his own self and exited the apartment.

As Mojag was leaving the apartment, he was not even trying to contemplate his concern that his roommate had perhaps envisioned his further steps in life in a different way than his own. No, pondering over an anxiety of such an origin would have been way too ungrateful, for regardless how far Wematin would be, they would always be bound by those four years when they became brothers.

Wematin was perhaps *the* only person in the world that knew as many things about the flamboyance of Mojag's life. That rather tall, slim figure with a blondish hair was genetically unrelated to Mojag. In fact they looked completely different, but their bond was far stronger than a relationship of two brothers. Wematin was perhaps one of the rare breed of people that could unselfishly endure Mojag's eccentricity at any point of their life while living together in their shared apartment. And he was always Mojag's best companion in the course of those four years.

Wematin was a couple of years older than his younger roommate, but they never failed to understand each other, never failing to *be* there for each other. Mojag thought of himself to be a good person with respect to others, and some might have said that he was. But, Wematin was a person way too good for the undeserving environment, and there was not a single one that could not confirm that virtue of his. Four years ago, Mojag left his family but in the course of that same extraordinary period that has been mercilessly passing by, Wematin *became* his family. And without any reasonable doubt, and if not for anything else, if Mojag would have been given a chance to go back four years in time to reevaluate his decision of his foreign journey, he would always choose the same road only to reconnect with his *brother*.

The joy of giving a finishing touch to Mojag's studies was backed up and greeted by the beautiful sun. As he was coming out to the outside of the apartment building, he was faced with the church in front of him, everyday reminding him of the existence of God. Many times he praised and thanked God for the positive turbulences in the years that had passed by. He now smiled thankfully and continued to the five minute road leading to his university. Those well-known five minutes have never lasted longer as they did that day. And this time, as opposed to rainy days, or usual lonesome Sundays, the sun and Mojag's ordeal got the best out of his memories from the past four years, converted in positive and fulfilling thoughts. For the first time, he was able to spot an enormous, and surprising to his seemingly shady thoughts, positive change in himself. Many times before he had gone through these alleyways, but only this time, he started reflecting that with every other time taking that same path, he was actually changing. He seemed to have learned how to be a different person, starting as a scared boy obeying the rules of the foreign institutions, to a man confident in himself, in his actions, and ultimately, in his success. It seemed that four years were quite a long period for a well-established personal change. But it was not those four years that had changed him. It was the ultimate and diverse experience gathered in those four years, making him adapt to all situations available, and as he remembered, there were indeed many of them. It takes a lot of courage for a person to acknowledge and accept change, especially on a personal matter, and it appeared as if he was well prepared to accept any change.

"It seems I have successfully overcome the many animosities of my old self. I feel strong and secure. The ultimate human battles are not those shown in daily newspapers, but the battles within a human itself. It is much more difficult to fight against yourself, but existentially important to succeed in constantly killing the outdated person in you. Only then can mankind live together", Mojag's thoughts abruptly faded for the moment, caused by diverse voices spreading through the university's hallways. The dominant *Southern* language at the university was giving life and spirit to that object's money making hallways. He was already inside the private university, the big city's only building he was emotionally bound to, despite being a symbol of the capitalist world's soft power.

The excitement of his last exam in there did not make him less excited about the constantly new casual talks among his friends and old acquaintances, and certainly among the university girls, who were always, mostly unsuccessfully trying to conceal their urge to be explored.

Most of those people constantly hanging around the smoker's corner were familiar with Mojag's final exam and most of them expressed feelings of melancholy that he would rarely come back again to smoke a cigarette with them. But perhaps, many of them were only too careful not to show their indifference. However, Mojag was firmly focused on wrapping up the final touch of his last exam, so at the moment, he was too occupied to allow himself to be bothered with other people's hypocrisy.

"In any case, you should be very happy. You have your final test today and you don't ever need to come to this stupid place anymore", was the overwhelming comment of the crowd directed at Mojag, to which he immediately replied.

"It is strange because I am satisfied I am completing my degree, but certainly not happy that I am leaving. This place, and not the institution, as stupid as you consider it, means much more than a simple degree paper to me. It means experience and friends; it means life to me. You have to get out of the box and start using your university years. Don't throw them away as they open up the path to some new and more enlightening horizons. Only then you will be thankful that you were once here."

The confused look in most of the people's eyes confirmed Mojag's assumption that some people would never realize that living, not improvising, is what makes you real.

"Good", he continued, "it's time to take the test. I have never been this relaxed before an exam as I am now. And I guess this will be the first time I will actually be in time for a test."

He smiled and walked towards the hallway leading to the exam room. He never felt any sympathy for the students that arrived half an hour before the classes start, waiting for the lecture and viewing the professor as some sort of a leper messiah. Sometimes he thought they were too frustrated in life from casual things that they were seeking shelter in the fucking institution. But not that day; that day he cared for his upbeat thoughts only and he was happy that he was able at least for once to be selfish and act accordingly. He took distance from the rest of the people and sat on the farthest desk concentrating on the exam on genocide that he was about to take. Awaiting the start, there was no other choice but to occupy his brain with thoughts.

"What is genocide? What are the claims of these institutions? What definition has the system accepted? Why only blame the *Orthodox* for the worst genocide in the once *Land of Peasants* in the peninsula of the hills, when the *Red and White* squares as well as the *Greens* had also a lot of blood on their hands and were equally savage? Why are they not mentioning the ongoing physical and cultural genocide taking place against the possibly genuine successor minority of the youngest conqueror ever in the land of the mythic Gods? Why some children of the Holy Land are denied a country? And ultimately, why is the biggest and starting point of genocide in history purposely forgotten – the one of the approximately nine million native lives victoriously slaughtered and still displaced? Ethnic cleansing? 1492's Conquest of Paradise marked the beginning of writing the manual for ethnic cleansing and mass exodus of innocent lives. Why certain genocides are justified, more important than the rest, and some are not even worth mentioning?" – So many questions bothered him; the world's injustice was always raising the revolutionaries in him. But he was truly aware that nothing could be done from within the air-conditioned classroom.

"Justice and freedom are conquered, never given", he anxiously exclaimed.

"Ok, class, I bet you are all ready for your exam", the professor cynically exclaimed as he was taking off his coat. Mojag didn't even notice the professor having entered the class.

As if when being drunk and losing track of reality, Mojag seemed to have lost himself, remembering only when the professor said:

"Half an hour remaining."

"No problem", uttered Mojag assertively. He was at his last sentence of genocide, and he was not to revise his test. For the first time, despite the arrogance, he was beforehand convinced that he had the best test. He was never one of the elite students, but now he was happy, sincere and real, and that gave him the ultimate advantage.

Unlike other times when finished writing, when he would immediately run out of the classroom, this time he stopped, took a deep breath, laid back in the chair and left his whole life flash before his eyes. He was looking at the whiteboard, and he felt he was watching the best play ever, and even better, he was one of the main actors.

His play originated in his 18th year. A small, seemingly innocent boy arrived at the filthy International Bus Station in the *Big City* with his mother; tons of suitcases and the instrument that helped kill his occasional solitude – his guitar. That night, the falling snow only increased his fear and anxiety towards the big city. Additionally, he wasted the last ticks on his battery's cell phone to a fellow stranger who equally desperately needed orientation. Mojag always had innate drives to help others, but he was still not able to think for his own benefit. But what could have possibly happened? Maybe that stranger really needed help much more than Mojag did.

He settled at the university dormitory at the unforgettable room 404, naively respecting all the rules of forbidden smoking and no alcohol inside the apartments. The insecurity stopped as soon as he started meeting new friends, interesting and appealing to him with their diversity and uniqueness, and some of them, with their devotedness. Many of them were constantly going away, but the beautiful memories and the everlasting bonds had never faded. Mojag remembered all the good and bad moments that the past detour brought to him, realizing that it all got wrapped up in a beautiful and extraordinary experience that started shaping his persona. Every unique person and every different moment lived through, had a great impact on his life. He strengthened his understanding of friendship, women, love, respect, success. And at that very moment sitting in the class desk, he was concluding that scenic chapter of his life. Always with his usual mysterious smile on his dark face, he led himself to the vast memories and experiences, sitting back and enjoying.

After that extraordinary session with his past, he stood up, head high, greeted the professor, and walked out of the classroom. He was unofficially eligible for the upcoming spring graduation ceremony!

Comprised as some sort of a well-known logical flow, the road led him to the student center in which he always contemplated the aftermaths of his exams. However, that didn't happen that day. He stood in front of the door, gave a fuzzy glance and turned away. He was too happy to share his feelings with people other than his closest and too confident to think of past exams; this time it was the future that he was trying to focus on, portrayed through present actions.

"What now? What follows? Have I achieved any goals? Where are the guidelines for my further actions? Is that it? Who has the answers? Or even better, who has the questions?"

So many people, so many voices arguing in his head, as if there was no sign of the long and anticipated psychological break that would eventually mean the reward of the journey.

He took the usual route to consolidating himself, whenever he was in need of calming down and identifying his thoughts and what those voices meant. It was the one road to the *Blue River*, the same place where he and his mother cherished the big city's beauties four years ago, when he was still that scary kid on the outside, never alone, but always by himself.

He sat on one of the anchor look-alike stones at the brink of the river, not even noticing the bored fishermen and the lovers that were abusing the calmness of nature. The urge of smoking a cigarette was unbearable, the joy of it even stronger. This one he really deserved. As he was smoking, he started noticing that all the crazy thoughts from moments ago had vanished; the poison of the nicotine was effective. He even failed to identify what those former thoughts were about. He was happy, a true achiever of the day. It was truly inspiring how his *Blue River* always helped him get through such unidentified moments.

3 THE MOST BEAUTIFUL CHAPTER OF LIFE

7 Days Later

The fundamental value of a human being, highly incompatible with today's misunderstood and highly hypocritical concept of liberal democracy and modern capitalist demands, is family. It is exceedingly ungrateful for a person to forget the people and the environment that enabled him to be the person that he currently is. Education is acquired in school and through life on the streets; true values are obtained through a healthy family. Appreciation of one's closest to an individual is the reason that makes that same individual love his neighbor and the world surrounding him. The critical feeling of belonging, deeply carved through a healthy childhood is a crucial part of one's life and one's identity, until at one point it falls apart and the individual gets disillusioned of family values that made him a seemingly valuable contributor to society.

* * * * * * * * * * *

The local civilian helicopter, which was circling around the borders of the big city, spotted a huge traffic jam on the highway leading towards the city's insides. So many vehicles, so many nervous faces in their barely moving cars on the lanes; some late for a meeting, some listening to a strange music, and other distinctive people impatiently waiting. There was only one car that seemed to enjoy every bit of the moment, adopting a momentary Zen mindset not to bother about things that cannot be controlled. And surprisingly enough, one of the followers of that short-lived philosophy was Mojag, a person that instantly and regularly lost his grip when similar situation occurred. He was one of the people in that happy car headed to the big city. The other two were his most valued people, they were his parents. After that last exam he had taken, Mojag could not wait but to go home, share his immediate success with his family, and then take them to his other, foreign lair, and share all the beautiful moments of the preparation for the long anticipated event that made them come to the big city for one time as a *family*.

The night was already approaching, and there were still 72 physical kilometers to overcome in arriving to the now cozy and warm apartment, where Mojag's sister, his brother-in-law, and his 3 months unborn nephew were already waiting.

Mojag never felt better coming to the *West* and at the same time leaving his childhood homeland. This time he didn't even put up a thought about it; his family was there with him, and they were all united. All of a sudden, mental life seemed so easy to cope with.

The annual *happy* fair of the district in front of *Mojag's family apartment* seemed as if it wanted to notify the surrounding of the upcoming happiness prescribed to pure persistence and major family effort. Mojag was to receive his university honors in front of his family, and for his achievement, every member of the family had its own unique contribution. In practice, and in today's dynamic world, it is perhaps not such a big deal to finish university, at least for the people that were given a chance. The biggest deal in it is the opportunity of the *achiever* to bring joy to his family.

As beautiful thoughts were constantly flying in his head, Mojag opened the door to his apartment, and for the first time in four years, there was somebody waiting for him. He was so glad to see his sister, that dark figure with all-seeing eyes visibly excited for the ceremonial preparations.

"Sis, going back to my high school years, I am pretty sure that nobody expected that such a day would come when you all would be proud of my education...but I was always saving my potential, never wanted to differ too much from the rest", started Mojag, with his recognizable, and sometimes annoying irony of his *humor*. "But doesn't matter", he continued, "Please make us coffee because we left our strength on the highway."

As he was speaking, the front door opened, and his parents were rushing in to the narrow hallway of the apartment, along with Mojag's roommate and his parents.

"Wematin!!!" shouted Mojag, "I don't believe this. This is the first time that all you people I am bonded to are here. As pathetic as it might sound, this is truly heaven on earth...I just miss my girl, who always prescribes as my fault the objective technical issues that sometimes prevent her from coming to me. But anyways, we have come this far, and that is what we are going to focus on."

"Yes indeed, brother, I didn't drag my family here for nothing. We are going to show them that all those times that they couldn't understand us, were for a reason. And tomorrow, we are going to uncover that reason..."

The next day, 7.35 AM

The joy of waking up that morning was immense. And surprisingly, Mojag woke up a couple of minutes before the infamous phone alarm clock went off. Even his body clock was directed towards the main event. The upcoming phone call raised his self-awareness even more than usual. Mato [6], his good *Eastern* friend that graduated the year before, who was always finding ways for exploring new businesses, called in the early hours of that revered morning. Cutting the usual talk that two good friends normally have, Mato initially called to congratulate Mojag and his roommate for the success they had achieved. The most motivating words his friend said, directed both at Mojag and Wematin, were the following:

"Dudes, *today is your day*. It is all your past efforts that put you on today's main stage. You truly deserve it. You are the stars of the day and you will never forget the experience that these moments will bring to you. It is your day, and today, you do nothing else but enjoy it and share it with the ones that have helped to shape you to who you are today."

Mato was always embracing the charms of philosophy but his words were never as enlightening as they were that day.

---

[6] Native American male name of Sioux origin. Its meaning is *BEAR*.

After the usual morning day revival, Wematin and Mojag put on their sharp suits to mark their reserved place high in the bright day. They put on their shining shoes, took their ceremonial graduation gowns in bags and were set to leave as the taxi was approaching. Their preparation was followed by Mojag's father, Hania[7], who was making sure that everything ran smoothly in the start of the day. Always punctual and reliable, he was awake long before the graduates were. He took his camera and literally escorted their way out.

Visibly excited, though silent, the three of them left the apartment to embrace the shining sun outside. As in a *Southern* movie, Hania was constantly taking pictures. His professional touch was never questioned. Two freshly shaved men standing proud and tall, seeming larger than life, side by side then and always; Mojag with a light black suit with almost unnoticeable silver stripes, white shirt and a beautifully elegant silver tie in addition to the discretely shining black shoes on one side; Wematin in a light blue suit, shirt in many striped colors, and an orange tie matching the carroty shoes. That is the depiction that forever will be carved in their memory. No other photography had nearly a value as the one described. Too ordinary? No, extremely fulfilling.

As the taxi driver was reaching the horn to remind them of his existence, they parted with Hania, but only for a few hours as he was also preparing to wake up the family so they can all witness the long awaited ceremony.

---

[7] Native American male name of Hopi origin. Its meaning is *SPIRIT WARRIOR.*

"You are stuck in a beautiful moment, use every bit of it!", Hania told them as they were entering the taxi, which seemed like the most luxurious limo at that point.

"We don't even try to think otherwise", they replied in one voice with a beautiful smile on their faces. They closed the doors of the back seats, looked at themselves with their usual funny smile, and as in an authentic version of Cinderella, they simply told the driver:

"To the *White Castle*, please."

* * * * * * * * * * *

The *White Castle* was the former royal summer residence of a once glorious imperial dynasty, having a great historical value to its people as well as to the whole *Western* heritage. The vast land that was initially occupied for the *needs* of the luxurious life of the rulers in the past was now at display for all the people that were formerly ruled, to enjoy the beauties of the creation. The beautiful natural habitat, the mysterious mazes, the zoo and the resting point on top of the hill made it complete and an elegant relaxation spot. And besides, it seemed that the sun was always shining there and the calmness was simply too perfect to be ignored. In fact, the *White Castle* 'complex' was "one of those" places Mojag was sentimentally attached to. He had so many beautiful memories there with his family, his girlfriend, and with his friends. And now, along with his other friends, he was to be the star of the castle, and almost everybody that meant everything to him was there to witness it.

9.10 AM

The taxi stopped in front of the huge iron gates of the castle's main entrance. They paid the driver, gave him the deserved tip and proudly walked out of the car. They were either too confused or too excited, or both, as they were wandering around for a while to find *their* stage. The steam of people coming in and out of one of the many supporting entrances attracted their attention as that was the only place alive at that point of the day. It had to be it – the *White Castle's* Orangery, one of the two largest Baroque orangeries in the world. They immediately rushed in there and they were not mistaken. The door entrance was full with those blood sucking office rats from the university's administration. And yet again, they were doing their dirty money collecting jobs, checking payments of the tickets and of the graduation gowns. They knew of no other value but the one of a worthless paper, and Mojag always felt his usual disgust when talking to them. But as always, his profound family education prevailed over his temperament. He greeted all the people there with the utmost honesty and appreciation. The huge hallway leading to the main ceremonial room was impressive, adding up to Mojag's excitement. Wematin was catching up.

And there it was, the main stage already prepared along with the now empty seats for the respected audience, and of course, the inevitable high ceiling to ensure unprecedented acoustics. The eastern side of the Orangery and the beautiful weather guaranteed the presence of the sun and its stunning positive effect. The overall setting could not be described short of perfection. Nothing could ruin the moment.

The backstage was already full of Mojag's friends. As he and Wematin were getting closer, they could hear a mixture of familiar voices: "There they are and I am even amazed they made it in time," was Nikan[8]'s comment on seeing the two roommates entering.

"Hey, you are not bad either," they smiled and hugged his presence.

Nikan was the third piece of the friendship, a friendship that was to stay forever. A person coming from a well situated family, Nikan was somebody that you could grant your life to and you would rest assured that he would look after it as it was his own. A short dark hair, and a misinterpreted indifference in his eyes constructed the noticeable parts of Nikan. A friend for life, he was someone who rarely allowed his emotions to penetrate the outside. Nevertheless, he never failed on showing the real friend he always was; a friend that he always would be.

The three of them moved on to the backstage where the rest of the crowd was engaged in their uniform for the moment – the graduation gowns. They met with the rest of the scattered crowd and shortly exchanged positive remarks on the day that seemed magical, though real. Most of them were already prepared for the ceremony. Besides the ceremonial details, the girls looked more ready than ever, all polished and sparkling. And that day was to be the last when that particular group of girls was in town, leaving the famous saying in place: *Vrime prolazi; ko je jeba, je jeba!*[9]

---

[8] Native American male name of Potawotomi origin. Its meaning is *MY FRIEND*.

[9] Time passes by. For those who haven't used the moments, it is forever lost.

After many talks with the now former university mates, Mojag put on his gown, despite the growing heat in the room. The graduation gowns were a nice and formal way to institute the change; no matter how horrible they looked, all black and nasty, resembling some sort of an ancient dark sect, and without any other choice, their purpose was consciously embraced:

"After all, they are not as bad as they seem," said Bemossed[10] with his unique smile that was part of him no matter what his mood was. Bemossed was yet another part of the group of good friends in which Mojag was its member.

"*Cimeru*[11]," referring to Mojag, "the pressure is starting to get on. Let's go in the garden for a smoke."

"I thought no one would think of that my friend; my nicotine level is getting very low in the midst of this anxiety. I can see Wematin, Nikan, and the girls sitting out there. Let's move", replied Mojag and they both headed towards the beautiful, sunny garden. They came right in time as the girls were preparing the ground for a group photo to mark their collective success and closeness of the past few years.

"To all the beautiful moments spent together! Cheers!" said one of the girls just in time for the sound of the camera.

They all stood in the corner, too nervous to sit. A big cloud of cigarette smoke started to spread. The look in their eyes gave away the ever present nostalgia that one day they would all have to get apart. And as fulfilling as that day was, it was the one that instigated

---

[10] Native American male name of Algonquin origin. Its meaning is *WALKER*.

[11] Roommate

their separation leading each of them to different and unknown paths. They were all too aware of that. And it took one of Mojag's somewhat inappropriate comments in such an uncomfortable situation:

"Look at this grandiose building. And what I can't stop thinking about is how much the former rulers were fucking in this kind of an environment. Imagine all the orgies with their maids and unknown queens going on down here."

"Oh my God, what are you thinking..." said the girls accompanied by the usual laughter of the group. And besides, they knew each other very well to give out any signs of artificial disgust.

"Ma, please, don't tell me you've never thought about it. But ok, I was just testing you", Mojag started laughing as he continued. "In any case, we were making many plans that at some point we are going to make some sort of a graduation trip, but let's face it, we are never going to do that. You all know I'm not as reliable as organizer, and the rest of you will be busy chilling on the coast, which is perfectly fine. My point is that today is our last day in this shape we are in, so I just wanted to remind you of the responsibility we all have today. We stay together until we all fall down."

"There is nothing else left to be done besides that. The cherry is waiting to get popped," Nikan colorfully explained as if talking for all of them.

As the chat continued, their eyes turned towards where Mojag was standing, though they were clearly not looking at him; as if they wanted to say something in order to notify him. While figuring out the origin of the new development, Mojag received a gentle touch on his shoulder. He turned, and there she was –

Keegsquaw[12], more beautiful and more charming than ever. His usual animalistic desires almost immediately transformed into an honest smile.

"Hey, Keegsquaw, how are you? I've been looking for you," he said and gave her a friendly kiss.

"I feel great; I was there in the back helping my friends to get ready. Everybody's mood seems to be as positive as it gets down here in the castle...Mojag?"

Mojag was out for a few moments of a second, lost in the beauty standing in front of him:

"Wow, you are beautiful," he started thinking out loud, and he could not avoid noticing the shy smile on her blushing face revealed by his comment. He then turned to his friends and said:

"Ah, this girl's smile always makes me helpless...It still seems to be early morning but that is not a reason why I shouldn't get something to drink. Keegsquaw, let's get something to drink".

They both went inside and grabbed a few drinks for themselves. She had juice; he had something inappropriate for the morning. Not so many other people were eager to start the day finishing off the host's drinks, but that was even better, since it gave them some sort of privacy. But, for the irony to be as senseless as it usually is, that privacy meant nothing that day. Because it was the next morning she was flying to a place Mojag could not even spell out correctly and possibly returning when things would be much different. That privacy would have been eventually useful some time ago. But in a sense, they

---

[12] Native American female name of Algonquin origin. Its meaning is *VIRGIN*.

were both very complicated in the way their fragile bond had progressed. He had a long and an almost overseas relationship with a beautiful girl that considered him the center of her world. And above all, his desires were changing very frequently. Keegsquaw, on the other hand, was a type of girl, truly innocent in all aspects, who would never go into an open adventure if she did not have all the expected details guaranteed. Many times before, when they both talked about themselves being together, it seemed as if she was trying to buy a car, trying to plan what she might expect in the future. However, understandably, and at that point, Mojag could not guarantee anything close to that, bearing such a huge responsibility. They were talking about many other things and plans in the small drinker's corner, but they were either too proud, or maybe too weary to touch that subject again. The passionate sparkle in their eyes was that of a happy ending, but the circumstances dictated otherwise. It didn't take them long to start realizing that most probably, their time was gone forever.

The lost conversation between them was suddenly interrupted by a voice, resembling that of a shepherd trying to bring his herd together. In fact, the picture did not seem much different as all students gathered around in some sort of a queue inside the hall. The thrill was far too high to keep track of time, as the running clock on the adjacent wall was mercilessly killing the time, at that point being stuck at exactly:

11.56 A.M.

It was becoming even more apparent that the big event was about to unfold. The backstage was filled with a formation of almost two hundred familiar faces in black, trying to smooth the human line they were orderly creating. Many glances to the main hall discovered hundreds of curious relatives and friends who found their way in the meantime. The hall seemed completely full, and the butterflies started their usual run in the stomachs of all contestants.

Mojag was completely bedazzled for a couple of moments, trying to embrace what was actually happening. He smiled as if he had agreed, and quickly found his marked place in the queue, and so did the rest of the herd. The flag carrier was at the top of the hill, the music was set, and all the participants seemed prepared for what followed. The final countdown was approaching its opening seconds. And that was when the inspiring and triumphant music started. And then, like warriors coming back to celebrate a glorious victory, the orderly crowd of people started moving along the prescribed path, one by one, entering the main hall. As the first dozen of people were leading the way inside, it was becoming too apparent that the atmosphere was getting electrified, and the excited voices from the official crowd started echoing across.

Mojag was somewhere in the middle of the line as his turn was hastily approaching. Strangely enough, his stomach was serving him well in the midst of the thrill; he seemed prepared for what followed, exchanging sharp but happy glances with the changing environment. The second before entering the threshold, his body was unwillingly conquered by the shivers of the moment; the victorious music playing with his fast beating heart. It maximized his desire to find the looks of his dear family to share that imaginary moment. He recognized the voice of his sister coming from within the crowd. He was relentlessly looking for the place where the voice came from and finally his family appeared almost in front of him. Their eyes met vigorously, and Mojag could not help noticing their joy and pride caused by his sensation. He could not stop the moving herd to hug them, and at the same time he was successfully fighting his tears that were showing his strong emotions towards them. He did not even realize that his marching brought him to his seat.

The fusion of feelings teasing his heart and mind made it unconsciously difficult for him to be calmly seated. However, even the ultimately heated and strained atmosphere was, for that one time, a beautiful experience. The opening bell's cling marked the proper start of the grandiose ceremony. By that time, all the active participants were seated at their fixed places in the ever existing hierarchy. The play was opened by the officials of the ceremony, giving the usual opening template with the one important difference. At that moment it felt much more valid than any other. Mojag was following very intensely as the hosts were commemorating the appreciations to the university staff who were in large part responsible for helping him find his way through life. Apart from commemorating the respected academics, however, much of useless blabbering was going on at the stage, with the capitalist lords not losing even this beautiful moment to share their irony and justify their war and destruction of *Babylon*?! But they were not to be blamed; they were just petty puppets following instructions. For God's sake, it was too probable that it was even part of their salary as university administrators. After a several booing from some of the conscious students to the respected and too talkative a guest, the digression from the main event was cut short.

"It seems that we are all hasty for the event we were all waiting for – the inauguration of the new graduates. And that moment is finally here with all of you", exclaimed the university's Director, as the sighs of the gathered instantly increased volume.

"There is one other very important part, though, that needs to be addressed before we get going with the main event. And for that occasion, students, please all rise", he continued.

All students rising resembled as the front line of a royal guard with their apparel and caps firmly in place, having their eyes fiercely fixed at the director's figure.

"During my university years, as many of you now, I was financially supported by my own family to finish up my expensive studies, which were naturally, very quickly draining the family's budget. And there was one time I went to a friend's house, a friend who was the same social class as I was, with the only difference being that his parents despised overtime work and at the same time they were maliciously jealous of people who were hard workers. They never missed out exclusive vacations in the year, and lived life with less care and independently of their children. One time, sitting there at his house, his father asked me a seemingly innocent question, whether I would mind that my friend joins me at the university abroad. I embraced the idea as wonderful, but soon became disillusioned by his words, spoken in an insensibly envious way, the words of a father: 'that is great,' he said, 'But tell me, where can I find the money required for my son's education?', as if putting the blame on me for his pitiful parenting. I had a huge respect for that man before that, however, from that incident on, I felt sorry for him, although grateful, because he reminded me of the true value of my parents and the sacrifices they were making for my success. And from that time on, I have never blamed myself for my envious situation in comparison to others; it was just that their parents had much less courage to make sacrifices for their children. And you here have the privilege to enjoy what you have achieved, however, never forget that you only made it here because some dear people were fighting for you. For most of you, being here is due to a wonderful and strong support of your parents, both financial as well as emotional. Therefore, I am asking you to turn around where your parents are seated and give them your best gratitude."

As he was speaking, many of the students felt their happy tears sliding on their cheeks. Most of them felt as if they were reliving the experience that the host had just described. Mojag was on the verge of an emotional crackdown, thinking that this ceremony was the least thing he could do to repay his proud parents. He, along with the rest of the students, turned back and stood for a whole minute with enormous ovations to their parents. Mojag could not directly see his parents through the crowd, but he applauded as hard as his hands clapped as he felt his mother and father sharing his pride and enjoying *their* precious moment.

Waiting for a few moments for the atmosphere to cool down and the emotions to get consolidated, the host continued with the announcement of the highly anticipated moment:

"And now, students, it is all set for your deserved recognition. Please follow the right hand side of the stage and follow the alphabetical order as I will read out each of your names. As soon as I read your name, you would be one step to getting your Diploma", he finished and he placed himself in the center of the stage.

The executive "orders" were happily embraced by the students, who organized themselves in the arranged, systematic fashion despite their increased excitement. Mojag could not put away his excited look in his eyes, but his everlasting smile portrayed his self-confidence. He could vividly identify all the details of his road to that beautiful moment he was stuck in, yet he was still wondering whether it was really happening. He put all the work of his brain to focus on an eventual pronunciation of his name; nothing else seemed to matter but making his own success – his family's success. And that is why he probably missed out his roommates name on the main speaker, even though he was extremely proud to see him standing tall on the stage, embracing his well-deserved diploma, and being walked out of it with huge ovations from his family and all of them extremely good friends that followed him. Mojag's contemplations kept him from remembering that his turn was the next on the list. His thoughts were swiftly, almost in an animalistic manner, cut off when the main speaker continued:

"Mojag!"

His hands stopped shaking and similar to his other peers, he wasted no time to shine for the opportunity of the moment, which momentarily seemed quite glorious. He climbed up the ladder leading him on the stage, followed by a prolonged applause from all the people including those he loved and all those seemingly innocent girls he had sex with. And that meant many clapping hands in the air and within. The delirium was reaching its highest levels. His world was experiencing a culmination. He walked up to the director and shook his hand firmly as he received that piece of paper that made his parents proud of his son; it was like receiving the fucking Oscars.

Standing tall, he smiled for the photo, gazed at his parents and galloped his way down in a victorious march, closely scrutinized by the inevitable Uncle Inteus[13] who was mercilessly taping every bit of the interaction. Mojag even forgot that the ceremony was still going on, his impressions being even strongly diverted to acknowledge otherwise. He somehow found his way back to where he was formerly seated as he mutually exchanged positive energy with his fellow students.

The sweat was gone. The ceremony was entering its final step – moving the cap's tassel from one side to the other, officially marking the transition to the new, graduate status. As exciting as they had said that transition would be, everybody, and with no exception, were much more eager to mark the tradition of throwing the caps in the air above and marking the initial step of getting rid of the increasingly annoying gowns. And then, all of a sudden, almost before the official permit, the air was filled with square objects flying around. No student seemed to find the same cap afterwards. All irrelevant!

The ceremony finished with the caring words of the hosts, which with all due respect, no one was interested to hear anymore. The herd of people followed the same

---

[13] Native American male name of Algonquin origin. Its meaning is *HAS NO SHAME*.

line backwards to the backstage where they initially took off. Mojag abused the confusion that was occurring among the participants and slid away at the point when he saw his most important supporters waiting to embrace him. His joy transformed in that haven-like phase, resembling a weightless satisfaction of a junkie that had just received a shot of his favorite meal. For a moment there, he even stopped thinking of what was going on in there; the only real thing that was bolstering his good spirit was seeing his family happy. He knew that what he had achieved that day was only a fragment of what could possibly be done, and therefore he consciously resented being too pathetic regarding his appraisal. He exchanged his hugs with his family and immediately took them to the drink he was focused on at the last moments of the ritual.

2: 00 P.M.

The outdoor setting, safely guarded by the everlasting sun could at least be described ideal, sufficing to a combination of pride, positive feelings, and a daily alcoholic drink to, ironically enough, maybe soften the growing melancholy. Melancholy was always the other part of human species; especially because it was the day when true friendship and brotherhood were, unwillingly, to start fading away – all of them, even the lesser involved were to be spread out in different places of the world. And that is where globalization fails; that is when different life paths make the most sophisticated transportation systems obsolete – simply, it is one phase back to reverting the globe's size to its natural, and that is of a huge volume and full of physical and emotional boundaries.

Along with the rest of the memorable characters, Wematin, Nikan and Mojag were exhausting their friend's cameras to make sure that they would always come back to what seemed a precious moment for them, vowing not to forget what they once were. And for the sake of it, at least momentarily, the busy day made sure their honesty was not severely challenged by any glasses containing the charms of ethanol.

And then there was Mr. B Wahchinksapa[14], head of one of the university's departments. He was Mojag's admirable professor and an inevitable beer drinker partner at any important football match. He came up to Mojag, frankly congratulating the close-up:

"Mojag, I finally found you. Those girls are real helpers; they serve as road signs to get to you", he said in his usual accent accompanied by a meaningful smile, "Congratulations on your success, you are one of the best students I have ever taught, and more importantly, you are an extremely good and dear person!"

"Thanks *Mr. Wahchinksapa*, I cannot express my entire appreciation for your words. Thank you for your guidance all these years, and above all, thank you for being a friend!"

"Oh", Mr. Wahchinksapa seemed to contemplate his response with an unusual frown on his face. "Before I thank you on your kind words, there is one thing that we need to clarify." Raising the surprise level even more, he suddenly turned to Mojag's parents by cheerfully saying:

---

[14] Native American male name of Sioux origin. Its meaning is *WISE*.

"You have raised a very good boy, always polite and always keeping the right words for the right time. You ought to be proud of it."

His parents gave him the appreciation nod, bearing in mind they could not understand a single word in that strange language to them. Mojag's confusion was crystallizing when Mr. Wahchinksapa turned his focus back on him, taking a single moment as if recalling where he had previously stopped:

"Ah yes, the thing to clarify...You have just earned the degree of an even more respected citizen, and technically, at this moment I stop being your professor. I know my age," his fake frown turning into a huge smile, "but if once again you call me Mr. Wahchinksapa, I'm gonna kick your ass."

Mojag accepted the "suggestion" with a warm laughter:

"Sure B, I thought you would never say that", he smiled, "I do owe you a beer for this one. But thanks again for everything and I wish you all the best to you and your family."

Besides their strange involvement in the conversation, Mojag's parents were following the talk trying to understand what the professor was saying, and again, the inevitable Uncle Inteus was there to translate the message to their well understood language of the *South*. They seemed to be overwhelmed with pride and to an even greater satisfaction to Mojag, his mother came up to him and said:

"Son, when you were in high school, my ears were ringing of bad deeds that your professors were prescribing to you...well, I believe they did it for a reason", she smiled, "but this time, and to our great honor, my heart is overwhelmed with pride derived from your achievement, the respect you have earned with your professors and the beautiful friendships that you have made."

"*Miks*", he replied referring to his mother with the nickname he had invented for her, "I wish I could be as half as good a parent as you both were in raising me. No education, no street skills and no book could ever replace the healthy upbringing atmosphere that you and dad have provided me with. My success is nothing without both of you and my sister. I love you so much!"

She seemed to have difficulties hiding her happy tears as Mojag hugged the three of them. Of all the flashy ceremonial parts, that was the peak. That hug was his personal graduation; that part was the one that really mattered and always would.

The celebration was coming to an end, and Nikan, Wematin, and Mojag were the only ones to stay together, just as they always did in the past years. This time was even more special, since they had organized lunch for themselves, along with their families and friends, although at the other end of the old city. They rushed to the many cars parked on the outside and within fractions of an hour, they finished chasing the road that led to a panoramic view of the ever-inspiring *Blue river*. In the heart of the riverbed, there was a restaurant hidden for their current cause only. They all gathered around, numbering at least twenty people. The restaurant looked really boring in its setting of chairs and tables, and the whole atmosphere seemed to be sterile. It was one of the many examples of plan-less exploitation of natural resources, but it was the special guests that really mattered.

They all got absorbed by the nature surrounding them, falling deeper into that situation of an immediate affect. From that time onward, and with a couple of carry-on whisky bottles hidden underneath the table, what was happening in that setting in the hours to come was essential. The family's warmth and the spirit of friendship were greater than ever before. A *substantial* item that would mark that beautiful moment forever could be prescribed by the one song that came out of Mojag's guitar as he was playing, a song that would be the hymn of the day, one they were all singing, and with a realistic irony, one that Mojag felt portrayed his further roam. And as the show went on to the elegantly posh-y ball in the *Flashy Hotel* in the heart of the city, the song followed them. And as the ceremonials of the day were officially ending, they all gathered around the hotel's entrance and to the amazement of many of the hotel's guests and other people insignificant to the moment, they started finishing in one voice:

"Tisina ko sidro veze mrak
 U meni polako kopni strah
 Oblacim kaput i odlazim
 Da sve zaboravim

 I opet Dunavom plove brodovi
 A ti vise za mene ne brini
 Ko lisce sam, vjetar me raznosi
 Vukovi umiru sami"[15]

---

[15] Silence ties the darkness like an anchor
  Slowly the fear melts away in me
  I put on my coat and leave

The follow up of the night meant cementing the glorious experience of the day. The parents left and Wematin, Mojag and Nikan lead themselves to the girls and the alcohol, which was already making that shaking sound in their veins. Probably they did not even have time to properly depart, since the rest was unknown and happily saved on the occasional photos that others might have taken.

That day Mojag was at the peak of his happiness as he was enjoying the true values of life in those special moments. He even forgot why he was celebrating in the first place. But what he would never forget was the blessing of having a good portion of his lifelong friends by his side, and most of all, the blessing of seeing his whole family transparently happy by his side in that alien world.

He was too happily overwhelmed to ruin those moments by thinking of the uncertainties a future usually brings. It was only the sad chords of the song shouting in his head that was stressing the upcoming reality – the old friends were leaving. Making new friends was becoming even more difficult as he was constantly losing faith since everybody that he would

---

So I can forget everything

And again boats sail down the Danube
Don't you worry about me any more
I'm like the leaves, wind blows me around
Wolves die alone*

*(*Vukovi Umiru Sami* - Boris Novkovic, Eurovision 2005)

get close to, was leaving to other paths destined in life. And he was indeed happy that all of his friends chose what was best for them. And he was not afraid that he would have to manage life all by himself from that point on; he had accepted that ordeal a long time ago. His only fear was that he would lose contact to the beautifully cherished friendship, as many times before. And the song went on:

"A sad adio, a sad adio
  I ko zna gde, I ko zna kad…"[16]

* * * * * * * * * *

The new dawn was chasing out the completion of the previous day/night combination. The cross on the adjacent church reflected the early rays of the sun. Mojag, happily tired with a momentarily distorted sense of reality, hugged his bed's most faithful companion – the little pillow, and let himself to the necessities of sleep.

---

[16] And now goodbye, and now goodbye,
    and who knows when, and who knows where…
    *(*A sad adio* – Zeljko Samardzic, transcription)

Memoirs of a wanderer

4 COMFORTABLY NUMB

Present Day. July 2005.

It appeared to be incredibly early in the morning as the heat of the apartment was increasing to disgusting heights. The alarm clock was mercilessly interrupting the beautiful moments of the silent dawn, even though the bed in the sleeping room was empty. Mojag seemed to have fallen off the bed as he was laying asleep, thrown right there on the floor. He must have had his recurring dream of the orgy with those sinfully blonde girls as they were never as easy to handle. The alarm clock came up to his dick and he was ready to wake up. Surprisingly enough, and even though with just a few hours of sleeping time, he was inconsistently fresh and calm for such an early morning precedent. It was to be his first day at work; his first day at work *ever*. And as possibilities of the third world implied, living, not survival, should be seek far away in foreign worlds only. And realistic prospects, and perhaps an agreement among the stars entailed Mojag in a journey to professionally explore the opportunities of what they called – *the West*.

Mojag rolled out of the carpet and before engaging himself with the daily routine, he turned on the volume to the highest of what was *To the Unknown Man*, a masterpiece composition by *Vangelis*. Half naked, and fully craving for the morning cigarette, he sat on the couch, gazed at the church as smoke was coming out of the accompanying cigarette. He dared not to think for a moment. He smiled in consolation and said to himself:

"Ah, it's a wonderful life!"

The rest was irrelevant to keep notice of. It was only moments passed as he was already following the road to what his mother always wanted to be his workplace. And that day, her aspirations were fulfilled. The curious structure of the tall buildings, incredibly unusual for the city, seemed more like a tourist attraction than a functional place. Nevertheless, the high speed elevator directly levitated him to *his* office. It was quite unusual to see him all suited up in an office *administered* by his own conscience. He had been continuously at odds with such people in the seemingly forgotten past, and yet, unconsciously, he was becoming one of them; he got incorporated into *the system*, another analogy of his apparently crushed rebellion. For good or for bad, he felt delighted with his current initial status.

One of the critical issues that helped him immediately fit into that system was the amazing people he was to share his work with in the following months to come. The group consisted of great enthusiasts, each in their own distinct way, and with no hidden intentions. The immediate friendly atmosphere was with no doubts highly appreciated by Mojag, although truly unusual for an increasingly foul world that had been created out of greed.

The first one to greet him was Viho[17], one of the group's most valuable components. And besides, he was a person that Mojag owed all the thanks in the world for being there. Viho was a real person, both on and off work. His honesty and straightforwardness were on the highest possible level. Never selfish, he was always sharing his vast knowledge and ideas not only for the benefit of the group, but also for the benefit of all its individuals. His perfectionist zeal was no utopia, always doing the right things in the most sophisticated and most durable ways possible. And above all, he was Mojag's mentor and somewhat a role model.

Viho briefly introduced Mojag to all the other members of the group and at the same time giving him overview of what his duties would look like. They were chatting for quite a while in what resembled a professional environment on a higher friendly tone. Leaving the other members of the group back to their tools, Viho escorted Mojag to the office of *the boss*. Mojag had gotten acquainted with him before, even though, the stakes were much higher at the time, since he had direct and paid responsibilities under the supervision of a morally profound boss. According to the somewhat complex and arrogant corporate structure, Howahkan[18] was rarely credited as a boss outside the small group. But for Mojag, Howahkan was the only real boss that he ever recognized and unquestionably appreciated.

---

[17] Native American male name of Cheyenne origin. Its meaning is *CHIEF*.
[18] Native American male name of Sioux origin. Its meaning is *OF THE MYSTERIOUS VOICE*.

Howahkan appeared to be a very authoritative person, always holding firmly to what he believed in. His strong voice always inclined to the listeners that his words should be taken all seriously. In line with the philosophy of the *South*, Howahkan seemed never to have taken life for granted and his mysteriousness reflected a life fully embraced.

Mojag always had a great respect for that man, accompanied with a certain dose of a healthy fear. And that is exactly how his first encounter with Howahkan as a professional worker was portrayed. They shook hands in an authoritative but friendly manner, thus marking their working relationship of the contracted period.

Mojag humbly and actively listened to the words of his master as his responsibilities were freshly being served to him. Judging by his previous inexperience in the real world, Mojag stood well, in a very self-confident manner nevertheless aided by the unusually parental approach of the boss when communicating his duties and privileges. The conversation was abruptly shortened as there were self-proclaimed important people coming to see the boss. The opening conversation he had with his boss was very informative and enlightening conversation that seemingly boosted Mojag's low self-esteem. In spite of that, Mojag felt relieved that it was over so he would be able to reflect upon that morning and all the events that were happening, as they still seemed surreal. He left the room and headed back to the office with a familiar label at its entrance – his own name. It was much easier for him to manage his way through the complex structure of the building than stop being strangely aroused by that sticker that actually identified a spot for him within the maze of people.

The gleaming view from that office on the 25th floor was carefully fulfilling. The sensation it was causing was truly inspiring and Mojag unconsciously overlooked the setting of the apparels in the room and mechanically escorted himself to the three big windowpanes that revealed the fascinating textures of the big city. He knew the city's streets well from the inside, but the view from above usually was accompanied by a false pride. In that tiny moment, he felt big. He could still not grasp the whole of what was going on, but it felt damn good.

"It all seems perfect from up here; it all seems much easier", he mumbled.

Suddenly, it did make sense to him why oppressive architects of people's fates assign unimportant value to lives of ordinary men. They always *work* from above and from such elevations that all *other* men look the same, small and vulnerable.

Mojag stepped away from the window, sat back in the chair and started a silent monologue to reflect upon this new environment. He didn't know where to start; his mind was still far away from understanding his fresh position. All the protocols were unknown to him and at the same time he seemed ambitious. It all felt interesting and amusing to a certain extent. He turned on his tool at his desk – the computer – and the mail client popped up immediately. It was his first day at work and he already had an unread message. He discretely opened it and it was a usual letter of welcoming a new employee. Mojag was aware that it was only a template formality, but the effect it had was only increasing the pleasant confusion that obsessed him. He was in a state of mind in which he forgot all the important things he had thought before would be obstacles to his lonesome return to the big city. Days ago, he was headed back to the city with a sore heart depicting a world of pain in which he was to hold on with the comfort of no one. In fact, he had returned after all the people he cared for in that city left to other directions. His home friends and family were also far away. His girlfriend was understandably not pleased with his decision to go away once again. After all, it was no one's but *his* own decision. In spite of the former reality, it was something in the whole surrounding that day, which promised that he would be able to overcome his sentiments and start a fresh, independent life. For a moment there, he forgot about all the things that had bothered him in the preparation period. Those first moments of his journey made it look all too easy.

It didn't take much for Mojag to get acquainted with the room that would consume most of his time in the working weeks to come. That day was his first day at work, and he was theoretically allowed to get familiar with the entire building without the need to find excuses. But he was partly uninterested to do all of that. The only detail that he immediately wanted to get familiar with was something he wanted to do the minute he entered that huge architectural complex. There were close to one thousand employees in the whole working system; he was only interested in the portion of the prospects of beautiful women that could help him get through. There was a high probability, he thought, that the place he got himself in, served as an inexhaustible pool of potential sinners.

In that period, he was even more falling in love with his girlfriend that was impatiently waiting for him many miles from the place he now lived in. His thoughts of her were the hope that in reality kept him strong. They were separated along many borders to cross, but nevertheless, after all those crazy years, she still seemed to be the one for him. And yet, ungratefully, he still had the dignity to think of other romantic opportunities. But there was no harm in it; because at least for the moment, he was only targeting. And besides, whenever his brain strongly focused on a beautiful pair of legs or a perfect scent of a woman's body, diminished NOT his feelings for the one he really loved. And after all, with the family and friends not by his side, what else could reaffirm his faith in life better than a soft touch of a woman? For most, the answer was to be philosophically elaborated and thought through. For Mojag, the answer was: *nothing else*.

The approaching sound of footsteps distracted Mojag's practical thoughts as he immediately sunk into the papers on the working desk, staging an improvised working environment. He was really interested in the responsibilities lying ahead of him, but it was only that he was momentarily too comfortably occupied by other strategic things. The sound of the walking shoes increased to the level that the sound stopped. Mojag acted occupied, pretending he was unaffected by the silhouette of the person standing at the door of his office. He played his busy act for the usual few second period, and only then looked up, recognizing a familiar face.

It was Chayton[19]; another member of Mojag's closest colleagues. They knew each other indirectly through the others even though they have never properly met. Chayton's eyes were discretely giving out an impression that he had experienced life to the fullest. Or at least, that seemed to be his story. Always managing things in a concealed manner, Chayton was a figure that in many ways reflected a true person of the *South*. According to the wedding ring on some of the fingers of his right hand, he seemed to be married; his posture revealed that the woman was the boss in charge of the house.

They quickly introduced themselves and after a short, meaningless conversation, they immediately felt a strong connection between them. In actuality, it seemed that they both looked slightly similar in their appearance and behavior. But that was only a small part of it. They were both fighters, dreaming of a healthy revolution benefiting all of humanity. How pathetic, as they were both wary of the road that they had chosen since it contradicted all of their guiding principles. Pure existence was their main, and probably justified excuse. Philosophies aside, Mojag was happy to discover that Chayton was a chain smoker as well, as they were forced to go out of the building any time they felt the urge to smoke due to the corporate discrimination of smokers, which was often difficult to resist. In that spirit, they walked out of the building to lit up and take a coffee, at the same time continuing

---

[19] Native American male name of Sioux origin. Its meaning is *FALCON*.

their pleasant discussion about that hot girl on their floor.

The coffee from the machine tasted like shit, but the view on the outside was stunning. Probably for a reason, Mojag felt like he was king of the hill. There was something meaningful in the air that day, something that boosted his pride to previously unknown heights. Or maybe it was the fact that the powerful surrounding of the company envisaged that the world's order was being designed in some of these particular corporation's basements; it was obviously a created illusion of a failed project. Chayton also seemed somehow astonished, even though he thought he had managed to hide it as much as possible. Nevertheless, as two strangers who are destined to work together, they both tried not to find out a lot about themselves, but covertly to figure out the weights of their personality – to figure out if they were both worthy of trust.

After the interesting encounter, it was obviously difficult to say that they were friends at the moment. But despite their age difference in favor of Mojag as well as their different social situation, they discovered many similarities between them. They were two people with overlapping innate drives. Mojag felt as if he had known Chayton for a long time already. He was usually skeptical of making new friends, as it was always a long process of trust, but the bond that developed there in the smoking yard promised to be the start of a true friendship.

By the time Mojag acknowledged his thoughts, he realized that it was time for a scheduled meeting with a machine. As obscure as it did sound indeed, that was what he was told and he was too serious to show his confusion. All of the working people who were aware of Mojag's existence did not challenge the fact that he was privileged to have a shorter day. Those were the rules, and frankly, there was nothing much to be done at the moment aside the required bureaucracies. Ah, the machine.

The machine was an instrument of history's great necessity to control. In a very common and a very shallow fashion, it was used to track down and neatly record the time of the corporation's subordinates. It was somewhat a fascist model serving as an insurance policy that workers would not be able to fuck around with their delegated time. Clocking in on arrival, checking out when leaving. Simple, though effective way to balance the deficiencies in human decency. In spite of all those "benefits", Mojag's perception of that pride depriving device was that it only added another layer of chains in his life. Going back to his childhood place seemed even more difficult at that moment. He felt that his own actions were not anymore his to control, giving up piece by piece of his freedom, the one he considered existentially fundamental. His freedom was something he always fought for, and yet, he was once again destined to witness that crushing blow of freedom being something that other people design for the rest; in fact, freedom meant a constant observation of required behavior.

"I wonder if I would have to tell them when I'm going to take a shit", he sarcastically commented.

That machine was nothing short of a big brother in the perfect meaning of the word. The concept of big brother did not start with the Orwellian description of the eye of the beholder. In fact, big brother never stopped being active since the invention of mankind.

But who could possibly contain the beast otherwise, had there not been preventive chains?

Mojag's *meeting* with the hated machinery went very well. Despite his brief dissent, he stood there naively, nonetheless firmly believing in the validity of control. And what was disgustingly diligent, he got all the instructions he needed to report his daily life.

The office moments were expiring for the day. Mojag went to his office to give in some thought of how he could organize his working time in the most effective way. In general, many times he acted adolescent, but at the moment his motivation to use the opportunity given to reveal his potential was larger than anything else. He was still unaware of how he would best achieve that since one of his major personality flaws was his lack of appreciation for time. He never wore a watch as he always thought he could dictate time and that everybody would be waiting for his immediate moves and eccentric wishes. It was fairly certain that in almost all the cases he had been proven bitterly wrong, and thus far, he had never stopped. Sitting there in that cozy office chair, he knew that he would need to fight for a change in himself if he wanted to justify the huge confidence that his boss had invested in him.

There were many modern computerized tools providing help to get organized, but he always reverted to the old fashioned ways of a careless notebook and an old pencil. He perceived it as another resistance to those damned machines he worked with, those same, unworthy of trust, machines that he despised. He unleashed the notebook papers and started abusing the white space. In less than an hour, he was set out with his plans. And as he was doing that, his belief only grew stronger as he insisted on firmly following the schedule that he had just outlined. It seemed much easier to get in line with the foes of time, when he was managing a working time frame that was no longer his.

The slope of the sun just now started to move in its natural downward direction.

"The sunset must be amazing from these heights", Mojag thought.

But it was too early and too boring for him to wait for that precious moment. He had finished all the requirements of that first day and he was already starting to feel uneasy. He wanted to be alone so he could reflect on what was in fact going on with his life.

With a certain dose of respectful fear, he knocked on the door of his boss. The affirmative answer from the other side of the door only increased Mojag's anxiety. His boss seemed eager to meet him yet another time as he was curious of the way Mojag would try to handle his huge responsibilities. Debrief started shortly. With surprising self-confidence, Mojag explained all the issues he had already prioritized, showing both his understanding and value of each assigned task. He earned a well-deserved relief as soon as his boss' satisfying smile was becoming visible. It seemed as if it would be a start not only of a great working relationship, but also a personal, sort of a parental relationship bearing in mind the bare youth of Mojag's years. As a consequent reward, he induced a blessing from his boss to take off early that day. Mojag humbly thanked the respected person on the other side of the desk and left out in a polite rush. Once again, he expressed his huge gratitude to all his colleagues and continued following the exit signs.

The outside looked much shinier now as he was about to enjoy the generously granted, fake freedom. His thoughts were too occupied to get a glimpse of relaxation alongside the fountain right there at the departing point. Nothing seemed interesting to him at that instant. He was too confused to acknowledge the environment and the annoying strangers surrounding him. And then, that very first day he was leaving his workplace he saw something so intriguing that it would add up to his determination to coming back. Right there, as he was ultimately finding his way out, in the distance he saw the most amazing woman's figure. It appeared to be a gentle, though untamed girl with a matching behind and well nurtured breasts. Her maroon hair was glowing in the air, lightly falling on her strong shoulders. Mojag could not stop staring at that beautiful face that was slowly and unintentionally approaching towards him, a look that she purposely hid well to increase the tension. She was well aware that she had cornered the views of all the people present. There seemed to be lack of breath when she was walking. Each side of her seemed to offer a sinful joy in the attentive audience. Mojag could not care less about that day's working experience; he was becoming even more poisoned as he started touching the scent of that mysterious woman. As they were headed to opposite directions, the walking distance between them was diminishing. She ran through her soft long hair with her sexiest fingers as if heralding that she would reveal her shiny look to the mortals. Mojag was mentally prepared for what followed. In what seemed to be an impatient year, their eyes finally met. They both looked pleasantly surprised of each other's awareness. Her eyes revealed the most beautiful experience a woman could offer. In those few seconds, their eyes were fixed to one another as if testing each other's thoughts. He could feel his breath fading away as he was trying to move his lips in sign of salutation. No words could come out. She gifted him with a sexy smile and an unseen flirty look in her eyes. He felt a burning sensation in his stomach as his sexual drive rose to unimaginable heights. There was something in that beauty that caused a thrilling chill and an amusing chaos in his heart as well as his hormones. He smiled back, and pierced through her eyes with his look as if trying to expose her. Both with their heads leaning back to see the other, they were slowly distancing from one another. Mojag felt speechless and at the same time guilty of the missed opportunity. His stupid pride did not let him go after her.

"Fuck, I'm such an idiot, maybe I will never get to see her again", he thought, even though his trusted senses implied the opposite. He went out on the outside and immediately reverted to his cigarettes for a possible relief. His mind was still frozen at the sight of that charming smile.

He had already forgotten what she was wearing, but he would never forget the way she looked. In any case, he knew he had a professional responsibility to get back to work; now he had yet another reason, a personal responsibility to explore where would that gorgeous smile lead him to.

* * * * * * * * * * *

As if totally lost in an imaginary world, he failed to comprehend how he had possibly found himself unlocking the door of his apartment. He seemed alcoholically intoxicated as he apparently could not remember how he had already gotten at the footsteps of his apartment hallway. And yet, he had not enjoyed a single drop of a distilled temptation. His strong self-confidence from the day quickly started depleting as he realized the unusual silence of his place. Many times before his place looked like a gypsy camp as there were so many dear people that had passed through the rooms of that apartment. That place could never be quiet, and yet now, it was the entire world's discouraging silence Mojag was left with.

He immediately got undressed and rushed on to the paused music's playing device. The heavy guitar sound was on its way. Familiar music started mixing with his feelings, helping him cope with the indecisive reality he got himself into. He sat on the dirty couch and refused his thoughts for as much as he could afford. That was always a costly thing to do, as thoughts never faded away while relaxing, but they only grew stronger, becoming even more fucking destructive. The tension kept on rising as he realized he could not let go. The numbness was steadily unwinding with the sense of reality increasing. Deliberate theories and thoughts rushed involuntarily to his head. And for the worse, most of these thoughts were difficult to understand at that fragile point. The one thought that overshadowed the whole pile of submissive thinking was the one that brings humans to act. It was *fear*, which always, and with no exceptions, was the first one to come to surface when no other awareness seemed known. For he seemed scared as never before, not even like the innocent times when he thought Freddy Krueger would disrupt his sleep through the insides of his guts. There was nobody in that damned big city to get a hold of; nobody to help him bypass his emotional weariness or to share his first work experience. He looked at the phone and started cursing the people who irrationally spent so much money on advertising those oppressive devices, when they did not even consider ringing in the most difficult times.

He crawled up to the fridge and to his utmost amazement, he found a couple of unopened beer cans. The cigarettes were with him too. His happiness was as high as it could get in the whole dizziness created. He quickly changed the music as his masochist instincts were instructing him that he needed something that could tear him down even more. Because only in such moments, he had proven to be able to realize what was actually happening to his sentiments. He came across a copy of a memorable concert performed in that glorious *Southern* city by one of his favorite groups. The chill of the first beats of the music of a forgotten past was in the form of a cold spiritual breeze. In spite of that, he started taking hold of himself. And so did some of his thoughts start becoming crystallized and slightly more civilized.

Objectively, Mojag was in an extremely envious position. With God's will and with a huge help from a couple of incredible people, he was employed as a high ranking worker among the scarce youth of the company. His salary was numbered to be as high as most of his country mates would unfortunately never see in a course of a full year, and certainly not in one month. He had a beautiful girlfriend whom he loved, and who was dedicated on leaving her home as well in order to join him in his quest of life. His honesty and devotedness brought him many extraordinary and diverse friends from all over the world. His parents were proud of him and supported him in all his actions and deeds. And for what was worth, his complete independence seemed to finally have a chance to taste freedom's flavor. It appeared as if he had no valid reason to feel crushed. At least that was what the resentful low lives would have said.

All people he just thought of, people he cared for, and people he was sure cared for him even more, was what brought him that little remaining satisfaction. But despite all those dear people sharing their mutual love, he was alone. That was what counted; that was what bothered. And there was nothing that could replace that bitter feeling. There was no possible comfort as all his dearest friends he had met in the big city were already spread elsewhere. There were even moments when he thought those people loved him because he was so fucking isolated from them. They rarely were in direct contact, and *"probably it is normal that they forget me as time goes by. It seems that I can never hold on to all those people I love, as if I am intentionally pushing them away from me. It was my choice to come here and leave everybody to explore the real challenges of life, but at what cost? I am not sure if I would like to lose the integrity of my own self in the process. And besides, even though this is only the beginning, nobody knows where and what the end is. And what would happen when I eventually return home when both the dates and the people, and even the innocent roses would be a lot more different to recognize. For God's sake, I will be the one difficult to recognize! I would probably be one of the usual strangers passing by, with no relevant history by his side. Something similar to what I appear to be here. But if I quit on my pursuit and go back now, maybe things will be easier to fix…The only problem is that I don't know how to quit. Until the day I die, the South will always be my home, but right now, I find it too difficult to distinguish a home. I have been in the big city for the past four of my most beautiful years and I have raised my self-awareness here at levels unthinkable of before. A large part of me was virtually formed in this organized city; a large part of me will always live here, and so I am on a crossroad to nowhere. No decision seems to be an option now since I am also attached to these dead sights of this Western city. This is where I came out of the shelf. And besides, what the fuck am I going to do in my beautiful South, in that unfortunate, failed country with deceitful people? And what would my parents feel seeing me there wasting my future? What about my girl? What would I do without the confident thought that she is always by my side? I feel so painfully empty. But here I will have so much money and live like a king as some had already zealously noted. And so what the fuck that money means if I cannot spend them with the ones I love?! Don't you fucking people understand?"*

So many related, but unorganized thoughts were abusing the fragility of his chaotic confusion. And it seemed to be only the beginning of an unbearable reality with a high tendency to get even more painful. The melancholic music only alleviated the company of his despair and the *modern conservatism* of his belief.

"It must have grown to be an extremely inhumane world when being an old fashioned conservative means great affection and appreciation towards family, love and friendship", he concluded with no substantial solution.

His present feeling of fear was derived from the thought that he might lose the ones he would uncontested die for.

The bathtub was bursting its final bubbles as water was almost starting to come out of its prescribed place.

The hot surrounding was patiently waiting for Mojag to help him forget about reality altogether for the moment. It was always a place full of trust and relief. And as if sensing the need for it, Mojag had turned on the water ahead of the contemplation so it could be ready to embrace and sink his thoughts. The music had to be changed once more to reflect the instantaneous functional changes in his mood. It was fully instrumental in order to avoid any unwilling thought distortion by reverting to any sort of remembrance of dear and at the same time lost past episodes. There was something in that bathtub that always prevented his hazardous thoughts from coming to surface and out of its shell.

As he was enjoying the gentle breeze of water pouring in all pores of his body, his mind was free. He seemed to have forgotten all previous slaughtering forces that poisoned his head. He seemed at ease with the whole situation as if cowardly giving in to the pressures of his personality. The momentary awareness whispered to him that he was supposed to fight in different fields, those that would bring him prosperity and not devastation. And besides, it seemed comforting that he could find reliable friends at the new workplace to drink beer with. Uh, and the encounter he had with the girl that boosted up all the parts of his ego was even more motivating now than when he felt her perfect scent. His senses were surprisingly overwhelmed with calmness that he did not even thought of the usual, sinful, physical self-satisfaction.

While he was preoccupied with the sacred thoughts of a *Southern* village with the world's best natural habitat, he was almost unconsciously sinking in the magic of the stream. He seemed too comfortable with his illusionary situation as his cowardly escape from reality almost made him drown while enjoying life of which the debt he had not yet settled. It required a Joan of Arc in a shining armor to pull him out. And in the odds of the moment, there she appeared in the form of a forgotten ring tone on Mojag's phone.

By the lengthy time he pulled his head out of the hot water and realized what was going on, the phone did not even show any signs of stopping its intention.

"It must be my girl", he thought. "She is the only one whose persistence is usually due to sometimes justified lack of trust of my actions."

He was not even closely mistaken. He picked up the phone and ran into the exciting talk of his loved one. It was quite strange that she did not even ask how he was doing because she seemed to have some inspiring news that she immediately started with. She simply said she was coming soon enough to visit him for his forthcoming birthday so they could go to the zoo and feed the squirrels *together*. As damned a personality Mojag had inherited, he did not even express as much of the delight to her as he was feeling. Regardless, he was the happiest person in the world. He got out of touch with the water, leaving his body to dry to the mercy of the summer air. He was too excited to feel anything else but love. Nothing else mattered as his major reinforcement of love was coming to get reunited. Rarely had he looked as happily aroused as he commenced appreciating his gratitude to the stars above. Judging by his wild motivation, his girl seemed to be the last resort of *hope* in that bitter and indecisive world he found himself caught into.

5 HOPE, SUBMISSIVE

Hope is the most deceitful flavor to a man's life. It is something often associated with a God given endurance to life's miseries, but unfortunately it is nothing but an increasing indicator of failure and obsolete dependence. It always sneaks in various forms of subconscious actions, giving fake strength and belief to a pitiful human's life. Nevertheless, hope heals only then when it is positively balanced with its opposite part – reality.

Love, when stripped down to its fundamental concepts, in many ways resembles hope. The one major difference between both is that the pursuit of love is sacred as is true love itself. There is in fact no doubt about that. However, such rare, unconditional love is often equally misunderstood by both the woman and the man involved. True love is found at least once in a lifetime by every single one of us, regardless if we see it or not, whether we accept it or not. And love, when stripped down to its fundamental concepts, is love no more.

* * * * * * * * * *

The properly organized airport in the big city never looked as happy as it did that day. The moderate sunny morning in that beautiful July season was only extending the joy. What was even more atypical was that Mojag was happy being there at that aerodrome that traditionally reminded him of the sufferings he was willingly enduring each time he would arrive after previously separating from his family and home. But now, not even the arrogant officials at the terminals were something to reflect upon and grumble about. The simple reason for such a drift in Mojag's emotional philosophy was boosted by the arrival of Aiyana[20], his long loved girlfriend. Reasonably pathetic, she seemed to be the only person that could bring him joy in his destined quest of loneliness, at least temporarily.

The plane with Mojag's carefully awaited passenger was already parked in the docks some quarter of an hour ago. It was only a few moments more that she was expected to come out of the port. His anxiety was steadily increasing as people started coming out. He was by now picturing her posture and her emotions to their brief reunion, already feeling her soft touch. The gate opened once again and there she was, looking wonderful and even gentler than how Mojag had envisioned her. Without delay, she left her luggage on the floor and ran quickly towards him. He was fully prepared for the moment as he sincerely embraced her body and started kissing her lips. They were so fucking soft, leaving him with no option to stop. They hardly uttered a word as they were too busy enjoying those

---

[20] Native American female name of unknown origin. Its meaning is *ETERNAL BLOSSOM*.

increasingly rare moments they were in each other's arms. No wonder why it is said that a kiss is an encounter, the most beautiful of them all; the one that marks the bridge between a man and a woman.

"I love you so very much that it's difficult to explain. If you just knew how much I miss you..." Mojag selfishly thought of those sacred words as he dared not to speak.

"I never want to be away from you again. Please", Aiyana said, almost in a demanding way, like she was reading his feelings as she melancholically wrapped her arms around him.

Having no immediate and sincere answer, he only nodded in guilt and profoundly avoided the answer:

"I know, baby. We will work something out. Let's get going now to *our* apartment", he charmingly replied, looking at her smile, exposing her satisfaction of Mojag's reference of his apartment as *their* place. Aiyana couldn't agree more. She trusted the luggage to Mojag's bell boy skills and they both took on to get the bus back to the city.

It seemed the bus was exclusively waiting for them since they were the only ones to pursue the ride to happiness. They sat themselves and started the usual chat about the missed pieces of their lives while they had been apart from each other on different sides. A story told was certainly not even close to living those moments together, but no other options were available to them. And sadly, they resembled more like two good friends that had not seen each other for a long time, than they resembled a definition of a beautiful couple in love. But in spite of those technicalities, there was still that ever present flare in their eyes revealing the unreserved love they nurtured for each other. In fact, their glances were nothing short of that same passion when they kissed for the very first time in that memorable setting of the old cinema. Mojag forgot everything about his ill-fated thoughts haunting him for many of the past days of painful loneliness.

Aiyana told him all about her plans to come to the big city and moving in with him, so they could finally enjoy their love together. It seemed that everything was prepared except for some bureaucracies, which at the moment were too irrelevant to be considered an obstacle. Despite sincerely in love and despite the fact that he could not make it through without her in those difficult moments, Mojag was secretly unsure of the idea of living together at a time when his youth and enviable position provided him with the chance of exploring the inexhaustible beauties of life in what he perceived as a gateway to freedom. He never dared to think those sensitive concerns out loud, as he was also heavily reluctant to shake Aiyana's self-confidence and ultimately reluctant to destroy that beautiful relationship. He ungratefully wanted everything; she simply wanted his presence.

The bus started entering Mojag's neighborhood. They were both excited to be arriving as they were lustily striving for some moments away from everybody; some moments only for themselves. The bus driver was kind enough to stop almost in front of Mojag's apartment. The two passionate passengers rushed out to embrace the soft rays of the sun. Aiyana, already acquainted with the surrounding from various times before, was guiding the way while Mojag was carefully carrying her load. Naturally, she did not have a key to the apartment, but her posture implied that she took it literally when he said the apartment belonged to both of them. They entered Mojag's place that eternally had this repelling odor of cigarette smoke embedded in its walls. But they were indeed too aroused to bother with details. In a wordless atmosphere, and with the occasional sweat on their bodies, they engaged in a commanding scene of sex, properly reflecting their apparent abstinence for couple of long weeks. It was only the sinful moans and sighs that were to be heard up to the neighboring apartments. With every inch further, their spiritual bond was growing stronger. And none of them seemed to care about time as the morning was long gone when they finished testing out all corners of the apartment. In essence, they were forced to abuse those precious moments together as it was usually very short until they would have to part again.

That whole week, while Aiyana was in the big city, was filled with nothing but joy and happiness. They were stealing every precious minute of the day to focus on each other.

Mojag didn't mind that he was acting like her ultimate servant, for it was her that was always his owner. He was doing everything possible to satisfy her and to make sure that they both cherished each moment together to the maximum. And surprisingly, though probably temporary, Mojag praised the idea that she might be moving in with him very soon. The thought of them living together appeared not so frightening anymore. On the contrary, it felt comforting and it gave him a sense of being safe with her. She reaffirmed his shaken self-confidence, bringing it back to its normal heights. In return, she strengthened his belief that she meant the whole world to him. And indeed, even when they were not physically together, separated among many worlds and borders, the mere thought that she was there waiting for his call always gave him hope to stop being desperate and nostalgically confused. She was his link to his dearest memories, the only one person carrying the hope that she could possibly save his spirit.

* * * * * * * * * * *

I don't like birthdays...at least those in which I am the one getting older. And it's certainly not the passing years that I feel sorry for, because as some great man righteously said 'life is not how many breaths you make; it is how many moments take your breath away.' But perhaps it is because I always felt lonely on my own birthdays for no justified reason, even though I was never alone most of the time. Or it's maybe because such days selfishly, though hypocritically put the focus on that one person, implying marginalization for the rest. But in any case, before I start to get into the agony of my frustrations, I guess I don't hate my birthdays either.

The day of Mojag's birthday came very quietly while he was still delaying the recognition of the event. Nevertheless, very shortly, his disaffection was abruptly interfered when Aiyana presented him her beautiful smile to him, her lovely words, and the usual morning love-revival. But as Mojag had noticed, it was everything but usual. That day, it appeared, that he was not obliged to request any permission for any specialties he wished for. He obviously felt quite comfortable with the privileged treatment. And besides, Aiyana was understandably eager to be unconditionally nice as much as possible so as to strengthen Mojag's fragile determination even more for their moving in together. And now she unquestionably had the perfect shot to *blow* his mind even further.

As expected, and certainly not due to usual bed laziness, they missed breakfast, although unexpectedly, they missed lunch as well. The missed calls on his mobile's screen and a lot of template "Happy Birthday" messages were shockingly piled up as Mojag listed through the names of thoughtful people, which apparently ran into programmed reminders of his birthday. Yes, the day indeed looked special in itself, so they didn't rush into arranging any pressuring events to make it look special; instead, they left the social events for the night. And for what it was worth, they were furiously in love. Aiyana made some snacks so Mojag could physically keep up with his daily dosage of nicotine. It was mainly junk food, but she made it with style, and that was what counted. And besides, he was never such a big fan of food as he never learned that meals are to be enjoyed unconditionally, especially when at least one third of the world's population were forced to eat every second day. He perceived eating as something that has to be dealt with very quickly as to be able to continue functioning and proceed with other activities. In that spirit, he instantly stuffed himself and became much more prepared for the alcohol that was designated for consumption that night. For he had already arranged an event to prevent a potential boredom at home.

A lot of his friends gave him the pleasure of honoring his birthday; *none* of them were there in the fucking city to share Mojag's day. In any case, it was merely his birthday, and his girlfriend was there to balance a lot of inconveniences in his emotions. But there were Mojag's colleagues, which were extraordinary people as well. And they were all in the city that particular weekend. His colleagues were actually the ones that Mojag organized the dinner for the night of his birthday.

* * * * * * * * * * *

Long before needed, he took his girl by her hand as they were already instantaneously trying to find their way through the overcrowded place of the night. The one empty table was always there waiting for him. They overcame the stomping crowd and got themselves seated on the upper floor, to the right of the wooden staircases. The chairs were commonly uncomfortable but that was never a problem. Due to many valuable experiences in that beer shop, it was Mojag's second, maybe even third home. And where better to celebrate a birthday then at *a home*? Well…probably at a pre-paid strip joint.

Mojag's disaffection towards time had always prevented him from actually being on time, regardless of the occasion. His friends were sometimes saying that he would probably be late even at his own funeral. But surprisingly, that night, he was in place before the others were booked to come. Shortly after Aiyana was getting comfortable with the setting, the others started coming in. It was all of Mojag's closest colleagues and one dear friend from his school days. They all came in one run. And unlike all his other birthdays, this one seemed particularly odd. He immediately noticed that all people about to be seated on his table were paired. He already knew all that and he was happy for them, but as he was introducing them to Aiyana, it evoked strange questions in Mojag's mind:

"Wow! I love these people but this looks like a married couple's social event. And for what is worse, I am the one greeting the guests, with a loved one by my side. And with all due respect, most of these people are much more mature than me and they have a justified cause for engaging in such events. But me? "

And while he was occupied with existential questions, Aiyana logically seemed to have loved the fact that she was in such a coupled company. She immediately related to the girls as if preparing the grounds for her recurring arrival in the big city. Nevertheless, they all got absorbed in many interesting conversations and Mojag's initial doubts were almost gone. He even started liking that way of living. And as the beer continued pouring in, it started unleashing new dimensions of life. He was very happy indeed.

Aiyana was already making shopping plans with the girls and at one point she tried to be amusing by sharing her burning desire that she and Mojag should have already been married. Following some usual jokes from the people, Mojag's grim expression on his face marked the point when Aiyana should stop feeling *that* comfortable. He never understood why she always rushed into growing old and build a family when life's mysteries were still to be discovered.

Mojag was already into the magic of the beer. He loosened up to the point where he unconsciously started staring over at the adjacent table directing his focus at an average blonde with big boobs. Too bad his girlfriend never drank alcohol; she was always too sober to miss out on such *deviations* of Mojag's behavior. She pinched him under the table reminding him of a painful lecture that would certainly follow up at one point.

"And I am still thinking of my belief of freedom", his sarcastic smile reflecting his thoughts.

The last quarter of the night started approaching. It was probably time to leave. And unlike the usual practices of the *West*, Mojag paid the whole bill. In fact, that was the least he could do to show his appreciation to his colleagues that honored him with their presence. He was indeed very joyful to share the night with them; they were quite pleasant a company. They parted in a nice way and subsequently, each took on a road on their own.

Mojag seemed very satisfied as he was walking on the cobblestone road, holding Aiyana firmly by his side and singing some cheerful tune. Above all, she was the main reason for his happiness. And he didn't even regret the fact that he would have to get serious and change his comprehensive attitude towards life. He was simply way too much in love to care about anything else. And besides, the alcohol was sneaking under his skin, adding up to his bedazzlement. The alcohol also guaranteed his current thoughts until the morning. But it was also sucking his blood out of the essential veins. And that was not a good sign, as his conscience still required him to pull out a good sexual stunt. And sex was another very important feature, especially when in a relationship. Not only because of the priceless act itself and its potential medical benefits, but also because of the act's effortless access.

The cab arrived at the familiar destination as both Mojag and Aiyana were feeling the mutual waves of burning desire. As soon as they opened the apartment door, the extent of time needed for them to take off each other's clothes was virtually instantaneous. And apart from such lust-craving initial encore, the body communication was too sensual to be put in words. In fact, it was exceedingly absolute to be called anything less but *love in the making.*

After such a perfect harmony between their spirits, Aiyana wanted to mess it up with her usual cuddling. It was easy for her not to fall asleep without any toxics in her body. In fact, she insisted to hug. But too bad Mojag was already asleep to contemplate her redundant wishes.

* * * * * * * * * * *

The day after was reflected through a chilly July's dawn as Mojag and Aiyana were watching the romantic sunrise over the calmness of the river. It was also a bit more of a chilly day because Aiyana's bags were already packed for leaving. But almost everything was rearranged so that she would come to Mojag shortly after again, and for all time. Mojag *"remembered how she said that (they) would meet again some sunny day"* [21], giving him mythical strength to endure his battles.

And love is a tricky thing. It doesn't choose where and when it is going to strike the most. And once two people get so deeply involved, they do things that others, even the ones in love, cannot quite understand.

Both Mojag and Aiyana were too young and naïve deciding their future. And their options were not many. It was actually that one option, the one that Aiyana would sacrifice her home and family for coming to the big city so they could start living together. Such step clearly had serious implications and

---

[21] *Vera* – Pink Floyd, "The Wall", 1979

responsibilities for their future. The other, preemptively discarded option that Mojag would come back to the city where they both grew up was not viable simply because Aiyana would not permit it. For she never wanted to cut Mojag's dreams as she was aware that in the probable future, he might regret his decision and blame it all on her. She didn't want to carry the burden if something would eventually go wrong. And now, the decision had been made. In less than a month, she would come back again, but this time with all her belongings.

In practice, Mojag was admittedly scared of the level of closeness that they were going to have when she would move in. And not only that he was scared of commitment and responsibilities, but he was also concerned about Aiyana. His concerns developed from a hypothetical scenario in case something went wrong and they decided to go their separate ways. That would be a severe blow to Mojag, but to his girl, who leaves her friends and family, and her whole life just to be with him, would be a crushing defeat to her eternal motivation for life. But regardless of all those things, he was even more frightened to speak up as she might think that he was unsure of his love. And he could not afford risking the opportunity to be with her at any cost to his freedom or to stupid future hypothetical calculations. He was too happy with the unfolding chain of events.

Mojag escorted her to the airport and their departure was much less painful when believing she would be back for good. He firmly embraced her body and *kissed her goodbye*.

6 INTERLUDE

It was a usual day at the office. The dull atmosphere was occasionally disrupted by Mojag's gloomy smile provoked by his sometimes defeated, but insatiable motivation of life. He appeared to have consolidated his emotions and destructive thoughts as he was still under the positive impressions of the short visit of his girlfriend some week before. He seemed ultimately satisfied and calm about his life. The one thought that enabled his naïve smile and kept him going on was simply the one of his girlfriend coming back to live with him. Ironically, his ungrateful consciousness had constantly implied that he was never quite in favor of such a step in his early stages of development, but his perception grew differently as his seemingly pointless life started becoming unbearable. And through that, and with a deficit of the usual abundance of his best friends, his love for Aiyana only grew stronger. Now it was only less than a month that he was expecting his love to be reunited for a longer and for once, a stable period.

The morning coffee was taking its toll, as Mojag's stomach was becoming usually irritated by that black substance. That meant reading time. He printed out the latest developments in the sick world and headed towards the toilet.

Typically outraged by the materialistic actions of the assholes who ruled the frontiers of the world, he came back to his office, at least physically relieved. He must have been reading for a longer while given that he noticed six missed calls on his phone. Strange, he thought, because receiving so many calls in a quarter of an hour was indeed a rare, if not a forgotten privilege. His observation was justified when he inspected the latest intrusions of the phone. All six missed calls were from Aiyana, each of them in a span of six minutes. He immediately got covered with that morbid, feverish sweat of storming "what if" questions.

"This cannot be right", he started, "and she knows I am in the office, which gives me a reasonable alibi, so it rules out the usual control that she is obsessed with. What the fuck happened? What if something happened to her? I hope they are all fine. She's ok, she has to be ok. What if she's pregnant?!!! Yes, that's the only explanation for her impulsive tension. It must have slipped when she was here."

He started reliving those moments of mutual lust, carefully following all the details that might have led to a pregnancy, biting his nails to the bone.

"No, but I was careful. It couldn't have happened. Oh God, I hope it is all fine. I love her, and she's coming here, but I am not ready for any additional shock at present. Fuck, it's eating me up. I have to call her. No, but what if it's true? What am I going to say?!!"

His legs were shaking with the creation of the sudden fanatical frenzy in his mind; his throat too dry to give out a sigh. Anything else might have helped him comfort but the sudden buzz. The recognizable melody implied yet another call from his girlfriend.

"I cannot talk here. I can't let anybody see me weak. I'm going outside so I can also accompany my anxiety with a cigarette. Ok, calm down. I will call you in five minutes" he said to himself.

His self-created lack of reasoning made him as pale as he could possibly get, expressing his intense eyes even more. He was instantaneously on the outside and got himself together for a while to be able to see what was going on. The suspense generated by the beeping sound of his outgoing call to Aiyana only increased the number of butterflies in his stomach. She finally answered. She was in tears. It was not a good sign.

"You are never there when I need you. What took you so long to get to me?" she started shouting at Mojag with an unfamiliar hysteria.

"Sorry baby, I was with my boss. What's going on, why are you crying? Are you all right?" he tried to calm her down.

"What do you think? Do I sound as if everything is fine?! And you are always too busy for me, enjoying your life there while I struggle with *our* problems."

"Aiyana", Mojag already losing his patience, though still calm, "please stop it! What is wrong?"

"Everything is wrong. But don't worry about your usual selfish fears of getting me pregnant, because it's not that. I'm already bleeding", she stopped for a moment only to continue with increased melancholy. – "Ah, Mojag…I love you so much", she barely uttered those words and immediately burst into tears again.

It should have been a relief for Mojag as his self-created fears were not reflecting reality. But he got even more puzzled and scared than those moments before. It seemed that something was really wrong.

"I love you too baby", wishing she was there in his arms, "Tell me what happened..."

"Mojag, it feels as if everybody is purposely working against us. Today I received a call from my boss regarding my transfer to the franchise company in your city. It was not good. They say I would have to wait up to one more year until I would be able to transfer. Some bureaucracies prevent me from transferring now. And all that means that we cannot be together."

"No, no, it must be some idiotic mistake." Mojag screamed in agony. All his hopes were turning into dust. "Please don't cry, we will find a way to work this out together. But just in case, I will call my father now to ask him if he can help bypass those procedures through his people. We will be together!" he said in desperation.

"Don't call anybody please", she said with difficulties taming her tears, "I asked my father and the issue is already too pumped up in the firm. It could have even bigger consequences than this, having in mind that my transfer at this point would be illegal regardless of who makes the sacrifice. The thing is that I am contractually bound to be in the firm until the project is finished. And the project was intended to be completed shortly after my visit to you, but now somebody has requested additional changes requiring another six to twelve months. But it is irrelevant to talk about things we cannot change; I don't want to think about it...I've been thinking of you the whole time... Mojag, what are we gonna do? I can't take it anymore to waste my most beautiful years without you. Like this, we have each other, but in fact we have nothing."

"Don't say that", Mojag exclaimed, irritated by her comment, sensing a burning sensation under his feet that reflected his helplessness. He could not afford a development unfolding, such as the situation implied.

I need her to be here with me. What am I gonna do without her? I have to find a way to do something; otherwise I will lose everything I had hoped for. And there is no way I can succeed here without her love by my side. I would have nothing in this stupid city; a half dead wanderer with a broken spirit. I cannot cope with that anymore.

A tormenting silence opened up. Not even their breaths could be recognized.

"I will return for good!" Mojag's heart now opened up. "Yes, I will. And then we will be together forever and a day. That is the only way to…"

"No", Aiyana unpleasantly interrupted, "I will never allow that, and you know it. I cannot live with the fact that I was the one who cut your dreams of *your* glorious freedom. You've been dreaming about the place where you are now and beyond, since that first day I met you. And I fell in love knowingly."

"Ma what glory? What dreams? The only thing I want is to be free, that we are free! And do you think I care about my dreams if you are not in there? And besides, I could have never made it up to this point without your unconditional support. And for sure I will not be able to function normally here without you. And I would not go back only to repay all those things you have provided me with for what you call it success, but I would go back because I love you and I want to be with you."

"Stop it, Mojag, please. I can't let you do that. You said it yourself. I was always there to help you in your pursuit, and that is the reason why I cannot be the one standing in your way. And after all, here in *your South*, there is nothing for you. You will only go back to despising all those envious people in this Stone Age you have carefully managed to avoid this entire time. I love you too much to let you do that."

"But you are not listening. It is my own decision that I am making myself. I've made many sacrifices in life before, many right, many wrong. And I really don't want to regret this for the rest of my life if I don't make the right choice in the vitality of this decision. I am fully aware of the consequences but I know it is the right thing to do; it is the only thing that can be done to make this whole thing work!"

"No, you listen! I understand all of that, but as arrogant as it might sound from my side, I refuse to listen to anything that resembles those stupidities you call decision. It is not a solution and I am sure you will realize that one day. If you dare to return, I promise that I will break up with you the moment you pick your bags at the airport."

"Aiyana, what's wrong with you? Are you crazy? What other options are there for us?"

"It seems that our love is not meant to be."

"Don't give me this sarcasm! You think it's so fucking easy for me, being here the loneliest person in the world? The only one hope that I have to live a normal life is the thought of you coming here. I am not quitting on you, so don't poison me with this attitude."

"I don't know Mojag, do something."

"Are you mocking me? I just set out my view on how things will be solved for good, and you rejected it without even giving it a second thought. And you are asking me to do something. It appears that whatever I say or do turns out to be wrong for you. I really cannot understand you. What is it that you want?"

"I'm sure there are other ways that you can make this work. And you know it."

"No, I don't. I wish I knew an easier way. Listen, maybe it will work out just fine. For the time being, until your situation is settled, I will come every weekend to you and we will be together. I have a good salary so it's not a problem. It will be difficult for both of us, but that is at least something so we don't get apart."

"That's your solution? What about the week, it is five days each week. What am I supposed to do when you are gone? I'm sick of not having you for myself."

"Ma please, what should I say? You at least have your family and friends to hang on to."

"Don't get lost in your illusions. You know that I'm not accepting anything less anymore. And besides, you also know that such a development would explode one way or another. One year is a long time."

"Then quit! If it is illegal for you to get transferred in the same company in a different city, I'm sure you have the possibility to fully abandon the firm. I know it's a good position and you are happy with your prospects in there, and it is maybe a little egoistic of me to ask you for it, but I think it's a possibility. And we will live together from my salary, until you find a job. It really seems like a viable option. Don't you think?"

"Well, actually I was thinking of it", she immediately changed her voice; as if she was patiently waiting the whole time that the conversation would eventually lead into that direction. But it was rather strange that she did not bring the subject upon her initiative.

"You were?"

"Yes, I was, but it's too risky for me."

"I guess I understand. I'm sorry to ask you to leave your job. It was selfish indeed", he humbly admitted.

"No, no, I was not referring to the risk of quitting my job."

"Then what is it?" his confusion turning into a blunt uneasiness.

"Well, let me put it this way. If I quit my job, besides leaving everything here, I would be headed into a totally unknown world. And what are the guarantees I have that you wouldn't leave me if it's not going to work out?"

"Listen, can you please cut out the rhetoric and tell me what you really mean? I sense that you are playing with me. And apart from all, why do you even think that it's not going to work out equally nicely?"

"No, no, of course I am not saying it's not going to work. But I am just looking after myself. I mean, God forbid, imagine something goes wrong and I am left there all alone having wasted the most valuable period of my life. I mean, you've been there for almost four years and you at least have your network there. And what would I be left with if you suddenly consider you have made a mistake moving in with me far away from home? Not even a shoulder to cry on! And that is why I think it is the right time to make decisions for our future", she suddenly shifted her tone as if it was a totally different conversation; her conspicuously chilly and arrogant voice implied lack of reasoning.

"First of all, my networks, as you call them, are spread all over, but here. So I am also alone in this serious stake. And besides, we've had these conversations many times before and I never thought that it would not work at any fucking point in time. If I did, I wouldn't have even insisted on it. I know I had some doubts and fears in the beginning, but you also know they are long gone now. And if us, living together far away from everybody doesn't appear serious to you judging by the age we both share, then I really don't know what you are asking me to do!"

"The thing I've always dreamed about since I was small is to become a young mother. And ever since the time I kissed you, I realized that you are to be my prince. And I know that you always feel edgy when I bring out the subject, but I think that it is currently the only way that will ensure our relationship. I'm already growing old. And honestly, I am a bit disappointed that you haven't already acted upon it."

Mojag was momentarily stunned. He seemed to be faced with an ultimatum he could not even think of abiding to, especially not because he was just enjoying the first years of his second decade. And furthermore, she explicitly knew that he could not grant her wish, as obscure as it was at the moment. But still, she simply threw it all there at Mojag. After a speechless motion while he was consolidating his furious mind, he fiercely spoke:

"Aiyana", exclaiming almost hostile, "I really admire your dreams as I admire your courage to ask me that. But can you hear what you are fucking saying?! Growing old? Are you sick with your ideas?! For God's sake, you are only 21! And how can you possibly think that getting married is going to provide you with the damn security you request? You are not buying a washing machine to obtain a warranty, you are in a relationship. And marriages, especially such, which are irrationally rushed into, are the ones most likely to burst shortly after. Above all, you knew my reaction is going to be exactly the way I now described and you still dare to ask me that. I'm not discarding this option right now, because you know I have already discarded it long ago. It is too soon! And why did you start crying again? You knew how it was going to develop even before you asked me that question."

"Yes, but I was always hoping, Mojag. You say you love me, but you cannot make such a *minor* sacrifice. And what difference does it make since we are going to be together anyway. But it seems that you would never be ready for such a step!!!", shouting in vain.

"I don't believe this...I don't fucking believe this! I've been an asshole many times before, but I've never been as ungrateful. And I've never even imagined that you could fill that infamous void. And what's more, it's really funny how you consider your greatest dream to be a minor issue, making it absolutely worthless."

"Great, now my dreams are worthless to you..."

"Please listen to what you are saying, baby", he said as if trying to save this dead-end conversation, "It seems that we both need to cool down. Let's sleep over it and we will talk about it tomorrow. Please."

"NO! I CANNOT WAIT ANY LONGER! It's now or me and you is never going to happen. It is no one's but your decision", she senselessly replied.

"Don't even dare to put all the pressure in the world on me for something that makes no sense! None of us is ready for that, and even if we were, a marriage would certainly not make things easier when you came here. In fact, it could only ruin us because we are too young for that. Marriage is something sacred that has to be done properly, and not because it has to fix something! Let's revert back to the much better options we had prepared."

"I don't have the nerves anymore to hear your viewpoint. I'm still waiting for your decision", she calmly, almost indifferently said.

"Good", he tried once again avoiding the subject, but her planned intention implied otherwise.

"What?" her awkward fury still keeping her from getting calm.

"Ma please, I love you so much without any grain of doubt. We don't need to take such steps to be together. Please think about the…"

"Then show me you love me!"

"It is much easier when you transfer obligations, isn't it? You don't want to feel the pressure and be the one who's saying the ending words, right? Is that it? I really don't understand what you have in your head. After so many years together, you are testing my love this way? And during those many years we have laughed and cried together, there was not even a moment in which I doubted my love towards you. And you know it better than I do. And what you are asking me to do is something I cannot do at any cost. At least not now. I never had such great dreams of getting married as a fucking teenager, but I reasonably thought that you and I would be there at a later, more instinctive time. I can't do that, I'm sorry…"

"Then I guess we are not destined for each other…I guess this is it…"

Those words…they sounded so unbelievably real. Mojag felt as if someone was cutting his intestines.

"No, no, please don't say that. We cannot make it without each other, please don't do it. Don't make me beg, please", he cried.

"I'm sorry Mojag. You left me with no other option. I can't take it anymore. We did frequent symbolic break ups before, but I guess we have encountered the end of our line. I love you."

"I love you too. Don't do this, I'll do anything but that...Please reason yourself..."

"I'm sorry...Goodbye Mojag...Please don't call me...I love you..." her weep growing even more destructive.

Mojag's ear was glued to the phone even minutes after she had stopped following from the other side of the line. He had experienced a lot of events before that were difficult to handle, but this one immediately seized his whole body and mind. He was unaware what was going on inside of him. And he was unsure if the feeling would go away; it seemed as if he would never wake up from the nightmare he got himself stuck into. Nothing seemed to be changing the course of his misery. He felt the coldest breeze in his stomach with that immediate vomiting urge. But he couldn't care less about himself. The words of Aiyana were still ringing across the cells of his affected mind. He was so damn painfully sure that she was gone forever this time.

He closed the phone, his bloodless hands trembling, looked above into the sky, whose sudden clouds were reflecting his awful state of emptiness. His silence scared him even more than usual. He looked at the phone with the utmost life-ironic humble smile on his face, which was unrecognizable even to himself, and smashed the phone onto the cobblestone pathway he had found himself at. Multimillion atoms of that fucking device spread elsewhere in the watchful atmosphere. It only reflected the state of his heart and his soul, torn apart to the base of their ultimate pieces.

The shadow of his reflection grew to unimaginable proportions while his weary silhouette was disturbingly trying to find a way out. The agony was mesmerizing. Nothing was important to him at that moment. And not even Mojag himself knew where he was headed next. He only wanted to escape from everybody, not least from the despair of his own self.

7 RECOLLECTING THE PAST

Past is the ballast of a human's life.

A worn out saying tells us that what we do in life echoes in eternity. But that enlightening phrase forgets to mention that what we do in our past, lives within us the whole time until we turn to dust. Eternity is something that some new kids will judge, but our present is the one that we need to live against. And regardless whether it was a good or a bad experience that had happened at any point before, it is a man's instinctive duty never to permit those past tensions to arise again. Naturally, we are never going to be able to relive or change the past, so why struggle with it? No time machine could encapsulate or reengineer the emotions that we have once experienced. The quicker one learns to instantaneously kill the past as it is happening, the easier it would be to embrace the present in its every precious moment. Sometimes it would seem impossible; most of the time it would be absolutely vital.

Deep Purple once shared their realism that "somewhere there's a place in your heart where the wounds never heal"[22]. It was a song of love. But it could have been a song of life as well. No matter what the wounds are, they will always be there. And you are, willingly or not, obliged to learn how to live with them. But trying to pretend as if they have never happened will only assemble them stronger, spreading all over and swallowing your thoughts like cancer. It is difficult, though necessary to embrace them so you can be at ease with them. And that is why sometimes your history gives you no more than two choices – either stand up to the constant emotional challenge, or drown in the misery of your own projection. And there is no living psychologist that could tell you which of the paths is easier to follow.

* * * * * * * * * * *

This fucked up, evasive concept called hope…

Mojag's world had never been as fragile. The love towards his most valuable half was the only thing that had been giving him strength to endure his aching struggle. And now, when his love was even stronger than ever before, he could not get consciously adapted to the twisted reality that his love was no longer part of his world. In fact, those moments signified the ultimate blow, delivering the imminent collapse of what he had called *his* world, something he sacredly kept even from God Himself. Drained by his agonizing thoughts, he felt all the bits of his heart falling further apart; all those precious moments from the past slipping away right in

---

[22] *Love Conquers All* – Deep Purple, "Slaves and Masters", 1990

front of him. Emotionally, he could not afford losing it for his past was everything he had. His future was meant to be projected upon it. At least that was what he had always believed in. He was sadistically and probably even willingly choking on his own misery. He could not afford to let go. And in spite of the deflated value of his praised history during those undefined moments, it was ever too valuable to let him focus on the much more important present.

What next to be done? How to continue with all those rotten remnants of life? It was already less than a month that Mojag had experienced the sudden conclusion of his love story. He had not noticed that so much time had passed since. He wasn't aware of the total elapsed time as he was counting the seconds only. And he exactly knew the content of every second, as each meant a painful excursion in reliving his dark thoughts. Each second also implied an improvised projection to an irrational strategy in order to cope with the next moment. Above all, his time was virtually absorbed with thoughts of Aiyana. Even though she made an unfair offer to him, more of an ultimatum that she knew could not be fulfilled in her timeframe, he was the one biting his nails down to their bones, accepting a huge burden of blame he righteously didn't deserve. But at the same time, he could not dare to put any blame on her. After all, it was him who for whatever reasons, rejected an "offer" that could have saved them. Even in historical terms, he would probably be regarded as an immoral character that deserves the death penalty. Fuck such history where you have to suffer in order to be remembered!

A lot of times, including many in which he was not under the enlightening effects of a strong alcohol, he would call his now ex-girlfriend and each time she would never pick up the phone. With every call, he was expecting to hear a familiar voice saying just a few words he so much needed. But with every call, he could only hear his abandoned breath striking back in that damned device of hope, making his agony grow deeper and deeper. Mojag knew that even now, Aiyana loved him much more than he was imagining, but it seemed she wanted to forget. What was most tearing him apart was the thought of her contemplating that Mojag was the one not loving her. But he had never loved as much. And it seemed uncertain to him if he ever would again. She was his first love, and he knew nothing besides that, except for a lot of meaningless experiences on the side.

His senses were sharpened to the point where he was even able to spot the sound of the dead leaves detaching from their base. Every noise reminded him of Aiyana; every beat of the usual healing music now meant memories lost. And every occasional phone call he received, reorganized his organs as he was always childishly anticipating her number on the display. It never happened. For Mojag's sake, it was inevitable that he should avoid making a whole science out of his sorrow, but he was already becoming an advanced expert in the field. And how could he not, when none of his friends were in less than a thousand kilometers from him, friends he shared everything with. And without them to seek comfort and accompany him in the purifying moments of the alcohol, he was broken and ferociously tired.

From the day he started working only some months ago, Mojag experienced the misused Germanic words that *Arbeit macht frei*[23] and reaffirmed his beliefs of hard work. Judging by his usual heavy laziness, no one seemed to believe that he actually enjoyed working. But he did. He didn't even mind waking up each day in those early hours of the morning. And it wasn't the money that interested him, in fact he hated money, but he was interested in exploiting his mind and body to serve life's purpose.

As much as he was fighting, it seemed that in many ways, during the time of those never-ending destructive seconds after his world was no longer, the effectiveness of his work increasingly dropped. His brain was too poisoned to focus on relevant issues. Sadly and unexpectedly, not even the tempting smiles of the *Porchellas*[24] at the workplace received any credibility in any of the two mental hemispheres of his brain. Perhaps he wasn't even noticing such moments that he had used to be driven by.

He was avoiding unnecessary contacts with people as he was not in the mood even to talk to himself. Understandably, he had that vacant expression in his eyes and silence in his mind for people he barely knew, since they meant nothing to him. The whole surrounding meant nothing to him, the people only sudden passengers running separate and obviously happier lives. Mojag always had respect even for people he had never met, or even unimportant ones, and therefore, arrogance was not the reason of his estrangement and sudden disgust of talking to people. He was not even afraid that someone could notice his weakness. He simply seemed afraid of people. He

---

[23] Work liberates

[24] A female pig, referring to "dirty" girls

perceived all of them as threats, as if working against him to prevent an even moderate smile to be painted on his face. His paranoid thoughts made him believe that everybody was looking strangely at him, although none of them probably noticed his existence. He carefully guarded himself using the Chinese walls of his shadow. And logically, in the end, his crushed will marked out the power of communication. He never felt as indifferent towards life. He even stopped fighting his mindless insomnia. It was only his dreadful fear derived from many things, inexistent sense of belonging in particular, that kept him going. It kept him going in an unknown direction, but it was much more than what he could possibly ask for at that moment.

Regardless of the technical calendar, every other day was the same blue Sunday to Mojag, "cause there is something in a Sunday that makes a body feel alone."[25] Any time he was not bound to stay at work, he was constantly wandering through the beauties of the city parks. And all those times he would sit on an abandoned bench at some forgotten corner of the nature, only to partially find shelter from other people, if not from himself. While there, sitting and thinking on that wooden partner, he was constantly trying to reach people his phone had memorized a long time ago. They were not quite friends, but merely acquaintances from the old days with which he occasionally had common, meaningless talks. He didn't necessary enjoy their gossipy company; he was only trying to exhaust all

---

[25] *Sunday Mornin' Comin' Down* – Johnny Cash, Transcription)

means that could possibly divert his thoughts into other directions. But each time he asked, naturally, they were all busy, having already plans that he was not part of. They were all saying: "Thanks for calling, but we could meet some other day. I'm having exams...I'm really busy these days. I'm working on a project. I'm flying on a business trip tonight. I'm sick. I'm out of town. I'm with my girl. I'm fucking my lover". Most likely, they were all valid and honest excuses, but then again, Mojag prescribed all of their justified selfish behavior to a greater conspiracy against himself. At that instance, they were all part of a *Truman Show*. The only difference was that he did not have the ideas and the tools to fight back, for it was Mojag's self-confidence that practically and completely died out. He was only a poor, anonymous spectacle, watching all those people sharing someone by their side, eating popcorns in the cinema, kissing under the linden trees, playing guitar to their loved ones, sharing a last beer with a good friend. Mojag's friend was the grass, the trees, the music and the inevitable wind which was undoubtedly his best and most reliable companion, as Mojag always followed its rebellious manner. And the wind always tried telling him to stay out of the pressures of the city and go to the river where he would be able to think without any obstructions caused by delusional lives of other people. His friend the wind, always brought him safely to the river bank where even the ducks were enjoying a silent fuck, and mosquitoes and various other annoying insects were harassing without disturbance.

The river. Not any river, but *this* one. That particular waterway was an important, if not an essential element to many of the composed songs and written texts of the

South. To many distinguished people of the self-proclaimed Land of Peasants, it was clearly an inspiration to a superior, romantic cause. Mojag didn't notice, but it was apparent that that particular, healing piece of nature undoubtedly became part of his life, unconsciously, yet strongly embraced by his romantic perceptions of life. From the very first days he left his home, smoking a confusing January cigarette with his mother somewhere in the midst of the then frozen river, that stream was a friend that not even once failed to understand Mojag's reserved self. Besides, the whole surrounding always provided him with an illusionary, but nevertheless, satisfactory peace of mind.

Strolling towards that special place of his, he walked past people at the pot-smoking corner and kept on moving to a peaceful green prairie in the middle of the river bank, and under the bridge. He usually preferred to go there because it was a place that offered a view of both sides of the stream, and at the same time, it provided a confined shelter from accidental passengers.

Mojag emptied his pockets of cigarettes and phones to manage some comfort. He purposely fell down, feeling the grass beneath him as he could fully stretch his physique and open up his weary mind. He always feared opening up certain disturbing concepts of his that were carefully locked up in many different chambers of his brain, but he had no choice given that ever since the past couple of weeks that he had lost track of, the locks were broken, and the single key master was dead. He had no other option but to lie back and bear vast memories of his life that were no longer part of his existence.

Unaware of the current positioning of his body, Mojag's structure was perfectly placed on the dehydrated grass, in large part resembling *a Vetruvian Man*. His position showed the perfect balance of a God's creation, but his mind was completely out of sync. The day was increasingly hot but he didn't care to take out the irritating sweat in the base of his balls. He even allowed disoriented insects to play hide and seek throughout all pores of his drained body. And the day was still increasingly hot, but the mirages of his past were provoked by nothing short of his succumbed state of consciousness. Everybody was there next to him, his best childhood friends and many other important people, his former roommate, his *former* girlfriend. He felt safe, regardless that none of them seemed to notice Mojag's presence. He started remembering certain moments, reconstructing each valued character only to make sure that those dear people are not only part of his experimental mind's eye. The trickery momentum reached a predictable peak when he started reliving a meaningful piece of his *Southern* past as it came flashing right between his eyes. In fact, it looked precisely reminiscent of something he had tasted before, but this time it looked more like an observation from a bridgeless distance. Everybody was present at the soothing episode.

Mojag could distinguish a familiar pool beside a fantastic house squared in a vast and well designed, *pueblo* garden. Some of the gathered were already abusing the calmness of the pool's water; others were too busy opening up endless bottles of Mojag's favorite beer. In the glimpse of the gathering of his *Southern* friends, the first one he took notice of, was expectedly

Shilah[26], his pale presence far too real to be discarded as an illusion.

Shilah was one of the purest people ever born. Too many times he acted over-realistic and super conscious towards people, and maybe that was the reason why he was practically always stressed. Sometimes he took life too seriously with respect to his age. In all cases, he was Mojag's best of friends, back-to-back their whole life dating back as early as their innocent days of childhood when they were eerily disrupting the fragile harmony of a *Southern* neighborhood. Even with a certain objective, but temporary halts in their life-long companionship, Mojag always considered him to be his best friend, as their similarity and dedicated connection guaranteed that they would be there for each other and unconditionally offer a helping hand when things get rusty.

And that was perhaps the reason why Shilah was the first to appear in Mojag's presence, while he was lying against the green grass. In that delirious moment, Mojag cared for somebody to understand his polarized brain, and not to listen to inexperienced advices. And many times Shilah had understood him, regardless that he could not be momentarily heard.

Many other friends from his old party from the *South* started appearing as they too wanted to break the single color of Mojag's loneliness. Mojag lovingly respected them all. Shilah's brother came, Chatan[27]; he historically dreamt of a lot of money and even bigger

---

[26] Native American male name of Navajo origin. Its meaning is *BROTHER.*

[27] Native American male name of Sioux origin. Its meaning is *HAWK.*

businesses; or at least that was what everybody perceived. Chatan was the usual manager of whatever was taking place. Then there was Istaqa[28], one of the laziest people ever born, with objective prospects to make a decent boss out of himself. But he was intentionally stubborn and often inexcusably discouraged to living, purposely killing the enthusiasm of his youth. Kusinut[29] and Ohcumgache[30] were the other parts of the once bigger group, both somewhat scared to experience change, though well fitted within the mechanism of the group. Mojag had huge respect for Kusinut because Kusinut never felt underrated when he was working several jobs that many would snobbishly cast off as low to their underrated morale. Ohcumgache was someone who often thought that nothing else existed apart from the blinding, aged relationship with his assertive girlfriend.

With the old friends there, with different intensity, and with different characteristics, Mojag felt as if the whole dear bunch was right there to divert his mind from the thoughts that ruled the dark chemistry of his mind. They were so freely enjoying the state of nature in which they had found themselves in. Their formation seemed much too familiar.

"Wait. I know what's going on. *They are making the usual barbecue fest. And without me?*"

---

[28] Native American male name of Hopi origin. Its meaning is *COYOTE*.

[29] Native American male name of Yakima origin. Its meaning is *HORSELESS*.

[30] Native American male name of Cheyenne origin. Its meaning is *LITTLE WOLF*.

"MOTHERFUCKERS!" Mojag jealously exclaimed, spicing it up with a dose of friendly irony. – "No, no...Wait, *there's me, or at least some kind of a dim version of myself, as if I had already happened. Ma, I knew they would never leave me out.*"

Mojag was indeed present in the arrangements of the setting, but it seemed as though no one could notice his existence. Nevertheless, he was happy watching his dear friends having that great time they always had; a great time *he* had always had with them. But this time it was an awkward rewind of a sacred moment with his friends. And even though he wasn't sure of his absence, he still did find some fake comfort.

But it was unusually strange that Aiyana was among them, for the group's girlfriends tried avoiding their presence as their breathing was always forgotten after the daring effect of friends and alcohol. But then again, many years ago, the first time when Aiyana was being introduced to the acceptance of the council of Mojag's friends, he took her to that very same place, and possibly at that very same barbecue. And she was there *now* smiling at Mojag as he was waving to her to show his passion for her lips. He ran up to her, but she still couldn't notice his charisma. Alas, he forgot he wasn't there, at least not physically. He enjoyed feeling her presence, but the initial and now former comfort of his friends turned into uneasiness as he finally admitted his absence. He became furious, but didn't have any strength left in his body to act accordingly.

Along with the inevitable hostility of his stars, Mojag could not stop fighting his pessimism. He would have done anything for Aiyana's recognition, even if it were to be discouraging, as he was frantically pleading for anything but disregard.

"Aiyana, AIYANA...." – she could never hear his outcry.

The storming, unexpected rain was already running full speed for the past ten minutes, but Mojag's senses were too occupied to remind him that his clothes were totally and thoroughly dripping due to the pouring shower. Now Mojag could not distinguish his tears with the water of the sky as he was painted blue. As nature's eruption grew ever more powerful, so Mojag's illusions irreversibly drowned.

So many friends, so many people he loved, so many people that loved him. And they were all so real and all so damn far away. That painful twist of reality was making Mojag feel so miserably abandoned by everybody. And unlike *Sisyphus*, he had neither the strength nor the will to push his stone further as his justified misconception concluded there was nothing left worth enduring for.

8 ALL AND ANY DECISIONS ARE WRONG

A worn out saying tells us that what we do in life echoes in eternity. But what we miss out in life goes straight into eternal damnation deeply carved within the complex pipeline of human cells. For it is much more justified and moral to regret about obsessions that we have done, rather than to regret about obsessions that we have never tried, obsessions we have ungratefully missed out. Courageous decisions failed to be made will always haunt every bit of the human being. The fear of trying is mostly poisoned by obnoxious reasons for which we tend to find inexistent excuses later in our lives, but none of the mediocre defenses could ever make up for the lost opportunities.

One British Somerset Mom once said: "When old, we regret about the sins missed out in our youth". Failure to dig out courage to act when the opportunity has presented itself will inevitably boomerang back as the highest remorse that a man can handle. A decision is never easy, it never has been. In fact, it has always been a historical evidence for even in the most reasonable decisions we have to give up parts of ourselves regardless what we gain in the process. But don't we nevertheless give up many beautiful things in the process called life, simply because of Mr. Einstein's illegitimate and daunting fourth dimension?

* * * * * * * * * * *

Hi, I'm Mojag and I am lost. I am lost in my quest of finding my place in the hierarchical oxymoron of emotions and modernity. In fact, I am nowhere to be found.

As far as what the official papers say, my story dates back some years ago, but what do those fucking officials know about me and my chronicles or whatever they call them these days? Wait, what's that annoying sound? ...Oh, it's just that same truck outside going in perpetual reverse. They always fucking beep. Just imagine the driver; he must have gone crazy a long time ago...And so? Fuck the driver, I was saying something different. It might have been some meaningful frustrations explicitly portrayed. But fuck that too; I guess I forgot what I was saying. I have so many things in my head that I am able to afford the privilege of forgetting some. But why not forget them all? Don't make me laugh. Nothing can ever be forgotten. But at least something has to be left out.

Mojag was sitting in the confinement of his room, unsuccessfully trying to ease his mind by emptying its insides. Floating beneath the pillows of the dirty couch, he was anxiously watching the dim shadows on the walls appearing so very real. They didn't frighten him; he was simply trying to distinguish their occurrences, whether they were genuine originals or actual things. But now, unlike previous times, he could not possibly determine the meaning and the origin of the illusionary silhouettes occupying the cigarette stained walls. It had already been almost half a decade since he managed to escape the obscurities of the grotto, and still, he could not put *his* pieces together. It was *Plato's cave* all over again, as if he had never walked out of there in the first place.

Shortly after, the apartment phone started ringing. Mojag couldn't care less. He wasn't motivated to hear any voice as he knew none of them would understand him. Indifferent towards the voluntary immobilization of his limbs, he wasn't even enthusiastic to check whether the call was really worth answering.

But the phone only broke the spell of Mojag's numbness. He started reaffirming the fact that he wasn't composed of broken thoughts only, but of thin flesh too. Regardless, he was all too lifeless to embrace God's most sacred gift – life itself – and to employ in it as an active participant, not the distant observer he had become.

Many times before, life had brought him to many crossroads that determined either his faith or the will of his own self. And all those times, he consciously believed in all his decisions no matter how difficult they insisted to be. But now, drowning in *a* dirt of his reality, at both ends of the crossroad, there was a dark abyss with an unpredictable end. Besides, he lost all he believed in, including the strong belief he always had in the reasoning of his own heart. In fact, now it seemed he was the last person he could have faith in. But he was the only choice he was left with. His most obvious inefficiencies were his strong, naive emotions, as he immediately attached to people he knew, to past moments of his life that didn't let him leave, moments of his life that didn't let him stay. Mathematically, it was all too simple. He had to choose whether he would go back to his home, to his warm *South*, or whether he would stay pursuing the unknown, adventurous realms of the outer world. Mojag never liked mathematics as it was simply overrated; it was far too easy compared to the complexities that life occasionally implied.

For the past five storming years, Mojag lived a matrix of two parallel worlds at the same time. And surprisingly enough, he had managed to hold on to both worlds enjoying all benefits of both lives. Perhaps he was successful because he could not possibly realize at the time that he was emotionally falling into the den of both worlds. He wasn't aware that the day would come when one of them would be torn apart to give way to the other to survive. Or at least, he never wanted to think about those things, cowardly discarding them as soon as they would start bypassing the permission to penetrate.

At the moment, he lost grip of both his worlds, one representing the innocent moments of the past and the warmth of a house that was always his shelter, a house in which he could always hide away; the other embodying potential freedom with an uncertain future, with both emotional and financial independence, in distant and foreign lands. Unlike previously, he completely lost all sense of belonging. His momentarily innate fear provided him with no helping hand involving the reasons to choose either world. He lost the girl that it seemed he would always love in many ways; he started believing that she was the one holding both his worlds together. She was the closest to heaven that Mojag would ever be. When she was not there, he was not anywhere. But it was quite awkward as it seemed that it was much more than the unexpected loss of his girl. His situation was a crossroad that would shape his life and his own guiding principles. But at the moment, he wasn't trying to mark a path; he was merely trying to gather possible indicators that would put him in any simple category that would tell him where he belonged after all those years.

* * * * * * * * * * *

The summer was still hitting hard at the buildings of the big city as its perfectionist structure had probably rules even for the direction of the sun. It was a bit awkward as the abnormal sun rays didn't overlook Mojag's building, since it usually couldn't help taming the inner cold that was destroying Mojag's body and soul.

It was Saturday. The early hum on his phone woke him up. And unlike his usual heated response when somebody would disturb his sleep on a weekend's morning after a lonely drinking session, Mojag immediately rose up in an embarrassed panic.

"FUCK! I overslept", he worryingly exclaimed, his gaze directed towards the colorful display on the phone. The letters revealed the name of Mojag's lifelong friend, in fact his best – Shilah – who was anxiously waiting for a releasing morning coffee. It had never happened before that some of Mojag's old friends visited him in the far away city. That Saturday morning marked a sweet and a much needed precedent.

Shilah came all the way from the *South* in a painful, daylong journey in a dirty bus, taking the chance to visiting his friend. In fact, he had already arrived since it was approaching 9.15 that Saturday morning. He had previously told Mojag to meet him around 8 o'clock after he had taken a shower at the hotel at the other end of the city. And while the phone kept on ringing intensely, Mojag shook his voice trying to sound as if he was already fully awake, and immediately ran out to the balcony so that the sound of the passing cars could eventually back up his comforting lie that he was already on his way.

"I'm on my..." Mojag immediately got interrupted by the friendly curses from the other side of the line.

"You fucking idiot, I came all the way here to meet you, I haven't slept for 24 hours in that disgusting bus and I'm still waiting for that coffee with you. You are still sleeping, aren't you? I know the way you breathe", Shilah correctly noted, readily prepared for the usual response.

"No, no, I'm on my way, but the traffic is jammed, and I'm trying to find that hotel of yours. I'll be there very soon. Hang on" he continued with an unwanted irony. He knew his friend was aware of Mojag's laziness and complete lack of organization.

"Ma! Do I have a choice but to wait?"

"I guess not my friend...Uf, I'm so fucking glad that you are here!!!"

"Spare me. I'll kill you when you get here", Shilah ended the expensive conversation in that usual friendly humor of the *South* that among many other *pueblo* warmth, the unworthy aristocrats will never understand.

Mojag felt the heat under his feet even more, knowing he would be even later than his usual, expected delay. He put on the topmost clothes of the closest pile that was thrown around the whole apartment. With the toilet still smoking from the morning cigarette, Mojag rushed to the streets with strong faith in the public transport. The transportation served so well to the critical point where it was up to

Mojag's feet to make up for the missed time. But how do they say: "Whoever doesn't have it in his head has it in his feet". *Don't pay attention to that phrase; it's just a bad joke I remember my parents used to tell me when I was younger.*

At last he managed to find his way to the hotel he was told to arrive at. The lobby had a strange setting, but not odd enough to gather Mojag's attention. He was looking for a best friend of his.

Walking towards the insides of the hotel, he noticed a familiar face, although with extreme shades of pale, even more noticeable than Shilah's usual lack of skin melanin. Without any doubt, it was Shilah, evidently tired from the trip, but readily prepared to roam the streets of the interesting city. Mojag firmly knew that this was not only one of those usual illusions, but a reality that was unselfishly happening. It was so amazingly real, that when he saw Shilah, Mojag felt as happy as if his friend was sent by God Himself. They embraced themselves in that usual *Southern* greeting, kissing three times in the cheek. Yes, in some cultures of Mojag's native region, even males kissed each other on in the cheek. It was that *Southern* comfort that simply expressed the closeness of two friends in a traditional way, dating back many years in history.

"Shilah, you are here. I still can't get used to it. But it feels very good, so very safe", Mojag even forgot his usual lame excuses of being late.

"I haven't slept for 24 hours. I am panicking for a coffee...I'm so glad as well to be here so we can finally drink that coffee together and you show me how you have spent all those years here."

Shilah's words seemed not to get through to Mojag as he was upgrading his sinful lust for women.

"Look at the beautifully shaped ass there on that dirty girl. She must be the receptionist..."

"Hello..." Shilah started impatiently waving so as to disturb Mojag's passion. "Leave those things for the night. Coffee now."

"Coffee..." Mojag said, getting away from the momentary sensation of thoughts, "coffee, ah, yes, that's exactly what I intended to do. Leave your passport somewhere safe and let's get out of here."

It was the first time ever that Shilah stepped into the civilized city, but he was too tired for sporadic sightseeing and Mojag was as lazy. A perfect situation. And how could it have been otherwise when two closest friends get together after a longer period without their usual everyday coffee and occasionally attempted foursomes? They constantly knew what was generally happening in their lives, as they had never lost contact, but it was so different when they were talking on a same table, so much better, each looking directly at the instant, revealing emotions of the other. And it was quite awkward, Mojag noticed, as he felt himself being the host. Technically, he was the host indeed, feeling more that this distant city had become his home those past years he had enjoyed its benefits.

In the midst of an awful lot of crowd of happy families and curious tourists, Mojag guided the way to the heart of the city. He was taking his friend to the coffee shop that he had spent all his university days in, enjoying a chit-chat with many of his friends at the time, while trying to spot a nice view of a woman's figure. The setting of the city's center was marked by two streets, each designed in a familiar setting, although placed in opposite directions. Both streets were enjoying large admirations among the passing creatures, however, only one of the streets offered a true inspiration to the soul. The most probable reason why, was because it lacked diminishing shopping malls, freeing up the street of unnecessary people, and giving way for absolute peace of mind. Even though the road was fairly frequent with foreign visitors and tourists at all times of the year, it was a place where all speed of the modern world was coming to an inevitable halt. The air too was filled with signs of peace and a sense of safeness. You could even feel a momentary lapse of being the king of the world when walking on top of the street's old cobbled stone. For Mojag, the magic of that particular street somewhat meant a source of life, in all the pathetic ways that his current life chapter accompanied. In reality and in common sense it could not have been such a thing. It was merely another illusion of Mojag, as many times his illusions had proven to be so abstractly necessary to get in touch with reality and survive the gnarled branches of a tricky human conscious.

But there was indeed something fulfilling in that street as Shilah too commented on the unusual calmness that a city offered. By that time, Mojag finished leading the way to the long praised coffee, as they found themselves in front of the sunny terrace of the ever-busy coffee shop. As the usual state of affairs implied, they had to wait for a place.

The coffee shop had arguably the worst setting it could offer. Different tables were too close to each other, which deprived any sense of privacy among talkers. The red color on the unnecessary umbrellas encapsulated certain resemblance of a summer *bordel*, and not of a peaceful place to enjoy the moment. Above all, most of the time the service was so very bad that none of the staff deserved extra tip. It was occurring that even the most constant guests waited forever to order. And the waitresses unquestionably had very little sex in the course of the year, as they were all too nervous and unfriendly. They only smiled occasionally, most probably after a scarce night when they had shared their lusty capabilities. Having all those deficiencies in mind, Mojag never missed a day out without having his coffee at the place whose design repelled him. The objectivity of the bad setting quickly faded away since the coffee shop was placed on *the street*. That was the main reason why Mojag hardly ever noticed anything else besides the usual good company and an occasional flirty look in some of the beautiful women's eyes of the abundant meat market.

Shilah already lost his patience earlier that day so he didn't mind waiting couple of more moments for the coffee that followed.

After couple of minutes tracking the most potent customers to leave, Mojag said:

"They are paying. It's a good place. Let's move"

"I'm already there", Shilah replied as he started walking to the now free table next to the transparent glass that marked the shop's borders, his blonde hair shining even more under the sun.

They finally managed to get seated. All seemed easier now, and it was immediately far manageable to think straight.

"So, what do you think? Was it worth it that I dragged you all the way here?" Mojag carefully asked.

"I had no doubts in you, having in mind that you are specialized in enjoying a coffee. Everything has to be perfect when you have your ritual of drinking that adrenaline stimulant.... Uh, I feel so tired, and the sun is killing me."

"Don't worry. Now we have a coffee, but we also have to drink some welcoming *grappa* so to make cheers for your arrival. I feel your disgust now for an early morning's alcohol, but you know the rules. I already ordered."

"Good! That's exactly what I wanted to hear, for I was afraid that you have already forgotten how it goes", replied Shilah with a decent doze of irony.

"Fucking dick, never. How could I forget all those things that I will always stand for?"

"I know, I know, don't get upset, just testing you", smiled Shilah.

"It's coming. A coffee and the inevitable complement of the fermented grapes", Mojag victoriously, even poetically exclaimed. – "Thanks", he turned to the waitress as she was leaving the goods.

"They are surely not stingy on the *grappa*", Shilah ambiguously commented on the big portion he just received.

"Ok, Shilah. Welcome here and cheers in good health!"

"Thanks. I'm glad I found you. Cheers!"

The ringing sound of glasses in their hands, given out by the appropriate contact between them, reflected the routine that these two friends enjoyed all times they gathered together.

"So, tell me, what's going on down in the old neighborhood? Anything new? Do you still go out as before? What about the others? I don't know what particulars to ask, so find a beginning and start talking", Mojag interrupted Shilah's peculiar, bitter face created by the animosities of the strong alcohol.

"You already know the story. Nothing is changing. The old bunch we once were is kind of falling apart. Each of the others is changing too fast in a different way, going in strange directions. Sometimes I feel they are taking life inappropriately. Or it is maybe I who has a different perception. In any case, we don't hang out the way we used to. But overall it is ok. The only danger is that the *South* is full of new girls. And the only problem is that most of them going out are below the legal age, even though they rush to appear at least five years older. You know how it goes; when you start pushing, they are too inexperienced to stay."

"Exactly. Here it is quite different. It is the older women that take your clothes off before you even start wandering what the fuck is going on. But I surely don't complain, and you get a free lecture on the latest *Kama sutra* moves. But I am very much unprovoked these past months, my friend. I feel a bit lifeless. I don't know if I have told you, but I broke up with Aiyana almost three months ago", Mojag couldn't make it without immediately bringing his worries out.

"No! Really? But why? You were together for what, five, six years? I got so used to both of you as a couple that I thought you were already naming your unborn children. What happened?"

"I'm sure she already had names for our unborn kids, but I guess she made the list too soon. But honestly, I'm not quite sure why she broke up with me. And I really behaved and cared for all my actions towards her. I guess we had different perceptions of life. For some reason, she wanted to be older than she was", Mojag wanted to explain, but he tried to avoid talking about his bitter feelings.

"I'm not sure I can follow what you're saying, but I'm very sorry, man. How did you take it?"

"Well, I guess I'm still 'taking' it. I guess I feel better now, but it is healthier that you didn't see me those days when I still couldn't believe that she's gone and no one was here to listen. It's ok...Forget it, tell me something about what you are doing", Mojag said, trying to change the subject that was causing him agonizing uneasiness to talk, even though he lusted to share his thoughts with his friend.

Shilah understood Mojag's pain and unwillingness to talk about his obvious shaken state of reasoning. He looked at Mojag, only to make sure that he was not mistaken and then switched away, talking about many funny stories from the *Southern* district. Lots of stories went on, with Shilah vividly bringing each of them to the knowledge of Mojag. Mojag seemed to be only physically present. The mere mention of Aiyana, and a best friend who knew most of their history, gave him all but a decent peace of mind.

"Lads...lads!!", a familiar voice interrupted Mojag's unintentional absence in the midst of the surely relaxing conversation of his friend. A recognizable figure, almost tall, with a dark hair, appeared out of nowhere, directing its way towards the two of them. Mojag respectfully stood up, greeting the man and firmly shaking his hand.

"Good morning, *Uncle* Inteus[31]. How are you doing? This is Shilah; I think you met him at my sister's wedding this spring."

---

[31] Native American male name of Algonquin origin. Its meaning is *HAS NO SHAME*.

"Hello. Yes, I remember him, we had couple of drinks together", Inteus responded returning the greeting and shaking Shilah's hand.

"Please, have a sit", Mojag asked.

"Thanks, I will. I still have another half an hour until I have to meet my wife", Uncle Inteus eerily got seated in the chair, opening up the aluminum bar he brought and taking out one of his fine, Cuban cigars out of it.

Uncle Inteus was in fact no uncle of Mojag's; they were not even related. He was a good friend of Mojag's father as their friendly relationship grew out of their mutual work experience. The epithet "uncle" was merely a respectful way to refer to an older person; at least that was the *Southerner's* mentality. But Mojag's respect towards that man grew not only out of traditions. He respected Inteus because he was a very smart person, and one who helped him so many times in the course of many previous crises. Inteus was a very interesting character indeed, having lived in the big city with his family for a longer period of time. His personality embedded a finest sense of humor as well as a metaphysical understanding of life. Mojag remembered the first time he and his mother arrived in the new world. Both were so lost, and the constant coldness of that early January morning was stretching their nerves in an unpleasant way. It was no other than Inteus that came there to pick them up and guide them through the modernized systems of the developed world. In fact, for a large part in those past five years since, Inteus was a true guide for Mojag, directing him in healthy and reasonable ways in many aspects of life. His philosophies were those of a man who had experienced life with all its difficulties, and that was perhaps one of the reasons why they were always so enlightening.

Any time he would sit with Mojag and his friends, Inteus never failed to comment valuable jokes with such huge content in the pile of words and expressions. Now as well, sitting there with Mojag and Shilah, he didn't omit sharing his wisdom in a funny, but meaningful way.

"So, where are the hot chicks? You both look too pale. You have to have a backup refreshment", Inteus started, lighting his cigar.

"They are too tired from the night", Shilah replied with a stupid anecdote.

"That's good, because there are days that come at one point, when you are the ones tired from them, and those days can be quite pride depriving. Do you know the only two times that a man blushes, when with a woman? The first one is when he cannot do it for the second time; the second time when he cannot do it even the first time", Inteus started again, followed by laughter from his focused peers.

Inteus engaged in a boring conversation with Shilah pointing out the benefits of certain companies over others. Mojag was dully listening with his eyes only, as he despised the inhumanity that businesses propagated. Only one thing that came out of the conversation would stay in Mojag's mind, forever guiding him to his unbreakable lust for freedom. It was still business related, but could as well be applied as a general rule. And it was Inteus again:

"There are only two ways in life. The first road is that you forever remain an insignificant screw in a system that someone else had already created, and that someone had already imposed the rules that you have no other choice but to blindly follow. The second way is that you make a system of your own, be your own commander and let others do the petty work, while you are getting a blowjob and smoking cigars in the Caribbean."

I still have to create my own system. Or destroy the current.

"In order to achieve that, you have to understand that life means a constant battle. And since understanding is never enough, you have to start acting as if being in a constant battle. Let me tell you a simple analogy", Inteus seemingly carried away with his lecture on life.

"Wow, this man never stops admiring me. He is an interesting genius" Mojag sincerely thought, but said nothing, waiting for the story to continue.

"The analogy is this, and I always abide to it", Inteus continued after taking a bigger sip of his coffee. "I always imagine myself being in the middle of the ocean. I have no freaking idea where the coast is, or where I am headed to. I only know that I have to keep swimming and stay on the surface if I want to survive. And that is what I do, no matter how difficult it is, or how exhausted I am. I see people drowning beneath me, I help some, I cannot help others, but essential is that I fight. I don't stop fighting and that is the only way to keep up with myself and with the deep, unpredictable waters of the ocean."

"Uncle Inteus, that seems a bit harsh and a lot more difficult, but you are so absolutely right", said Shilah.

"I owe you many thanks, Uncle Inteus", Mojag switched in. "These philosophies are too good, but very scarce to be heard anywhere else. Not so many people seem to understand it."

"I think you wouldn't be mistaken too if you embrace such a stance", Inteus parentally replied.

"Do you want to drink something else, Uncle Inteus? It's on me as I'm officially deprived of the former excuse of being a poor student", Mojag politely asked.

"No, thanks, I really have to go. If I don't go now, my credit card will be lighter since you know how women feel strong when they have other people's money at the shop's counter", he smiled and started leaving.

"Good. Lads, thanks for the time. And remember one other thing. Apart from, God forbid, happenings that cannot be mend, there are no obstacles in life. They are only obstacles chained in our minds. You can do all those things that you might consider ludicrous, or impossible, now. BORBA[32], lads!"

"Thanks, uncle Inteus, for everything. Send many greetings to your family. Bye", Mojag replied.

"It's been a pleasure. Goodbye", Shilah concluded.

* * * * * * * * * * *

After the much needed nap Shilah had to obey to, Mojag showed him the insides of his rented apartment, here and there revealing sweet portions of sins that have occurred there. The tour of the apartment was brief, and possibly uninteresting. That was why they skipped the details and went on to explore the city lights, which revealed the roads of the night in the known districts. Mojag wanted to show his friend the

---

[32] Battle

places, compulsory in the days when he was still a careless student. The beginning station of the night was obvious. It was that very same place where he celebrated his latest birthday with his colleagues, and Aiyana, his most precious and then current girlfriend.

The one empty table was always there waiting for him. They got themselves seated on the upper floor, to the right of the wooden staircases.

"Shilah, this is the place that consumed most of my liver's capabilities in the past years. In sickness and in health, it has always been there for me", Mojag expressed his odd pride.

Knowing no other place in the big city that he could compare it to the one he was in, Shilah sincerely commented:

"It feels very good here, very relaxed. Good choice!"

The place was some sort of a beer pub; they had the machinery there to make their own beer, a fine domestic taste. It was a beer pub, but certainly not a hole. Its interior was virtually made completely out of wood, which saved that embedded odor of cigarette smoke and the stench of the beer's fermentation process. But regardless how the place looked like, Mojag never paid too much attention to the physical structure of a place he liked to have a beer in. The setting of the current pub was decent, but it could have as well been a shithole or redundantly pompous. Mojag cared only to feel comfortable when he enjoyed his beer and he was rarely concerned to be at a better place only because it offered a fake prestige.

"Hi. One pitcher of beer and two glasses, please", asked Mojag, referring to the beautiful blonde waitress. She smiled, attempting a fake flirt and went on to place the order.

"Ay, she's hot!", Shilah passionately noted.

"They're all hot here. I don't know this one, she must be new. Or it's me, since it was a long time that I wasn't here. But for a new girl, she must be quite experienced or she must have fallen in love with you since she's already bringing the nectar", Mojag said in happy amazement as he was looking the nice working figure coming towards their table.

"Thanks! I never had such a fast service here", Shilah told the waitress even though it was the first time he set foot in the beer place.

"You're welcome", she said with an instinctive, if not mechanical smile and walked away to serve the rest.

"Damn cock teaser!", Mojag's frequently said remark followed.

"Don't ruin the moment, man."

"Exactly. Look at the sweaty beer. It's so cold, so incredibly tempting. Let's take it out of the loose chains of the pitcher", Mojag said pouring beer in both glasses. "Here you go", he continued. "Cheers! Let us live until we die!"

"You can't be wrong. Let us live until we die!"

The close friends engaged in usual conversations – friends, girls, beer. Such topics were to Mojag always the most favorite and easiest to communicate. He always had something to reflect upon in those beautiful areas. And they had already passed their tenth glass each, but Mojag was still unusually silent. He talked, but not as much as Shilah was used to. Shilah didn't mind, but something was simply not right.

"Dude, are you ok?" he asked.

"Sure, everything is perfect. Why?" Mojag tried to defend himself, as if he already had a prepared response, unsuccessfully hiding his emotions.

"No, you are not all right. This is the first time I visit you and the whole day I feel you so distant. Sorry, but I had to say it."

"No, I am sorry that you felt that way, I really am. Especially because I am unable to show you the happiness I enjoy that you came all the way to visit me here. It's just a strange period I'm going through."

"Well I could imagine. Five, six years is not a short period. Even if you have this glass sitting in front of you for such a period, it would be difficult many days after it's not there anymore. I'm sorry if it seems an example too simple, but I can imagine that it's still not easy for you after you broke up with Aiyana."

"I know, I know. But I don't know what to tell you. I feel I'm becoming much more different than I used to be. I started being unresponsive to life's challenges. Nothing seems important anymore. I guess it's not only Aiyana; in fact, I am sure it's not only her that is the only cause of my stateless self. It is many other things too that make it so difficult. But it's fine; I'm used not talking to anybody about this. I don't want to bother you with my shit", Mojag still ambiguous whether he should continue talking any further.

"Dude, fuck off, I'm not anybody. I'm your friend. You don't bother me, you fucking idiot. Don't piss me off."

"Pour me another one. I hope the alcohol will make me start faster as you would wait forever if you rely solely on me to initiate a talk about pathetic way of my own personal origin. Shilah, I really don't know how I can explain what I'm going through right now. I feel as if I'm becoming a shadow that has never existed. All my senses started dying when my *amigos* from my university days spread all over the world and nobody remained here. Apart from certain people, there is barely anyone I still know in this city. And undoubtedly, there are rare people that still know me here. It seems that everyone I know goes away in the end."

"Come on, Mojag, try bringing in some sense. I'm sure it's not as fatalistic as you have just philosophically put it. You must have *some* friends."

"Ma, I have all my senses ready, and I have so many friends, including you as one at the top of the list, but it is so difficult to talk to someone these days. And those friends I have here would probably never understand, never even try to understand. And who would listen to someone else's misery?"

"But ok, it's only a period. You're gonna make new friends. What's the problem?"

"That's not the problem. As I already told you, being without friends for life all of a sudden as opposed to millions before by my side, was already the start."

"The next chapter was Aiyana, right?"

"Of course you're right. She was my one true love and my only hope that I will forget other things that made me feel miserable, like the fucking, unbeaten nostalgia towards a life that I have chosen to quit long time ago. And the relationship would have become too serious if she had moved in here with me as was planned. But despite that, I still made a decision that she comes here so we'd start living together. But it seems that same moment I took my decision firmly, it was all gone. She wanted something more, something too rushed."

"She wanted you to get married?!" Shilah asked as if in a paparazzi shock.

"Doesn't matter."

"Sorry. But maybe there are still ways that you end up together after all."

"I'm hoping for that ever since, I cannot deny that I haven't stopped loving her. In fact, I love her even more than before, if that is possible. But she doesn't even pick up the fucking phone when I call her on occasions!" Mojag vividly aroused.

Shilah stopped for a moment, having nothing to say to calm his friend down.

"Actually, I forgot to tell you", he started, "my brother told me he had seen Aiyana at a disco back home. She was acting very cold, very much different than her usual warmth. He greeted her, asking about you. My brother said she had pretended not having seen him at first, and he said he didn't like the tone of voice she had replied with. It was very arrogant, saying: 'I don't care, I'm not with Mojag anymore!'"

Mojag felt a feverish electricity burning the pores of his skin, the beer already making its way back to the inside basins of his neck.

Who was she with? Was she smiling? Did she ask anything about me??!!! What was she wearing? Where did she go afterwards? I'm not with Mojag anymore??!!!

Mojag had so many questions strolling through his head, but he didn't have the courage to ask. Carefully concealing his raging interest, he said:

"If I am to be the one, tell your brother I apologize for her behavior."

"Ma, please! What the fuck are you saying? No one needs an apology."

"But have you talked to her at all after you broke up?"

"It wouldn't make a difference. I talked to her only once as she was too fucking kind to pick up the phone. We talked for half an hour, in which she only confirmed the willfulness of what she had decided before. And what she had decided was the end. If I go back to her, she would break up, if not, she wouldn't come here unless we get fucking married and legalize our relationship. It seemed as if she had already planned our entire life together, without my consult. She was colder than ever before. She sounded as if we had never kissed, as if I had always been a stranger to her. She only said that we should occasionally talk simply to notify each other about our lives. And tell you what, I said, keep you up to date with my misery?"

"Mojag, you have to take it easier, man. I haven't experienced what you are dealing with, but I assure you that it will be fine."

"Sure" Mojag ungratefully answered with an arrogant tone. He fixed his gaze absently at the adjacent wall for a few moments and continued – "All my nostalgia towards my family, friends, and our neighborhood was vividly reflected by her figure. She was the bridge to my past. And now that bridge is irreversibly destroyed. And it is not only the God damn nostalgia. I am so fucking afraid, having that awful feeling of being abandoned. I have unbearable crises of belonging and crises of identity, being torn apart between two parallel worlds. So many stupid, so many dark thoughts are eating me up. My work productivity went flushing down as I am too occupied with illusions. I have lost interest in everything that used to be so important to me. Don't get me wrong, but I'm losing my faith in friends. I lost my faith in love, in life for God's sake!!! Sometimes I feel I'm getting crazy watching shadows on the wall."

"Dude, chill. You'll be fine. Try to forget her."

"Shilah, I'm glad you accepted my torturing talk, but I sincerely didn't expect that you would understand, even though you did, many times before." *Why am I so fucking ungrateful?! Why do I make people I love feel guilty because of my incapability to live a normal life?* "Shilah, don't get offended and don't blame anyone for my problems, but no one understands. Even my parents think it is only my willful talk! But maybe I cannot portray in detail the feelings that I have, along with the ones that I am constantly deprived of. Nevertheless, I'm not even trying to forget her anymore. I'm solely making an effort to live", Mojag paused for a minute and out of nowhere started banging the glass on the wooden table:

– "Fuck all! I'm staying here in this foreign world. I've been thinking a lot about it and this is the crossing point. I am learning it the hard way, but I can never deny that this place taught much more than I asked for. I cannot throw that away. And besides, I have nothing back in the *South* that was once my hiding place

"I don't know what to say to your sudden determination. It seems bold considering how naked you feel in this world. And it seems you don't like it with that same enthusiasm you had in your university years."

"You don't need to say anything my friend. You are the only person I talked about this so much. And don't get scared by my thoughts. I guess it's just an extremely bad period. And I have to find all my strength to make sure that it stays a period, and not a living habit. I told you before that I have lost my sense of belonging and identity somewhere on the way. And I cannot and will not let myself lose my soul. Tonight, by being here, you reminded me who I am and where I come from. And that gives me strength to endure. Ha, I still remember the times when we were throwing rocks at anti-revolutionary vehicles passing through *our* southern boulevard. And if you ever have any doubts about my friendship towards you, please don't, because I will never forget what kind of a person is sitting in front of me this very moment."

"Thanks man, you know we both share that same empathy. I have no worries that it will always be the case. I'm glad you feel more confident, but I said nothing that helped you although I wish I could do something to be of assistance."

"You've said enough, my friend. You listened a lot. And that is what I appreciate."

Life goes on. I start realizing it's solely up to me to decide whether I'm going to live along.

9 EVERYTHING HAPPENS FOR A REASON. WHY?

Indeed, everything happens for a reason. However, no matter how mistakenly marketed as a comforting note, the reason within the phrase is not of metaphysical origin, but it is the same reason that you unconsciously believed in the first time you made anything happen. In its simplest definition, it is faith, and faith intrinsically differs from hope. It is the ability to believe in your own self that makes a reason happen. You don't make a decision waiting for the reason to appear. You make a decision because you believe you will exploit the chosen path and learn from it to be a better person. One way or another, each and every one of us pursues his own reasoning of the moment. Don't let impatience alter the fragility of your ego; for you will never understand the opportunity that arises right there in front of you, until you stop questioning the circumstances of your behavior.

* * * * * * * * * * *

Six full months have passed since I finished the unhealthy, but undoubtedly life-prolonging cycle of my university life. I guess those days are forever gone, and I'm still having difficulties adjusting to life's responsibilities; not life's responsibilities in general, but my own. Everything is happening so fucking suddenly; my friends are away, my girlfriend lost, my home forgotten. Is there any point left to share any responsibilities? Is there anything left worth fighting for? Is there any meaning left? I could die, and they would find out only after worms start feasting on my brains. Fucking Chronos[33], you put an end to everything, and that much I started accepting. But why do you always put an end to things at the worst possible time, time suitable only to your fucking self? I'm begging you, wait. Take a breath for a moment. I'm sure you can do it, for I've felt it. You always stop time when you are enjoying my misery, but you are ever too hasty to bring an end to the rarities of my happiness! Why don't you let me enjoy at least some of what I have achieved in the past few years? I have accumulated so many different experiences and perceptions of life from the very first day I came to this alien world, and I'm still not able to consolidate my own interpretations! All this passed time, my horizons never stopped widening, and yet I still cannot find a way to at least unchain the box I'm in, when I cannot get out of it!

"Hello...?" Langundo[34] started, waving his hand in front of Mojag's eyes, so as to see what was happening. Mojag was contemplating too strongly that he didn't even notice some of his thoughts were in fact slipping out. Loudly.

"What...? What happened?" Mojag replied, almost jumping from the chair. He appeared as if he was coming out of hypnosis, suddenly starting to readjust

---

[33] Associated with the (Greek) mythic God of time.

[34] Native American male name of unknown origin. Its meaning is *PEACEFUL.*

to the reality of his office he had already been in for the past 6 hours of the day.

"Are you all right? You were shouting something there for a moment", Langundo carefully explained himself.

Mojag started realizing that his thoughts were exposed; his dark tan concealing the blush on his face caused by an instant rush of timid blood to the head. But although he was briefly questioning his consciousness *what* words might have come out to the public, he couldn't care less that his colleague he shared the office with, or anybody else heard them.

"Don't worry, everything is under control, it's just that my thoughts can sometimes get a little loud", he answered coldly and resumed staring back at the blank screen of the computer.

I really feel sorry Langundo has to bear my changing moods; they must be so fucking annoying to keep track of.

It was Friday. Mojag's thoughts were everywhere but at the present moment. But it was Friday, a day for prayer to many peoples; a day of momentary joy to Mojag. In the *South*, they always said every day was God's day, but there was something inexplicably and sacred in a Friday that made it distinct. Perhaps it was God's favorite day.

Still staring at the blank screen of his office tool, he was doing absolutely nothing of what his task manager had recorded; he was anxiously counting the seconds to what followed. And for Mojag, what followed was not the patiently anticipated, planned weekend to many of the real working class heroes. What was about to commence was the traditional gathering at *the bar*, located in the well-known position within that same complex building structure. And not only that it marked time to appreciate beer – the drink of the Gods – but it marked the presence of a handful of some very special people. And for that matter, Mojag was immensely grateful to take part at their table. Among others, those special people were Mojag's boss and his people. None of them left him without unconditional guidance at any point. They were one of those rare breed of people that Mojag owed so much to. And he was happy that such great people were the ones he felt obliged to pay back what they had given to him whenever he would be in a position to do so. It was difficult to classify them as Mojag's friends, mainly because of the age difference and the different way of life that experience implied, but they were certainly a group that Mojag always felt safe with.

In those moments of Mojag's critical mindset, he stopped listening to what people were saying and all the advices they stupidly sought to enlighten him, as if they had any idea of what was going on in his mind. He stopped listening to everybody except for his close colleagues whose opinion and advice he valued even more than his own.

The working week was reaching its final moments. Mojag had preemptively cleaned up his desk and was fully prepared to feel free for that little time that filled his heart with rare joy. He would have already been at the bar, but he first had to pick up all his colleagues as they were still finishing the final moments of their current tasks. And unlike Mojag's childish perceptions, the start of their weekend was only a casual afternoon they unconditionally cared to enjoy a relaxing glass of their favorite drink.

He went on to pick up Viho and Chayton. He went to their offices; staying at each office for the additional couple of minutes until they got ready; he only wanted to make sure they would not recall they had forgotten to do something and unintentionally postpone the weekly bar assembly. They followed him to the elevator where Langundo was patiently waiting. The huge respect Mojag had for his boss prevented him knocking on his door the same way he did to remind his colleagues. Nevertheless, shortly after, Howahkan was there too.

Everything seemed flawless. Even the ever busy elevator served them well as they wasted no additional stop for people fighting to get in at every damn floor. As they were steadily approaching the bar, it seemed full, but some people were already finishing their drinks and the table was free to be taken again. Mojag immediately projected the best spot at the table so he could at any moment keep track of decadent girls on the other tables, having that firm grip on the beer bottle in their hands and sinful lust in their eyes.

It wasn't difficult to notice that they were regular customers at the bar, judging by the drinks, arriving almost immediately after they got themselves comfortable. They never had to bother ordering. As soon as the friendly waiter was aware of their presence, he would always bring the preferred drink to each person accordingly. He probably did that partly out of courtesy, and partly because those same regular customers were always very generous with the tip.

Every passing week Mojag learned about work and the related hierarchy as its basis; every other Friday he learned much more important things about life. Each of his coworkers shared valuable perceptions of the human's state of nature. They all shared similarities even though each was distinct and special in a different way. Chayton was one of the people Mojag spent most of his time with, while at the office building. The reason was not to separate themselves from the rest, and it was certainly not the case that the others were less worthy. It was just that their understanding of life was far too similar, regardless of the age difference spanning slightly more than a decade. The extent to which they spent their time together was visible in the talks of outsiders who confused them to be brothers. They even started looking alike. Both heavy smokers, every working hour they were on the outside enjoying the smoke and contemplating or complaining about life. Often unnecessarily nervous because of people who were dictating their lives, they were equally skeptical of servant's fake smiles in the confined walls of the sterile corridors. It seemed that so many changes were happening in Chayton's life that he was still unaware and unprepared to accept that his way of life would never be the same as it had been some years ago. He rarely lived a moment without complaining about many things that seemed momentarily irrelevant. They both lived to be free, but many times they exaggerated their situation and suffocated their cherished freedom by their twisted, and a concept far too idealistic.

Chayton always told me that I have to live life to the fullest, and waste no moment to use the opportunity at hand. I'm sure that wasn't the case, but sometimes it felt that he missed out on a few things in life that meant his freedom, and he could not wash away the regret he had accumulated. He was talking ever so passionate about his lectures of life that it even appeared as if he was trying to make sure that I don't make the same mistakes he might have done in the past. We were not related, and we knew each other for a short period of the past six months, but his philosophies of life's realism helped me a lot to act more assertively and start to take pieces of control of my own life.

I always followed both written and moral rules of society. And at the same time, I was frequently labeled arrogant, and irresponsive to other people's words. But despite my careless façade, I've always cared about other people's feelings. When I say "other people", I mean other people, not friends, not family, but unknown, unimportant people in life that happen to have found themselves in the same time and place as I have. And many times such naivety of mine prevented me from reaching the goals I had intended to achieve. Certain people exist to do exactly that, enviously distracting you from achieving your own dreams and praising your failure. And I sometimes think I've always been placing others first in front of my happiness. And I always felt disappointed afterwards from other people I've been trying to "satisfy", even when I knew it was my own fault allowing them to cloud my reasoning.

I remember Chayton saying to me once: "Mojag, listen. In life, you usually have two points related to any event. One is point A, the other is point B. You are currently in A and you want to, if not have to, to get to point B. The way you reason now, it seems that you think of everything else except getting to your intended destination, which is getting to point B. Never think of anything apart from your ultimate goal. Now, there are going to be many noises, many distractions, and so many fucking people that are going to try to prevent you to get to the finish line. If you stop at all of them, you will even forget why you have engaged yourself in a journey in the first place. And nobody will remind you. They will only be glad to have stopped you in building your own path. Never do that. Love your own, but fuck those meaningless, soulless people. You are to arrive at B and you are to arrive with style, and nothing else matters!" Beautiful, simple, unfuckable philosophy. And it is ever so valuable to hear it coming from a person whose opinion about life you value a lot.

Thank you, Chayton. Thank you so much.

Chayton always had stories of his own and he always told them with such a passion, that the whole group was frequently enjoying the caused laughter.

Then there was Viho, sitting next to Chayton, his breathing area filled up with smoke of the finest Cuban cigars. That was one complete passion of his. Momentarily full of shady smoke engulfing his face, but his real portrait was that there was probably no living person on the planet more transparent than he was. His honesty and openness were brought to a level, virtually painful to try believing it was true. But it was undoubtedly real. It seemed as if he had been born on a distant planet in which hypocrisy never existed. Ever a good critic and a good friend, he appeared to be the backbone of the working group. His advices were always listened to, and almost ever followed through. And the advices he gave to people in need were both professional and thorough, that even if one didn't like what the advice was, that person would certainly not discard it without giving it a real thought.

I don't like the way I am treating my life right now, and this emotional turmoil I'm currently in. But what I know for sure this very moment sitting at this table full of such good people you rarely meet, is that I am so very thankful for having been brought into the circle of these people. And for that matter, besides the Ultimate Magician above, there is one other person I would like to repay one day in enabling me to be working and drinking here. And that person is no other than Viho. He is one of those rare people who gave me the chance, usually difficult to get in the first place, to sell myself to the professional world and take hold of their knowledge. He is the person that smuggled me in that corporate organization so I can begin evolving. And he is yet another person I owe much to.

I am thirsty for knowledge, but I am far too lazy to prevent myself from dehydration. Viho, on the other hand is an encyclopedia of knowledge, ranging from turtles and their biological mechanisms, through computer systems and artificial intelligence, to the sacrosanct taste of beer and interesting scents of various women. And the clarity he expresses himself with is even scary at moments. I never doubt in anything he does; the inexistent faith in myself I experience, is many times overridden by his helping hand. I am not even feeling degraded I have to show my weakness. In fact, I always feel proud when I am being corrected by the master. And besides, he showed me the meaning of success.

What amazes me the most, is that I never heard him complaining, and I wish everything flourishes for him in the course of his life. He never found himself in a position to complain because he was always taking care of potential obscurities in a timely and so unbelievably efficient manner. And above all, this short period of time I am acquainted to him, he never failed to understand, and he never failed to be best of friends when needed.

Thank you, Viho. Thank you so much.

The atmosphere at the table got indecently loud. Howahkan had his head put down, impatiently stroking his forehead, as if trying to hold himself and escape in a place where he would not be distracted; Chayton and Viho were making indifferent jokes. Mojag observed. The usual was happening again. Langundo never omitted a designated Friday at the bar to continue talking about work. And it was not the case that he didn't get enough of it. It seemed it was simply his happy subject when work related issues are at any table. And every Friday, up to the moment when Howahkan would cut him off in a tacit way, he would never miss out on his passion. And the reality was that he was a direct ancestor of the indigenous peoples of the *North*, but having that in mind, he had an extremely good personality. His manners were on a level so high that such were virtually becoming extinct.

I got to know Langundo better by sharing my office with him. To be more precise, he was sharing his office with me. He was brought up in a traditional Catholic mindset, and that was why he sometimes seemed somewhat reluctant to show his affection towards the inevitable, earthly satisfactions. But on the other hand, I like the fact that he is taking part of his university's fraternity. I have no idea what that means, but I know that it's usually a place where you learn how to appreciate the magic of beer drops and it is also a good way to learn about the joy of a woman's body. When I think about it, he seems like a random person that you would occasionally go to have a drink with. Well, he is indeed excellent company for a drink, and fantastic beer drinking equal, but I could never oust him as random.

The extent to which he offered his help to me, absolutely unconditionally, sometimes really makes me think. The first time I was doing a project for free for the very same company I am currently in, I was actually trying to pass a test. If I succeeded, I would continue working, but for a lot more than working for free. The project of my responsibility was something completed with style. And for its completion, I could never take the full credit. I did become a paid worker, but I can never selfishly say it was solely my own achievement. Langundo is the person that virtually designed most of the project that supposed to be a task of mine. I was eager to do it myself, but my limited knowledge, lack of organization, and passion for women and alcohol implied I needed help.

In the end, my job came about putting the pieces together and presenting the project to certain people who were in charge of my destiny. And I remember as if it is happening this very moment, when I stood there to enlighten my superiors with my skills for the profession. They were satisfied, and I was the star of the moment... No, it was Langundo who was the real star. And what made him even a bigger person was that he never complained that he had been deprived of the momentary glory that he righteously deserved; he never reminded me that his help made me achieve so much. And can you tell me, how can I ever forget such an unselfish act from a person I know so little?

Thank you, Langundo. Thank you so much.

The energetic waiter stopped by to ask for the last round of the night, as the bar staff was already cleaning the inventory, preparing their way home. The seated group virtually never missed out on abusing the last call, and so it happened again. It was only Howahkan that usually bailed out. In fact, this was a very rare occasion that he stayed to the end, and when it did happen, it always filled Mojag with an additional pride as he always enjoyed the company of a great person. The most amazing thing about Howahkan, unlike other bosses, was that he always mixed with his employees, treating them as equals in the stone-set hierarchy.

Our working group reminds me of a revolutionary fraction always there for the ungrateful world, a fraction to which Howahkan was Il Commandante.

I will never forget the day when Howahkan engaged in conversation explaining his perceptions of what a boss is and what a boss should be like. And he was never a demagogue and had no double standards. He said then, that by default, a boss is an asshole, or at least that is the way a boss is initially perceived by the fellows under his grip. I remember I felt a little uncomfortable in a childish, shy way, as if trying to make him understand that I never had such an opinion of him. Regardless, that is not the point I'm making.

"Since a boss is perceived the way I just described, he has to work his way very hard to gain appreciation from the people he directs. And only then, when the hierarchy is mildly leveled, the authority can emerge and only then he can provide the basis for a worthy respect." That is what he said, and it takes a lot of courage and a vast amount of self-awareness, for a well-positioned person, to share such views with his subordinates. To fit him in the sentence of his own philosophy, Howahkan never needed to work his way to be appreciated because he was never an asshole. He's always been a real person and too good a boss. And to me, he is simply a person who makes you feel better, and guides you whenever he deems necessary. I always felt this perhaps unintentional parental approach that he had, and it felt truly enlightening. I am still in a state in which I am far too occupied with other things to think about life. Howahkan, without knowing my facts, always taught me about life and the things I need to become aware of, and take responsibility for the things I ought to do. Whenever I would talk to him, I had a certain dose of fearful respect, but at the same time I felt safe to the level that is difficult to express. That man helped me by giving me free guidance of my life at a time where basically I had everything else but a life. He gave me the basis, which made me emotionally stronger. Both professionally and personally, his advices were many times appropriate and always necessary to my development. At these times when my shadow is far bigger than my soul, this man helps me preserve parts of myself that I once stood for. And I strongly wish that a day will come when I will be able to repay at least some of what he has done for me. I will always be too grateful to forget.

In the midst of myself, and the seed of negative energy I was spreading, every other word in my sentences was "no, but". Instead, I accepted his nervous advice that I will go about better if I replaced those words with "yes, and". And as far as my situation allowed me to, I was feeling much better with that simple, but meaningful change. He taught me how to be much more assertive and to cut out on my stupid modesty, which was at many times perceived as a highest level of arrogance. The most astonishing thing is that he revealed so many flaws in my character that I never even thought existed. And it doesn't take a boss, but it takes a real person to openly say what your negative aspects are. For it is crucial that you identify the flaws you carry so you would be able to start fixing them. And Howahkan always told me these things not to make me feel bad, or to impose his authority, but he always said it to help me become a better person. Many times I would start being defensive when being criticized, but all times that I would walk away from his talks, I would realize that everything he had told me was in fact an honest truth. He gave me a meaning to everything that was happening within me and within the remaining walls of my inexistent world.

Thank you, Mr. Howahkan. Thank you so very much.

As each of them drank the finishing drops of beer, the Friday afternoon was coming to an end. It happened very rarely that they continued elsewhere in a similar setting. That day was not one of them. They parted as each of them had their own plans, and each of them was happy that the weekend had just started. Each of them, except Mojag, who had many plans but he needed someone else to make them reality. He despised the weekends as they were too painful to bear observing how they were being wasted away. He liked the working week a lot better since it gave him an occupation to forget about the perceived realities of his misery. Even though the working week turned his life into a framework of mechanic rhythms, waking up every day at the same time, catching the last bus to get him in time for work, working the whole day, coming home with full bottles of beer to be emptied by the end of the night and then off to bed. And nothing was changing the following day. But the weekend was quite the opposite, utterly worse, giving him all the unnecessary time to waste on his innermost thoughts he didn't like. And it would have been too much if he was to be drunk the whole weekend; there were many weekends to come, and he was devastated but surely not determined to throw his life away.

Shortly after the needed drink with his colleagues, Mojag arrived in the ridiculously hot insides of his apartment walls. As a usual manifestation of his depression mixed with alcohol, he wanted to break any of the things that would stand in his way, but for some reason, he always did stay quiet. He didn't even bother taking his shoes off; he immediately went on to one of the rooms and took out the familiarly shaped suitcase from underneath the bed. He opened it gently, and *she* was ever there for him. That piece of carved wood he cherished so much was almost as old as he was. His parents bought it for him for a lot less than its real worth. *Pink Floyd* got a grand piano to prop up their mortal remains; Mojag's remains were many times preserved by the chords of his guitar. Every time he opened that suitcase, holding out the precious guitar he was so emotionally bound to, he thought about the person that taught him the enchantment of the instrument, at times when Mojag was still a kid. His teacher was an older man, a friend of Mojag's father, which gave Mojag the power to create something that fulfilled his soul even at times when he felt like a beggar of the world. His teacher helped him master the sounds of the people. He showed him how to master the instrument not to play for keeps, but to play for preserving the integrity and the inner strength of his own self. In the now distant times while the other kids were playing football, Mojag was clumsily trying to produce a mesmerizing tone of his first chords. As soon as he learned how to do it properly, while he was playing the guitar, the girls were offering free blowjobs. And now, while he was having too many questions that could not be answered, the guitar always brought him comfort. *She* always understood him and rarely asked questions.

That is how he kept on surviving the moody moments of the weekend's loneliness. He was shaking the peace and nerves of his neighbors with the beautiful sounds of his guitar. He would play until the skin of his fingers was falling off, the strings getting red from his blood. Literally. When his fingers were in a state in which he was not even able to hold a cigarette, he would continue the rush of punishment running for hours on the river bank until his legs felt like stone. He didn't miss out on sacrificing his body as he occasionally felt he needed to hurt himself just to make sure that he could still feel. If not for anything else, the physical pain he was inflicting on himself got all balanced with the emotional burden of his life. And so life continued, living on a borrowed time, with no will to care for tomorrow.

I will not stop fighting until the night I prevail over myself.

10 SOMEBODY, ANYBODY...

The ugliest thing a person can possibly inflict upon himself is self-pity. When you start debating that your life is so desperate, and there is not a single thing that will bring you faith to survive, you reach the point when you deserve nothing of what you have. And in fact, when you stop for a while and look back on all the great moments you are ungrateful for, moments that you immediately forget when the stars make a turn to reveal the darkness of their other side, you will realize that you *possess* much more things that at any moment will make you complete.

It is a customary, damned tradition that we have so many expectations in others that we get disappointed if we do not get what we had intended right then, at that fucking, selfish outburst of a moment. And then the whole world is at fault. No, my friend, the world shares a fault only for the parts that concern them. You are the one who should be judged, and hanged, because it is nobody else but you whose fault you are not willing to accept. If we are not able to hold on to what we have, we will never learn to fulfill any of our subsequent desires.

* * * * * * * * * * *

Another Sunday was making its way through. Mojag reluctantly woke up to have his morning toxics even though he would have rather slept through a difficult day. He was ever at odds with a Sunday; it was the highest burden of them all. It was even difficult to distinguish between day and night as they were both equally and painfully unbearable. But there was something else that made that bloody Sunday different.

Walking nervously around his apartment, much more than usual, Mojag was too obsessed with thoughts that did not directly concern him, but concerned his happiness, and more importantly, the happiness of his family. Hitting the lightweight, plastic chair for many times against the empty wall, he would not let his fading cigarette finish until the other one was already lit. He was so fucking worried. It was at least twenty-five times that he called his father and his mother. Additional twenty-five calls he unsuccessfully placed to his sister and his brother-in-law. No fucking body was answering the phone. Something was wrong. Something was completely unusual, and it seemed they all wanted to hide from Mojag whatever was going on. The day before he received a call from his parents that his sister was detained at the hospital, and now nobody was calling. Mojag was so loud in half-destroying his apartment, that even if some of the neighbors, or anyone else came to complain, he would have peeled their skin off without even blinking. And how could he have possibly been able to blink when something was going on with his family and he was not there to bear the situation. His life was of no value at the moment. He forgot all about his grief and the pathetic situation he could not escape from. Nothing else mattered when his family was put into question.

Then, as many minutes passed by while Mojag was impatiently looking at the display of his phone, praying for familiar letters to appear, the phone rang. It was his brother-in-law. At first, Mojag felt an immediate urge to go to the toilet as all his guts went inside out because of the anticipation of the call's contents. He took a deep breath, which was of no help and went on to pick up the call that made his strength shiver.

"It's a boy! Mojag, it's a boy! They are both well and IT IS A BOY!!!" Mojag's brother-in-law screamed in confusion of happiness.

Mojag's sister had been in the final months of her pregnancy, waiting at any moment to burst and give birth for the first time. That moment had come. It was the first newborn in the family and it was a boy. The joy was God given.

"OOOOOOAAAAAAAAAAAAAAAAA!!!!!" was the only consistent sound that Mojag could make when he heard he had become an uncle. Happy tears of his were on the verge of bursting out; his body hyperventilating. – "Let it be in good health and let it grow to be a man guided by the genes of our family. I love you all, and make sure you tell that to my family. I wish I could be there so much…" he sighed, couple of teardrops already making their way to his dried lips, although he was trying to make sure his emotions wouldn't surface out to the other side of the line.

"Just don't call anybody yet, as you are now the first one that knows. I'm a father…I have to go back to the room, we'll talk later", the brother-in-law, still in moments of pleasing shock, ended the conversation.

Mojag could not get back to his senses, all the nerves in his body full of fulfilling tremble. Having a rare smile on his face, virtually staying aloft and fixed within the lines of his face, he did what he always mechanically would do in similar situations when he was not able to get even slightest control of his body and mind. He went to the shelf at the *southern* corner of the room and opened the best bottle of single malt whiskey he had. The shelf was basically designed to serve the purpose of such occasions. Such occasions were not so many, but the lack of dust on the wooden holder gave out the correct impression that the shelf was in frequent use. He turned the auxiliary, whiskey glasses on the other side and the drink started pouring down.

My sister has a baby and it's our first newborn in the family. I have become an uncle...I am an uncle!

And only for a breeze of a moment, he felt an enormous emotional change, which he prayed would last for as much as he had deserved it. Up until the moment of his family's generational advancement, he was living on that borrowed time indeed, with no will to care neither about the day after nor about a present moment. But it was different now, as he felt he had forgotten how it was *to feel*. The present was all that mattered, and a future to be shaped upon it. Having appropriate reflections running through his mind and body, he raised the glass high and exalted calmly in a gratifying prayer.

The second glass went underway.

Shortly after, both his phones started ringing like they had never rung before. His parents, the newly made, proud grandparents, were the first to share their utmost happiness with their son. Mojag was still trying to start a process of recovering from the beautiful shock as he couldn't even recall his parents' words seconds after they had finished a sentence. But he could feel their immense joy, and that is what he could never forget.

"He's so tiny, I can't wait for you to see him", his mother kept on saying.

I know, mother. My feet are burning to be there.

"We miss you son…"

I miss you all more than I could possibly explain it with words.

Mojag's parents practically never failed to get in touch with him, even though he was trying as hard as humanely possible to prevent his agonizing thoughts from being sensed by the ever watching eye of the beholder. And many times when they called, he could feel their worries about him. They might have not even had a clue; they simply knew it. Sometimes he thought they were trying to comfort him in order to distract him from making something he would regret for years to come. But all that comfort that they were trying so hard to put across to him only made him even more anxious. They seemed never to understand what he felt; and he never succeeded nor did he want to explain his life, not least because he didn't want them to worry. The consequent anxiety produced by seemingly naïve comments from his parents, especially his mother, made him feel even more estranged. And that was killing him, even though he knew the cause of estrangement was not the care his parents wanted to advocate.

"They don't want me anymore", he would think. *How could I possibly dare to think such crap?! What have I become?*

But that day a new life was born into the sincere, modest family. And family was the most important in the world. Mojag buried his baseless thoughts and once again realized what he really meant to the people that gave him life. And in large part because of their healthy efforts, another life was opening the eyes to the world.

The phone calls seemed to be getting exhausted. All important people finished calling and the room was beginning to go silent again, but the excitement was not even close to subsiding. Mojag hardly noticed that the bottle he opened a few moments ago was far from the level it had initially been. The crazed shine in his eyes was a lot different than the usual crazed shine he was carrying so damn frequently. This crazed shine was one of sobriety, one of happiness he so rarely had the opportunity to practice. He didn't hesitate even for one moment. He immediately took out the phone and started calling the inexhaustible list of family-like friends of his that he wanted to share his happiness with.

He started off with his (former) roommate and the best friend of his old neighborhood that never failed to understand him; he started off with Wematin and Shilah. *They would have done the same thing. I only hope they won't get scared of this sudden outburst of cheerfulness because I forgot when it was the last time since they had heard me as happy, especially in the midst of my fucking life that seems so unimportant now.*

And what other response from his friends were to be expected, but the one that unconditionally causes life to ascent to its celebration. For true friends are not necessarily those that offer their comfort when you are down and out, but true friends are the ones that enjoy your happiness as if it were a happiest moment of their own. And such were *the* friends Mojag had on his list. And such a friend was Mojag on their list. *Forever.*

So many positive talks with such a distinct selection of friends, added up to the motivating news he shared with them. It had already been little more than two hours after he had started envisioning all the necessary things he would have to pass on to his nephew. And after the frenzy of excitement subsided in its natural flow, so did the brightness in Mojag's eyes. He was happy. Oh, he couldn't recall the last time he had been so happy in his recent, yet overwhelming past. He was still happy, but he wanted to prolong such a rare state of mind as much as the circumstances allowed. But damn *Murphy* was about to be right again. They all cursed *Murphy* because of what he had invented, but no one had the courage to accept the reality of the *Laws* he had brought to their plate. And so was becoming Mojag's reality once again, a repetitive cycle of weariness.

Why aren't you happy, you sick fuck? What is it that you now want?

As he intended, he wanted to steal any additional moments that would preserve his joy, preserve his mind. His family deserved that. *How can I preserve my mind when I have nobody by my side to celebrate what I feel, to celebrate such a moment that requires it? They all know about my momentary goodwill now, but they all continue with their lives, and I'm only a forgotten part of it. Can't at least for once all be smooth in my favor? I have a reason to celebrate, not to keep on getting drunk alone with the all too familiar shadows on my smoke-stained walls. I can do that tomorrow, I WILL do that tomorrow, so why don't you fucking give me a break? Why don't you find somebody else to mess up, at least for a while, and then have me again?*

Don't you ever get bored of me, I hope that my misery is killing you, or otherwise you would not be the one they all say you are, whoever you are that you are rolling my film, the film that you have created; the film you so much enjoy grinning at. I am the loneliest person that has ever roamed the streets of mayhem, but for once, let my happy tears remain happy!

The silence now screening into all parts of Mojag's living cells, he was filled with anger. He was so full of it, that it was even unbearable to himself. The anger that lived within made him what he never cared to be. And he never omitted a moment to self-pity himself and his bare existence. That made him even more furious, but that was something that he gave up trying to control. It was beyond his reach as was the only thing he so idealistically lusted for in life – his freedom.

He tried once more to dial the phone. Nothing. The stupid answering machine was propping his mind and fueling his aggression. He simply put the phone away, hoping he would do no sudden movements. His breath barely going out, he spread himself down on the floor. It was the fourth, or maybe even the fifth attempt to reach a very good friend of his, one of the rare to return back to the city. That very good friend of his was special on his own, but what made him even more special was that he was in the big city, the same big city that was slowly swallowing Mojag's sanity. But he wasn't picking up the phone. *Why? What the fuck is he doing on a Sunday? It's not even mid-afternoon.* But then again, perhaps not so many other people left their days pass by along them. Perhaps other people were not as lonely. And then *Mr. Cash's* voice came along as if Mojag had fucking booked him for the moment:

"What have I become, my sweetest friend
Everyone I know goes away in the end
And you can have it all, my empire of dirt,
I will let you down, I will make you hurt."[35]

He didn't need *Mr. Cash* to teach him the meaning of those words. Those were *Mojag's* verses, ones that were infuriating his mind, reflecting the reality he involuntarily couldn't stop pursuing. *JR*[36] merely confirmed it.

I have become a host, a fuck body to a parasite that overtakes me so quickly. And there is nothing I do about it. There is nothing I can do it about it. But then again, I have to do something. What can I do? I don't mind being alone no more, I can always start talking to the introverted silence of my cactus friend, but now I need emotions, a companion that will be there to witness my cheerfulness for I am NOT this monster I have become. And it's not even difficult to think of adjusting back to the so very much familiar state of agony I am so much into. No, that has become a routine now. What is difficult is that I am alone on such a rare occasion, when I have a real cause to celebrate, to smile, to be full of positive energy which I lack just as I lack vitamins in my body. The reflection of his face in the vast window glass portrayed his sunken face, as he started at himself:

"Stop this ungrateful madness of self-pitiful, disgusting behavior."

But it's so difficult.

"Fuck you, get lost; get away from me."

In those moments of trying to find little order in the chaos of his consumed brain, he would have done

---

[35] *Hurt* - Johnny Cash
[36] A nickname of Johnny Cash

anything to help him find a fake comfort. He would have even phoned his girlfriend. *Fuck you, stop calling her your 'girlfriend'. She is your ex-girlfriend!!!! Why can't you fucking understand that, let it go!* And he did call her. In fact, she was the first one he thought about when his brother-in-law delivered the sacred news that made his day. He was hesitant to the point when he could not take it any longer. *I so much want that she hears the news, to be part of it all. Ah, she will be so happy!*

And besides, she deserved to know. It was a major thing that happened in Mojag's family, and no matter what the hostilities among the former lovers were, she deserved to know. She *needed* to know. And he was supposed to be the one delivering. They hadn't talked for what seemed to be a period of decades, and so the butterflies started running around Mojag's stomach, drying his throat, and reducing his oxygen capacity. He dialed the number he could never forget. Nothing…nothing…nothing…nothing. He was losing his patience; he could not afford another call on the ignore list. By the time he reached the level of total craziness, he waited a moment longer…and there it was, that clutching sound that marked the opening words of Aiyana's familiar voice. Mojag still didn't regret he had called. But not for long. She was happy for Mojag, she was happy for his family and there was no doubt about it. It couldn't have been otherwise. But then again, the coldness with which she exclaimed her excitement gave Mojag the coldest shivers he had ever experienced. He wanted to vomit. *She doesn't even care that I exist anymore.* And with all the unexpected stupidity that his bared mind often produced in the never ending period, he opened the scarce conversation to his EX, by exclaiming the most stupid and most inappropriate sentence ever said.

"I am an uncle", he said. "My sister just gave birth, it's a boy...! Girl, you have become an aunt because that makes you one!" *That makes you an aunt? What am I fucking thinking? What am I fucking trying to do? No wonder my state of consciousness is so difficult to preserve.*

Mojag's miseries perhaps would remain, but she would not be part of them anymore. Never again. The voice she relayed marked the seal to the box that was so difficult to close. It still was, but at least the turn on the crossroad he was already taking. *And why do I have to feel guilty for us? What are you, a fucking saint? You put the entire burden on me, and the most naïve part is that I had accepted it. No, let me talk, I don't want to listen anymore. What for? I don't even get a decent smile at least for my happiness if not for me? No, no, baby, I don't need it for you are free from the chains of my life. Find a husband that will treat you good, buy a big house where your children can carelessly run around and be the happiest girl in the world. And for once in my life, I say this without any intentions of offering my often sarcastic precision. And in case you are asking about me anytime in the following days, months, years, always remember that the song remains the same, and that the song would always shine with memories. And let me live, for I'm letting you live this very moment.*

And amidst all, Mojag finally concluded that she was a large part of the cause, but she would and could never possibly be again a part of his solution. The dream of Mojag and Aiyana, the dream as they had so naively and affectionately envisaged for themselves, was never fulfilled. And it was perhaps never meant to be fulfilled. *But maybe those dreams you keep in the closet to think of them your whole life are the ones worth the most.*

No, not this one; never this one for once it was far too valuable to only live with the thought of it. In this case, the closet was gone long before the dream picked up its turn.

It could take an eternity to finding and shaping your life around a person you might consider a soul mate. It usually takes one such delirious moment and all the revelations it brings to render it forgotten. *And perhaps that is the way it should be.*

Just as Mojag accepted yet another defeat to his inexistent pride, the phone started ringing and instantly killed the extreme sounds of silence. At first, Mojag looked at the phone, moving due to the planted vibrations, hesitant to talk to anyone. The first thought that came to his powerless brain was the one of his brother-in-law calling to say how sophistically drunk he was because of his recent membership to the club of fathers, an experience not even closely comparable to any other in life. But then again, it was too early for such a celebration, and he knew his brother-in-law was able, as many in the *South*, to withhold the effects of alcohol for quite a while. Mojag was right. By the time he decided to answer, the phone stopped ringing, but enough for him to get a curious glance at the letters written on the display. If his short term memory served him well, the dirty phone display spelled out the *Guyapi*[37].

Mojag, indifferent but happy, took the phone and started dialing back.

---

[37] Native American male name of unknown origin. Its meaning is *CANDID*.

"What the hell happened? You called me seven times! Is everything all right?" cautiously screamed the voice on the other side of the line.

"Don't worry my friend, I didn't realize that I called you so many times", Mojag started replying, as if embarrassed. "Everything's fine. But yes, something did happen, and I wouldn't even try explaining how happy I am! Just few hours ago I became an uncle! My sister just had a baby boy!" he said those words with a huge amount of pride that even amazed himself.

"Wow, that's excellent news! Congratulations! Let he be healthy and alive, and let his dick grow! I can imagine how the feeling is, and if you believe me, I share your happiness, and if I may, it made my day too", said Guyapi, his words abundant with sheer honesty.

"Thank you so much, I appreciate it a lot. I wish that you too experience this feeling when your brother decides he needs a smaller version of himself", Mojag said in the same honesty as did his friend moments ago. And that was not a matter of mere reciprocity, but it was a simple matter of friendship.

"So, what are you up to? Have you started celebrating...what a stupid question! I'm sure that whiskey you had at your place is slowly expiring."

"Exactly. But the whiskey is not only expiring, but it is truly mesmerizing my thoughts", Mojag started joking about what was in fact going on in his mindset. He then put on a different kind of voice as if making a plea to his friend without asking a question. "But to be honest, I'm getting a little tired celebrating alone, and I just talked to the other guys from my neighborhood to have a drink but you know that they need a fucking consensus to decide. And I didn't have the nerves to wait for their stupid excuses. As you well noticed, I was calling you so we could go together and continue this..."

"Say no more. I had plans for today, but the situation requires immediate attention so all my other plans seem irrelevant now. I roughly have an idea where we are going..."

"Thanks a lot, be sure that I will remember it. And don't mind that I will cut out the unnecessary politeness trying to "convince" you to stick to your initial plans," Mojag started, decisively smiling.

"Ma please, I'm not doing anything special, I only want to help you enjoy your happiness", his friend affectionately exclaimed.

"Be sure of it."

"So, when do we meet?"

"How much time do you need?"

"Thirty-five minutes?"

"So be it."

* * * * * * * * * * *

Lying there on the bed and watching the scarce stars in the cold month of November, reflected in the big city's skyline, Mojag's reflections were spread out unevenly between happiness and ethanol. And for the rarity of the moment, the effects of ethanol, regardless of the decent amounts he had in his body, were significantly subsided. He was still in the snowy shoes that got washed out in the streets of the big city, but why would he bother with details? He arrived shortly before the clock ticked its opening hours of the new day, and he could not even care to feel the cold breeze coming out of his balcony door. He felt good, and that was what he counted as success. He was roaming all possible holes of the night with Guyapi in celebrating the moment of his family's glow. Guyapi was a very quiet friend as opposed to many other Mojag's friends, whose passion for life was explicit. Both of them were different in many aspects, but both of them were the same in the most important one, the one that marked the true definition of friendship. As it was always the case, Guyapi's reliability as a friend did not fail, and it grew especially high in those moments when it was of utmost necessity. His being there, made Mojag contemplate that even when one feels as being the loneliest person in the world, one should perhaps think again, for he might not be the loneliest one after all.

For a slight moment, Mojag's thoughts stopped. Despite the drilling sound of the alcohol, his mind was all too clear to let anything fly inside the way it usually did. And whenever he was experiencing such a luxury, it meant that it was required that he did something of a momentary concern.

He energetically stood up and turned on that time-killing computer. By the time the system was ready, he was prepared as well. He engaged in the deceiving commodities of the modern world. The mediocre site of the *Southern* airline started opening. Shortly after, Mojag finished entering the sixteen digits in the designated place. He pressed the purchase button as another confirmation screen appeared:

"Please acknowledge the following information before placing your purchase:

Departure: Tomorrow, 10.50 a.m.

Return: Upon reservation

Would you like to confirm, or cancel your flight?"

Of course I would like to confirm, you stupid bitch, why do you think I would otherwise visit your idiotic website?

He pressed the affirmative button, which he didn't notice but was far more visible than the other, and printed out his ticket for his way home. No luggage, no burdens. And even though he was objectively bound to go to work the next day, subjectively, he could do that work the week after, and all the other weeks that followed the week after.

With a childlike smile full of satisfaction, he didn't forget to hug the pillow as he was already falling asleep with the thought of being awoken by the familiar warmth of his home.

I will not stop fighting until the night I prevail over myself.

11 WHAT WAS THE MEANING OF HOME?

"Moj dom je dole u predgradju
Od centra prema zapadu
Gdje Sunce sja kad zalazi
Gdje Sunce sja samo kad zalazi

Moj dom je tamo gdje si ti
Moja draga ljubavi
Moj dom je tamo, tamo gdje sam ja
Takva je moja sudbina"[38]

* * * * * * * * * * *

---

[38] My home is down in the suburbs
From the center to the west
Where the sun shines when it's setting
Where the sun shines only when it's setting

My home is there where you are
My dear love
My home is there where I am
That is my destiny*

*(*Dom* – Jura Stublic & Film)

It was already ten minutes passed since the airplane had landed on the *Southern* airport's asphalt. The engines of the machine gave out the familiar sound of being cooled down. The front gate opened as the unimportant passengers from the business class were already on their way out to the ground of *Mojag's city* outskirts. He had been seated somewhere in the middle of the plane, and was impatiently waiting for his turn to join the exiting row of smelly people. His turn came shortly after his thoughts and excitement. Giving his honest gratitude to the stewardesses with unconcealed fake smiles, he found himself onto the stairs leading to the ever familiar asphalt. Looking there from the modest height of the manual escalator stairs, he stopped for one, three seconds at most to grasp the landscape of the surrounding. There was something in the air, he thought, that made him feel special anytime he was arriving back to where he once belonged. Forgetting that his short stay would only add up to his envious collection of temporary illusions, he smiled in satisfaction and continued to the bus that was taking him to the usual bureaucratic procedures of the customs officers, which were far less efficient than anywhere else, but far friendlier than in a lot of other places.

Hey, it is about time for you to shut up. This is my home and I don't care to philosophize.

The handbag firmly in his grip, Mojag walked around the small airport barracks to reach the exit with a warm smile on his face. On the outside, as in some lawless animal farm, the exit was always full of taxi drivers that were virtually breathing in every passenger's neck to impose their services. And to any normal observer, that was not an over-statement. But at the moment, none of the surrounding was important to Mojag's attention. He was only trying to find the person that had never failed to pick him up from the airport, not even on such a short notice as was the unexpected rationale of Mojag's arrival that beautiful day. It was already four months that he had not visited the Land of his childhood, and the happiness when he saw his father waiting there, in a spot away from the other people, was difficult to describe. The son increased his pace with an even warmer smile on his face to approach his father and firmly embraced him.

"It's good to see you father", Mojag said, "And there's something different. I mean, you look even younger despite the fact that you are grandfather now", Mojag continued in sincere laughter.

"Be careful what you say, cause you are an uncle now, remember?" his father replied with tenderness. "It's a wonderful feeling, and I wish that one day you would experience the way I am feeling now...And I couldn't be happier to have you here my son...now, my family is complete."

"I can imagine, I'm still in fantastic shock from the beautiful news. So, start telling me everything that I have missed." Mojag expressed his eagerness to take part in everything that was happening.

Only moments after, they reached the car and they started making their way to the hospital where Mojag's sister was recovering from the most natural process of them all, and where her firstborn child was detained those additional three days until they prepare him for the outside.

Mojag's father, Hania[39], started talking in excitement to what had taken place, and how it all got unfurled. It was so beautiful to see his father so talkative and so happy at the same time for that rarely happened, if ever. Hania was nervous type of a person with dark tan and expressive eyes that were always revealing many stories. But in spite of those features, he seemed trained to conceal his emotions to the most sophisticated levels. And he was impeccable in it. Not even the most expensive translating device could even nearly spell out what his eyes were saying. However, that day was one of the few when Mojag noticed his father's emotions surfacing. And it was probably not a change in Hania's mindset, but only a temporary exposure of his true happiness.

As the car was approaching the urbanized part of the city, Mojag noticed a difference in the way his own emotions made his conscience react. Apart from all other times, when he would be very careful to absorb all details of the road and the city's static synchronicity, this time he was there with a purpose and that was all that mattered. Strangely, the city felt as a neutral ground serving as a physical stage of life, and not as an emotional duress as was always imposed by Mojag's subconscious. And all those once, and perhaps still, valuable memorabilia places of his life, were now only a blurry link to a life once lived. He felt like an observer of a past of a person he once knew, perhaps a person he once was.

---

[39] Native American male name of Hopi origin. Its meaning is *SPIRIT WARRIOR.*

The car was already well penetrating the city. There were almost no road signs, and those that were still intact from decades ago, were covered with leaves and tree branches of the wilderness that no one cared to tame. But all that seemed well planned, for additional "constraints", such as road signs, would possibly be an overhead to the current conception of the people and the environment they lived in. The traffic jams, nervous, inexperienced drivers swearing at each other and at careless pedestrians, tons of gypsies and beggars blocking the way of the cars for a fistful of dollars; those were the usual, everyday signs of the city's bloodline. Hania's car slowly started approaching the hospital as Mojag ironically, though silently observed that the hospital was only three hundred meters away from the place he knew so well for the past five or six years; the house where his ex-girlfriend lived. Times before, he would have felt guilty if he would not feel the usual suffering, but at the moment he arrogantly tossed his emotions away as they tried to suck him in. He wasn't even trying to distinguish whether that healthy emotional shift of his was only temporary or it would remain for many other times to come; it was only a mechanical movement that came along without asking for it.

The sound of the car engine abruptly stopped as they parked right in front of the hospital. Mojag observed that this time was the only one that he enjoyed going any near a hospital environment and its familiar, repulsive odor, despite the ever wet, penetrating fantasies of sexy nurses with their familiar and irresistible outfit. Mojag followed his father inside the facility as the well paid staff greeted them. One of the nurses, a slightly fat one, although cute, with a silver collar around her neck accompanied them. Mojag shook her hand in sign of respect as she went on to escort them to the room where his sister lived for those couple of days while giving birth.

How is she? How does she feel being a mother? What about my nephew, is he there in the room with her? How does he look like? Who does he resemble more, my sister, or my brother in law? How am I going to react when I see them? How am I going to recognize my emotions when they overwhelm me? Will I be able to control them? But how the fuck I could possibly think of controlling my emotions when I am so much looking forward to them? So many wary questions were testing the fragility of Mojag's patience, and as many butterflies were roaming the pipelines of his stomach.

They finally reached the entrance of the room. Hania thanked the sweet, but unattractive nurse as she was heading back to her post. Mojag reached for the door as his heart's stomp was rising unnoticeably. He was already inside the room and the usual warmth of the surrounding of his family was shining in the air. He admitted to himself that he was a bit confused that his baby nephew was not in the room as he had already been preparing for the encounter. But then again, it was quite normal that the small infant would not be able to stay with the mother the whole time in the beginning of his days.

"Where is he?", his thoughts started speaking instead of Mojag even when he knew the answer in advance.

"He's in the room with the other babies, just about to wake up. They will bring him in a short while", Mojag's mother, Rozenne replied in soft whisper as she approached the door to greet her son that she had not seen for what seemed an infinity. In the course of the embrace, Mojag had already entered the new phase of life in the natural flow. He was independent of his parents, both emotionally and materially, and he was old enough and capable to take care of himself and by himself. But not even in that phase did his mother omit to show her warmth and concerns for Mojag the same way she did when he was just a little boy.

"Congratulations, grandma", he said to her with a proud smile on his face. "I am so happy to see you all here", Mojag continued in an almost protective way.

"Thanks my son, I hope one day you make us happy with children of your own this same way."

Before he replied anything, he went on to his sister and hugged her carefully as she was still shaken from the humane operation. She was very happy that she softly started crying in joy. Actually, it was a strange mix of crying and laughing at the same time, because modern medicine drugs had a miraculously mixed, short term effect on the brain of the recipient.

"Ay, sis, look at you, a mother…is this for real? That girl, who was constantly shouting at me for practically everything I was doing in my puberty, that same girl that is my sister, has become a mother! Sorry sis, I still can't get used to it, even though we all expected it coming…" he paused for a moment and continued. – "And that makes me an uncle and what a happy uncle! Congratulations!!! I love you so much", he finished the sentence giving a careful hug to his sister.

She switched on, laughing uncontrollably as she started:

"Thanks, bro, it's not only you. I myself cannot get used to what is happening. And with these crazy sedatives, I feel I'm in a loony motion picture."

"Ma don't worry, just enjoy them. What about that little creature you got out of yourself? How does he look like? How did you feel when they showed him to you? When is he gonna wake up? Concentrate now and start telling me everything before I go and wake him up!"

She started talking as fast as her current state had allowed, frequently with flavored additions from Hania and Rozenne. They all started talking in excitement of what was going on. Basically, they were briefing Mojag on all details he had not been there to witness. He was so insatiable to know everything that he even posed some of the same questions for much more than two times. He had never taken any brain-altering drugs, but he appeared as bedazzled as if *he* was the one giving birth. His sweet confusion drastically increased its level when they heard a knock on the door. Another nurse had just entered the room. But this time, she came carrying a small robe that looked like an enormous bean, and there was this little head peeking out of the white cloth.

"Here is the big guy", the nurse said. Mojag felt his breath speeding up to enchantment. He stood there motionless, his gaze fixed at his nephew. It took him more than a couple of seconds to utter some murmuring words and approach the little one.

"Look at him, he's so small…Hey big guy, how do you like this world?" he spoke softly to his nephew as he was gently touching his mini fingers. His nephew didn't say anything back; he still seemed exhausted from the procedure that brought him to the world of his family. He was making some mimics with his mouth as if trying to say he wanted to have his prescribed dose of mother's milk. At least that was how

Mojag translated the baby talk to himself. Mojag's sister, Alsoomse[40] was carefully proud to hold her son as the nurse put him on her chest. It was such a fascinating scene guided by the most natural drives of humanity. Mojag looked at the mother feeding her baby boy. He then looked at his own mother and father. They were all so happy, including him, and he was the most grateful person in the world. And scientists don't have a clue what they are saying when they conclude that such a small baby is not aware of his surrounding because there were no doubts that he was happy and smiling as well. Not even a single doubt about it.

* * * * * * * * * * *

The night that followed that same day can be best described in a few keywords. It was a big celebration of the newest member in the family. The place was at the house of Mojag's brother-in-law. A special drink that was sealed the day Mojag's brother-in-law was born some thirty years ago marked its reopening. The atmosphere was delirious at its simplest description. Mojag was out of himself, much more because of his strong emotions for his healthy and happy family and just enough because of the extreme volumes of alcohol he mechanically swallowed with each of the many glasses that followed. He was indeed feeling free.

I feel so fucking free!

---

[40] Native American female name of Algonquin origin. Its meaning is *INDEPENDENT.*

He was fully focused on the biggest happening of the year, and was partly occupied with the usual silent processing of the thoughts of both hemispheres of his brain.

Whenever I am in the city that keeps my childhood alive and keeps most of my dirty teenage secrets hidden, I feel like the King Kong of the world. And even more importantly, I feel the master of my own universe. And at the same time, it is so difficult to relax because I know that my days in what I like to refer to as my city, are limited. I'm only a visitor now, rarely the host I once was. And every time I have to leave my city, my heart breaks. But I still leave.

My family and friends make my city the most valuable of them all, making each of my subsequent returns the most beautiful, real experiences to remember. But maybe that is only a sweet illusion that derives from my short stay, when everybody successfully tries to make me feel good because I'm not there most of the time. And that doesn't make it less beautiful for me, but it doesn't bring me to the everyday problems that my fellow people, including friends and family, are facing every day. Because I know that not even close to everything is as perfect as it seems every time I come as witness, back to my roots. For most of these two million people, surviving is the most they have been allowed to achieve. For me, the possibility to live and to be free has been served on a silver platter, although it takes a lot of courage and delusional moments in order to be persistent making it through. And no matter how difficult it is, and no matter how much more difficult it might get, I could not permit my bittersweet torment go away in vain. I couldn't allow the balance of loss and gain to be for nothing, along with the vast experience that was born out of that balance.

And on a more practical note, the greatest obstacle of mine is that it seems I have lost a huge deal of the entire connection with this world a long time ago. And I have never noticed it while that process was running in the background of my mind. I used to come here to my home, but now I make home wherever I lay my head. For my pursuit is somewhere else into finding whether I could live as a Bohemian of the world, where personal freedom can be touched and can be obtained as the ultimate reward for the everlasting battle of life. And that is why I cannot come back for good. Not now. Not yet.

However, this entire metaphysical demagogy doesn't kill me less, because every other time I go back to the warmth of my most sincere address and I see my parents getting older and my friends getting more serious. It is a natural process, they say, but I am not there to share my troubles and happiness with any of them. And that is where misunderstandings usually start off. But regardless, whenever I am with them, I realize how meaningless the outer world is; how sick the world immoral people rule is. And then it makes it so simple to openly say "fuck you world". Nothing is even remotely important as the well-being of the ones I love.

Today, when I saw my nephew and when I saw my sister, and my dearest parents so happy, that was all that mattered. No matter where I am in this world, even if I would be living with the polar bears in the icebergs of Alaska, the meaning of home will always be what it forever was when I was once the child I knew, the child that this fucking world is not going to destroy, this child that I will not allow myself for it to self-destruct.

* * * * * * * * * * * *

Lying in that old bed of his where he had sex for the first time many years ago, Mojag was not even sure that he was sleeping. But there was one thing he was sure of. Even while sleeping, the happiest smile on his face was bigger than himself. And a well-known song that marked the pain of his misery that entire time while he had been away, was coming out of the old cassette recorder. But even its descriptive verses that faithfully reflected his life and everything he might have lost, he now perceived as something that makes him stronger, and not something that his life would be consumed by it. And the song went on.

> *"Zaustavi se, vjetre, pita bih te nesto*
> *Vidjas li mi dragu i pita li za mene?*
> *Prolazija jesam krajevima tvojim*
> *Draga te jos voli cijelim srcem svojim*
>
> *Piju li nam vuci sa izvora vodu?*
> *Da li nam slavuji pjevaju u zoru?*
> *Vukovi se kriju i piju ti vodu*
> *Veseli slavuji pjevaju u zoru*
>
> *Vjetre s Dinare, hej, zaustavi se*
> *Vjetre s Dinare, hej, cujes li me*
> *Vjetre s Dinare, hej, poslusaj me, hej*
> *Gdje sam rodjen, tu ponesi me"*[41]

---

[41] Stop, my wind, I'd ask you a thing
Do you see my loved one and does she ask for me?
I have been over the fields of yours
Your girl still loves you with all her heart

Are the wolfs drinking from the water of our well?
Are the humming birds singing in the morning ?
The wolfs are hiding and drink your water
The happy birds are singing in the dawn

I will not stop fighting until the night I prevail over myself.

Hey, you wind of the mountains, stop
Hey, you wind of the mountains, can you hear me
Hey, you wind of the mountains, listen to me
To the place I was born, always take me there*

*41(*Vjetar s Dinare* – Marko Perkovic Thompson, 1998)

12 THE OTHER SIDE OF SIN

A sin is what makes any world go round. It's what I know, it's what you know, and it is what the hypocrisy of the silent priest knows. No one is a saint, and no one has ever become one in the course of our history and in the history of other worlds, no matter how convincing some books persist to sound. If we are to go theoretical, we are born in sin, and no one can deter that fact. What people, obsessed with controlling the behavior of others, are not willing to tell you is that an earthly sin can also make you feel alive in case you have forgotten the sensation. However, that should not serve as justification for engaging into it, for there is someone else, and not you, who is qualified to be the judge of your actions. No, it is certainly not a justification, for at least that much honor should be preserved. It is only a point of view derived from situations that make the blurry road to recovery ever so slippery.

There is always risk of having a bad after-taste in your mouth, but if you don't accept risk, you will never allow your life to change. Never be decadent for then you risk losing your faith and losing yourself because of insecurity towards others, and decadence has nothing to do with the innocence of sins we everyday commit. But never forget that your parents have changed many beds in a sinful act so they can start watching you grow nine months after. And that means that in order to discover the moral side of a proposed wrongdoing, you need to commit yourself into it first. For remember, all those imposed mysteries of the world can be uncovered by a single look of a passionate woman.

* * * * * * * * * * *

It is so inhumane how the human brain is designed to work. *And I'm sure you have noticed that, even though you might have never thought about it the way I did.*

Among other mysteries of its marvelous creation, the human brain is capable of many things that we are afraid to discover. And among those other things, the brain always remembers the good experiences in life so well, but its positive impact stays for such a short while. What about the experiences in life that have caused a bad taste in your mouth? Is that part of our brain so big that the destructive state of depression stays much longer and its bitter feelings never tend to go away? That is exactly what Mojag was thinking at that moment, sitting at the lonely table, in the bar at his workplace.

"It is so frustrating", he thought, "Only two days ago, I was witnessing the beauty of my family and I was my own king. Now I'm not even my own beggar. Am I so hopeless, so fucking weak? And I'm not even sure if it's my brain that fiddles with the order of my chaos, or it is my heart, which feels as if small people with sharp hatchets are tearing apart its inconsistent pieces."

But nevertheless, saying that the human brain is inhumanely designed to work, is perhaps one of the most ungrateful statements one could possibly exhale. The human brain has been created for us, and it is up to us to decide whether we are to force ourselves and learn how to control it and properly direct its unlimited, God given powers.

The day was sometime in the middle of the week but who cared. *Why should I drink alone at home when I can do it here? Do you think I feel bad that every day I am at this gruesome bar, greeting all people I work for? Oh, no, I don't give a shit.*

Mojag ordered the usual; half a liter bottle of beer. He actually ordered two bottles of beer. The waiter didn't look at him in a strange way since Mojag was sitting alone and was ordering two beers at the same time. It was only because the faithful waiter knew Chayton was coming along. Lately, Mojag and Chayton became inseparable; virtually every boring day they were sitting in that disgusting setting of the bar, whose atmosphere seemed to be stuck in the summer of 1983. But at least the terrace was still open, no matter that the outside temperature was inappropriate for it. It was a fine compensation and a satisfying comfort. And they were not the only ubiquitous customers at the bar, so they had no reason for feeling ashamed to have couple of drinks every single day. The other ubiquitous customers were retirees from that same workplace, which were in fact more alcoholics than retirees, but at least they filled in some of the empty spaces.

Finally, after some ten minutes or so, there was this dark skinned, bearded figure with understanding eyes, which appeared in the hallways that led to the door of the bar's terrace. It was Chayton, and he was even worse than Mojag in keeping track of an agreed time. He wasn't trying to look for Mojag's table; they were always sitting at the same one and so it was that time, and so it was other times even when other people had it already occupied. There was nothing special about that particular table. It was simply the best watchtower for the eventual presence of a group of flirty girls.

"Where the fuck were you?" Mojag greeted his companion.

"I just went to buy some cigarettes. That stupid machine took all my money and gave me nothing. I'm sure a woman had it designed", they started laughing together.

"What can we do when they rule our world...But don't worry, I have a full pack, I think it should be enough for both of us. Now pour that fucking beer because I dehydrated while waiting for you!"

"Ok, but you were not waiting so long..."

"Ma, doesn't matter. I rarely have all the pieces together in my head so I engaged in the usual discussion with myself", Mojag tried to be funny, but it was what he was actually doing while waiting for Chayton. Regardless, they started laughing again no matter how meaningless the conversation was. And that was why Mojag enjoyed so much sharing an endless talk with his older companion, for they could talk to one another whatever the fuck they wanted in such a relaxed atmosphere, as if they had known each other for so many years. And they could laugh at those stupid things that other petty people would ignorantly discard as barbaric behavior. *Well, my others, that is exactly why your wives are commanding your whole life, the same way your father did until the very last day you got married. But why am I fucking thinking about the rest of you when it is my own life that I cannot get hold of? At least you are not even aware that your life is not anymore yours to live.*

It was still day, in fact it was such a beautiful sunny day, despite that it didn't fit any of those myths they taught kids at school, for how the beginnings of winter are cruel by a fucking default. After all, maybe this scandalous global warming was not as bad as northern penguins persisted to advertise it. But as it was with the highly unpredictable weather of an abused earth, so was Mojag's emotions and behavior. For one moment he would be as happy as if he had all the reasons to be so, full of energy and positive thoughts. But only so shortly after, his head would be filled with nothing else but dangerous and unpredictable to himself, thoughts of destruction. His mood and emotions resembled those of a heavy drug addict that changed his behavior as often as he blinked. But he had never taken any such drugs, an invention of the profit-caring world. And why would he; he lived that sensation without the extra costs. The most difficult part, unlike the effects of drugs, was not even the fact that he was in reality *aware* of his crazy behavior. Oh no, awareness to pain was not a bother, for it had become part of himself. The most difficult fragment was that no one could notice his behavior changing, since he always kept it to himself. It was strange how he had not exploded yet. His pain could not have been read even by taking a focused journey *inside* his dark eyes. He never liked accumulating all the anger of his world, in fact that scared him the most, but his reasons were simple. Initially, who would possibly like to endure hearing about a misery of an existence?

And it was not that Mojag never tried to express what he had been feeling all that time. He modestly attempted many times, and people usually never listened. With some exceptions, no fucking body listened. Not his parents, not his friends, and especially not the girls he was finding provisional comfort inside of them. And it was not that they were a different breed, and none of them was even close to stupid. It was simply not easy for them to understand and no one blamed them for that, for their own fight was somewhat different, and their experiences much more static. But their response was ever so hasty as to discard Mojag's behavior as if he had been living a prolonged puberty phase of his life, another one of his flamboyance.

Their response was not what had hurt him, but it was the fact that most of them had unintentionally diminished his feelings in a cold-blooded and such an ignorant manner. And that was why he never tried talking about it to anyone, and that was why nobody knew the details of his life and *not* because of the ascribed arrogance to his character.

Among the rare who did understand, perhaps the only one, was exactly the person sitting opposite Mojag. Chayton seemed to have experienced similar things in life for he always had a method of relating Mojag's anger to his own, in examples that resembled each other. And the same was happening that day in the bar as the day before, and as Mojag's pattern of life seemed to be written in stone, it was probably meant to be happening many of the days after.

"Chayton, did it ever occur to you that sometimes you get this feeling when you want to destroy everything that's in front of you, no matter who or what stands in your way? Or sometimes when you simply can't stand any of the people around you, which have hypocrisy written over their fucking forehead?"

"Ha, are you joking with me? I have that feeling many times, it's normal...ok, I don't know if it is *really* normal but yes, it does happen. What can I do? What can *we* do?" Chayton replied with a smile that concealed a little pride in there.

"I hope that you are honest, because usually people don't have those sensations."

"Ma what are you saying!? Just tell me how can I not be like that, with so many fucking people that think to know everything, while constantly believing in the inferiority of the rest. And on top of that, they come to me and start breaking my balls for things I was doing when I was ten years old in the streets of my crooked city."

"I know, but I don't even pay that close attention to them anymore. Fuck them; they are nothing in my life. But it's not only that, sometimes I feel so nervous, all, but virtually all nerves in my body are shaking and I cannot find a reason why? Everything makes me so anxious, and I just want to break through. Even when I go outside on the streets, I have this awkward feeling that everyone is staring at me, monitoring every move I make. I hope it is not the case, but I spend so much time alone that I think I am losing contact with the world that is happening around me. And then, after a while, I become so indifferent to the world, even to my fucking self and to the importance of my life. And I get this fear that I can never determine why. Sometimes I am so scared, that I feel like I'm drowning; I feel like I can't breath. And yet again, I don't have a clue where this fear is coming from or why I'm becoming its slave. But I guess the fear is what keeps me going, what makes me fight."

"Don't ever be afraid, and don't ever let fear – any fear – consume your life, for that is the worst you could do", Chayton started in an almost demanding voice that was meant to be obeyed. – "And I know the feeling exactly and I know it's everything but pleasant. But you are young, you need to learn how to live with it, and control it at the same time. It's not something you can switch on and off, but it is the way your character is. I'm the same way. Analyze yourself and tell your brain otherwise."

"I have analyzed me my whole fucking life and nothing compromising comes out of it. And my own brain works against me. When I can define them, my brain is full of scary thoughts derived mostly from "what if" questions in which I debate the most fatalistic thoughts. So many things bother me, so many things I want, so many perceived injustices that fuck me up. And none of those fucking people understand that. They live their pathetic lives perfectly organized, always blushing when girls are brought into question, everything known upfront, and they never fail to bend over in front of anyone so they can satisfy the system. And all of them have the word emotion wiped out of their dictionary and their behavior...but maybe it is better to be like that, to be the obedient servant that opposes to nothing his conscious doesn't agree with. I guess being like the folks on the hill is the only way to be left alone and be satisfied..."

Chayton immediately got infuriated, his voice getting louder.

"Mojag, what the fuck are you talking about? Let me ask you something. *What if* we die this very moment? We die and that's it, end of story. But don't ask yourself what if it happens. For if something is meant to be and it's out of your reach, it is going to happen anyway. So don't put your negative thoughts to obsess you. Live your life until it lasts and share your happiness with people while they are still around. What if questions could bring you nothing else but painful regrets for lost time, caused by that same fear you just mentioned; lost time you can never make up. And do you really think you would be better off to be like the folks on the hill, whose world has nothing to do with reality?

"Ma, of course not, I just said it full of my usual and inappropriate irony. It is just..." Mojag got eerily interrupted by Chayton, as if he had forgotten to complete his previous thought of a momentary outburst of anger, when unworthy people were mentioned.

"Those fucking people are so full of shit, and so fake that I get animosities every time their existence is brought up in a discussion at my table. All those people tell you that they are too strong and they need not the generosity of others. But what they would never say, but can be immediately sensed, is that besides their words, nothing is real about them. For at night, they lock themselves in their closets, too scared to deal with the realities of darkness. They only go out when day emerges, when it looks so easy for them to consolidate their infamous bullshit. Don't get fooled by illusions of other people, Mojag, for many times you would have too many illusions on your own that would be difficult to cope with. And never forget the realism of your own reasoning and the authenticity of your own cause. And that is what makes you a better person. And that is why you should start appreciating yourself. It is difficult, I can't deny it, but it is one of the ways to reach self-awareness of your innermost reasoning and emotions, and understand the world in which you are brought up. But knowing that, would you trade your life with the one of those low lives that know nothing else but their mother's breasts and their wife's or girlfriend's demanding instruction?", Chayton rhetorically concluded with some relief considering his instinctive rush of fury.

"I know, you are absolutely right about everything you have just said. I would never trade any bit of my life with no one no matter how inconsistently difficult my survival is. That's the way I am, and that's the right way for me. *It has to be.* And thanks for telling me all that, for even though I know it, it is always good when you remind me", Mojag seemed to have completed his contemplations, since he looked much calmer than before, if not more confident. But he could never quite end his contemplations. – "The only thing is that I sometimes have so many thoughts that drill my brain, thoughts that I cannot control, thoughts that I don't want. There were even times when I'm having sex with a beautiful girl and I am thinking of stupid things, even when I have that perfect piece of curved body in my face. Can you imagine?" Mojag asked a question that was more an observation than a phrase that demanded answer.

"No, that I cannot", Chayton started laughing.

Mojag, trying to define the thoughts that only now came to his head when a woman's body was mentioned; he seemingly forgot about his fearful contemplations as he almost jumped out of the chair. It was as if a totally different person emerged.

"Oh, Chayton, I have to tell you about this girl I had last week. She sucked me so dry that I'm still in need of oxygen..."

Mojag was ever somewhat mysterious and always accepted the discretion of the women he had sex with. That was his general guideline, for he was the one who has having it good. He had never had a girl for the sake of showing off in front of his friends; he always had girls in order to satisfy his lust and his counter, and ultimately, to satisfy the girl in his momentary grip. Even on those rare occasions when he shared his experiences with people like Chayton, it was only because he or anyone else for that matter had never met the girls Mojag was talking about. That way, he thought he was protecting the insecure pride of all those beautiful girls. Mojag trusted Chayton, but he was ever too cautious to reveal the identity of his woman of the moment, for it is in human's nature of them all to sometimes say more than they are supposed to.

What else to say? Everything was as usual, all those similarly structured conversations among the two of them, along with an elevated dosage of beer. There was nothing special, nothing extraordinary that day that was worth taking an extra notice. And most probably, that same status quo would have remained unchanged if Mojag had not spotted *her*. It was *her*. *It is her!* It was that same girl he unofficially met for that small fraction of his first day he started working in that same place. It was a very small fraction of a moment that confusing day, but a huge impact that her scent left on his persona. Mojag was aware that she was the last thing on his mind all of those days after he had first seen her, but there were moments in which her scent he was able to touch in his fantasies. And all those times his blood switched on to boiling mode. Now, seeing her again, it caused an instant rush of sperm to the head.

She was sitting there with a bunch of people in what seemed to be a celebration of some sort. Mojag was wandering how he didn't notice them entering the bar as that same group of girls was already with their glasses half empty, or perhaps half full. But that was all irrelevant. As soon as he had spotted her, he never changed the fixture of his eyes. She was dressed in a red skirt that matched her stylish, red shoes. The top he couldn't define as he was focused on her curves in that part of the body, slightly covered by the gleam of her maroon hair. *But probably he would never remember what was she wearing that day, but he would certainly never forget the way she looked.* And the way she looked was nothing short of sexually enchanting. Mojag was in an absolute state of unjustified Aesthetic Arrest. He also noticed that she had some sticker, positioned on the side of her left breast, which meant that she was not an employee in the company, but an occasional visitor. *I can't miss the opportunity. I have to react quickly. Look this way, princess, let yourself read my eyes.*

And those very moments he was contemplating his strategy, she finished a conversation with her friends and gazed in his direction, as if she could feel the heat he was emulating towards her. Their eyes crossed and that was the one moment needed. The spark exploded as an Apollo going to the moon. She smiled affectionately as she immediately started flirting with Mojag. She was probably the best one in it. Mojag smiled back to her without moving his eyes from her gaze. Only at looking at each other, they were already French-kissing. Especially when she started to move her legs from one side to the other, signifying the burning sensation she was evidently feeling.

"What? What are you smiling at?" Chayton asked as he noticed Mojag irreversibly losing track of what his friend was saying. He turned back and he immediately understood Mojag's distraction.

"Ok, I understand that you can never stop at such an occasion, so I guess it's justified that I was talking in vain", Chayton answered his own question.

"A?" Mojag asked in absence and started coming back from the flirt of a lifetime. "Oh, sorry, I just drifted away for a little while", he continued, trying to avoid any questions that he didn't want to answer, pretending that nothing had happened. Chayton continued with whatever he had been saying before, but Mojag was already mentally away to the other table. Now all of a sudden, the mysterious girl's friends started looking towards Mojag's position and started giggling. There was no doubt that she had already informed her friends of her intimate "encounter" with Mojag, if they hadn't noticed her flirty eyes themselves. *Damn it, why the fuck do girls need to talk to their friends even before something happens? It only ruins opportunities, rarely promotes them. I have to react quickly.*

After a very short while, she left the table. *No, noooo!!! She's leaving. I have to do something.* Mojag's anxiety reached a peak. *Wait, calm down, this is a perfect opportunity. She's not leaving; she can't leave without her purse. It is right there on the table. And besides, stupid, she didn't say goodbye to her friends. There is only one explanation. She must be on her way to the toilet. Perfect!*

Patience was never one of Mojag's characteristics, but he had to deal with his anxiety and stomach in the next couple of minutes, his heart pounding. Those moments seemed cheerfully painful in which little luck meant everything. He waited exactly three minutes and 12 seconds. It was the perfect timing. He went to the toilet, erect, but revealing nothing of his vital disturbances to Chayton, who suspected that something was going on, but at least he did not receive any confirmation from Mojag.

The momentary road to the toilets was a blaze of glory for Mojag. He felt as if going to a battlefield in which he *knew*, not sensed, the outcome in advance. He not only felt he would meet her; he had never been as sure, but he was convinced she had already been won. Or perhaps, he was the one who had been won. And it was no arrogance of Mojag that he felt confident, for it was solely she who was driving his self-assurance. Such a look in those expressive, dark eyes of hers meant much more than a flirt, it was a whole story she told with that secure gaze, femme fatale in all aspects of the myth. The temptation of her lust was too strong to resist, and too sacred to forfeit.

Mojag wasn't even trying to do the usual adjustment to a strategy so well played many times before; he kept the same pace, not in need to slow down in order to make sure that he wouldn't miss her. Everything was unconditionally perfect and everything was so damn real at the same time. How could that possibly be? The stars seemed to be smiling, and so was Mojag as she started approaching in the near distance, in the same hallway where he was headed right into her. She had nowhere to go. And she appeared as if she did not want to go anywhere else but to bump into him. And that was exactly what she did. She touched him with her strong, but fine shoulder as they almost went away. In fact, the timing was so perfect that they didn't even need to get over a distance among themselves while looking at each other, for those were usually moments when the brain makes too many, too obsolete decisions. They had no time to think, as they nearly bumped into one another.

"*I'm all yours*", she started talking without speaking, her thoughts still silent but too obvious to conceal. She said nothing else for her smile and that deep look in her eyes said it all.

After moments of sensation, he started in whisper rather than a cohesive sound, giving her a sincere comment, keeping his smile on in the usual charming mode:

"Before I say anything else...simply...you look beautiful."

* * * * * * * * * * *

45 minutes later

"What are you having?" he asked, hoping that she would be thirsty even for a drop of water. Any affirmative answer was fine as long as he could go to the kitchen of his apartment and consolidate his thoughts.

"Red wine would do it", she replied without giving it a single thought. She appeared as if she had either planned the encounter or she was far too experienced to know otherwise. Mojag was convinced it was both. *My kind of girl. She knows what she wants.*

The proximity of Mojag's apartment to his workplace was ideal. It was only couple of minutes walking, so it was convenient in case any of the girls had extra time after work.

He went on to the kitchen, masterminding his next move. *She said her name was Hantaywee[42] or something like that, and she seems prepared to do anything that my occasionally dirty imagination would request. And the momentary occasion is such.* He popped open the new bottle of quality wine, originating from its designated region of the *South*. He didn't like the acids that a wine usually left in his stomach the morning after, but his apartment was never in deficit of unopened wine bottles... red bottles of wine. The reason was simple, for that was what girls perceived as a sign of passion and romance. And they were right, Mojag often admitted.

He already got back in the room where her thoughts were settled. He gently filled up the proper glasses of the wine bottle he had only now opened. He passed one of them to the girl that was sitting on the apartment's *legendary couch* full of dried, white, organic stains.

"To your smile", he started the toast exposing a delicious smile on his face.

She said nothing but returned the smile, even more desirable than before; her dark tan preventing her blush to be noticed. After the first sip and their connecting look full of passion, they realized they had nothing else to say to themselves; they *couldn't* say

---

[42] Native American female name of Sioux origin. Its meaning is *FAITHFUL.*

anything more to themselves. Mojag was already swept off his feet as he forgot to do what was usually his line, his move; he was consolidating his thoughts way too much. But she was as experienced to fill his momentary lapse of reason and kissed him.

Uh, the kiss. The kiss was a rare breed; it was probably the top of his list. It surpassed any scene from a romantic movie. He didn't want to close his eyes as he was examining the strong passion she was giving out. They were already into each other's bodies, as she took *his initiative* in her own hands. Everything was happening before their eyes could even flick.

1 hour later

Strolling through some of her slightly torn clothes on the floor, Mojag hastily went to the toilet to clean himself up. With his back against the naked woman, satisfyingly spread on his couch, there was only one thought he had in mind. *Please disappear.*

His counter just increased its number, but the sex was bad, or at least unfulfilling. The reason was not that she was bad, for he was certain she could do much better. It was the fact that she was quite reluctant to relax, giving away an image of being uncomfortably guilty of what she was doing. But at that point, there was no return for her; at least she did not ask for a preemptive stop. And now it was already too late. *What? Do I need to feel sorry for her? She comes here to fuck me without even knowing me, and I need to explore her feelings? Ma please!* The way of a women's guilt is to suck you into them without you even noticing. She had enjoyed every single bit, and now she seemed to pretend that she was a good girl. And obviously she had an undefined life, but Mojag wasn't sure that he was enthusiastic to know about it. There was only one tiny part of his subconscious that didn't match his style and the circumstances of the moment. Looking at himself in the mirror he saw that reflection of his mind that was giving away confusion. For a fraction of a moment, trying to push it away instantly, he recalled a sensation that had occurred to him. Despite the aftermath and the anonymity of the girl, he felt so unusually safe inside of her, for a moment back there. His thoughts were as weird to himself as they would have been to any objective observer. And besides, was it possible that there was anything different about her? She was as the same as any other girl during Mojag's period of undiagnosed insanity, too passionate not to give in, and too proud to admit it afterwards. Those things made Mojag strangely curious, at least momentarily, but he certainly wasn't eager to discover what was so special about the brief sensation in him that she had caused. Physically, she was mesmerizing, and that was the only side of her he was aware of. The other side went into far more complex, philosophical reasoning that was based on the inexistent scruples of that mysterious woman. Those were the only facts he knew about her, and they might have been insufficient to be judged upon. Be as it was, Mojag's state of life at that point of his own history stated that even if she was a princess, she would only be an additional constraint, a luxury he could not, and was not willing to sustain. One thing he felt sorry for was his tremendously frequent, changing sense of reality and the occasional actors in his life. A couple of hours ago, she was his goddess, the only thing that mattered; at this very moment she was an unnecessary burden that he couldn't wait to say goodbye to.

He reentered back to the room where she was waiting, his hesitance to be close to her made him taking more time in the toilet than he actually needed. She was already dressed again, wearing the clothes she could piece back together. It immediately struck him that she was not less mesmerizing than before, but there was something, a decisive change that was difficult to grasp. Her eyes entailed not even ruins of the fire they had revealed before; her eyes now portrayed an innocence that she couldn't justify in any way. On the other side, the expression in Mojag's eyes appeared more ambiguous than vacant. Very shortly after, in spite of her persistence, she realized that she would not be granted the opportunity to get close to Mojag, and she initiated her departure. And that was probably the best what she could do at that moment, as anything else would have quickly peeled off Mojag's fragile patience. She put on her sexiest red shoes and they kissed instinctively as she closed the apartment's door from the outside. Maybe they had talked something in between but it all probably resembled an irrelevant, all too familiar a cliché.

Mojag strolled to his favorite room where the deep, relaxing sounds of music were still running. Some late hours were approaching as it was almost time for bed; he didn't even try to take notice of that fact. He went on looking for what was a familiar box with a disgusting label: *Smoking kills*. He found the cigarettes in the chaos of the room, switched on to some mind teasing music and lit one cigarette. He wasn't tired at all, but he was trying to relax. The exercise was great until the moment his mind started functioning again, full of many things he wasn't willing to debate about with himself. But he had no other choice, but to at least follow his moods if he could not understand them. And only now, he started recollecting the conversations, if any, with that beautiful girl that he thought was already out of his life the same way she had come in it. They had talked about something for sure, but it was difficult to remember, not because he had not been listening, but because he was too obsessed with the passion that her eyes conveyed. There were many stories to be revealed in those eyes, and possibly that was what made him reflect on that girl he knew nothing about. From the limited pool of little facts he knew about her, he got to know that her parents were some diplomats that happened to have their current mission in the big city. That was the basic reason why she happened to be living there as well. She killed her time by working part time in some company making designer clothes. It wasn't clear whether she liked her life the way it was organized, because he felt her to be lonely as well. The fierce look in her eyes was too passionate, and even though she immediately exposed herself to Mojag, there was an instinct of Mojag's that was telling him she was not only a fuck body as she had initially introduced herself as. There was something in those eyes revealing that she had an immense amount of emotions to give, emotions she had been holding within for a long period. Once again, her parents were diplomats and that also meant that like almost everybody, she would be leaving in a couple of months when the ambassador's mission would change. But at that point Mojag didn't care at all about her plans or any plans of any other girl; his observations were merely a reflection on a life of someone who he had just met.

The passion in her eyes was something he could reflect upon, but he could not define. The one thing he could relate to and the one thing that had possibly created the subversive warmth in the caverns of his soul was music. Thinking back about their scarce dialogs, he realized that they were talking about music most of the time. And according to what she was telling before, music was a huge part of her life. And it was not random, meaningless music she was talking of, but real, meaningful music that she also understood at the same time, and in the same way Mojag did. And music was to him a very sensitive issue. Their taste was very similar, and Mojag could sense she felt the same emotions when talking about or listening to music. It rarely happened that he had found somebody that understood music the way he did, and she certainly was the one rare case he had witnessed. To Mojag, it seemed to have an enlightening effect, because to him, there was no religion but sex and music. And she seemed to encompass both revelations. Focusing there for an additional moment, he started reliving the passions of that mysterious woman, feeling her breath around his neck. He wasn't sure if he was getting aroused or simply spaced out in the product of his own imagination. *Who cares? Most probably I would never see that girl again, no matter the deceptions that my brain serves me with now. And besides, right now, I want to sleep, and that's good for those are the only moments when I clear my mind from thoughts, even while dreaming.* Forgetting to realize that he had given his phone number to the girl of his contemplations, he put a bit more thought than in any other, changed to his naked, sleeping uniform, and fell benevolently above the clean, but messy sheets of his bed.

I will not stop fighting until the night I prevail over myself.

13 DEFEATING YOUR OWN SELF

One of humanity's many fundamental problems is the belief that other people are bad, and other people are to be blamed for being the cause to all the dread and miseries of the world. In fact, almost all wars in history are waged because of such guiding principles; today's wars are just continuing the old tradition. The same analogy applies to an individual, and those in his surrounding. The one reason of such a behavior, with all its obsoleteness it accompanies, is the incapacitation of man to understand and accept the changes that are occurring within his own self. By winning the constant battle with himself, only then a man can start understanding and accepting other people in every aspect of their differences. Only by being able to change *your* world you would be able to start acknowledging the existence of other worlds. And that is the basis to achieving anything you desire, by defeating your yesterday self, your five-minutes-ago self. That is how you would start expecting less from the world, as it offers you only fake illusion of conditional help. However, when you see that help is on your doorway and you are really in need of it, don't let your fake pride deny it.

But nevertheless, no matter how someone can inspire vital faith in yourself, there is absolutely nobody in this world, but you, who can make the finishing touch happen.

There is no such thing as a winnable war, apart from the war you wage within, the struggle against the beast of your old self. That is a constant, inevitable war, and is happening whether you like it or not. The one clear way to experience defeat is if you make yourself an observer of your fall.

* * * * * * * * * * *

The usual summer look-a-like sunset was nowhere to be seen. It seemed as if the big city had swallowed the nature that allowed it to prosper. But the sunset was nowhere to be seen because it was already so dark despite the fact that it was only 3.30 p.m. on that working day.

There was nothing scarier than winter, especially because the newest century minimized the number of the usual four seasons to only two, summer and winter. And the transition from one to another resembled a flashlight turning on and off, nothing in between. The animosities that were opening up with the emergence of winter within different fractions of the human psyche, were so unwelcome and way too unpleasant. And probably not only in the confined borders of the big city, for the winter depression had inevitably become a global movement and of a global concern.

The big city, in winter in particular, served as yet another major thing to be bitched at, to complain about, and to get insane in it. As it did that day, and would be the same for many days to follow, the pessimism of the darkness was ever too hasty to cover the heart of the city and the soul of people who were still in possession of it.

Mojag was having his fifth coffee of the day along with his tenth cigarette, while taking yet another unjustified break from work. The setting was the usual, dull ritual; the confined and dirty air of the company's smoking room, cigarette, coffee replacing the alcohol of the previous night, and occasional people to greet. Mojag didn't always enjoy having coffee by himself, but when he did, he was observing other people, their moods and the obsessions of their whispering thoughts. That way, and with some success, he avoided his own, unwanted thoughts.

Two people sitting opposite each other on a different table caught his attention. They were not interesting at all; in fact they were so fucking repelling. And the repulsion was not because of their appearance but because of their conversation. They were talking in a language that Mojag could not understand, but the fanatically jealous look in their eyes while talking to each other, revealed much more than any of the words they were saying. For their eyes and body language clearly implied they were gossiping about other people's life. And not only that; they seemed to be gossiping as if their own life was in question, with the one difference that they were obviously cheering on someone else's misery, or failure, someone else's love story, or something like that. Perhaps that was the reason why they had no life on their own to reflect upon it, for other people's successes and failures seemed to make them happier and more thrilled. The most desperate part of it was that they were not even females, which made them even worse people.

Gossiping was one of the main signatures of almost all people working at that very same place that was paying out Mojag's salary each month. Gossiping was something Mojag rarely cared about, unless the lies of the circling rumors could damage the integrity of his friends and the integrity of his intimate girls. He rarely cared about what people thought of him or whether he was the center of an amusing topic to them. He rarely cared because he frequently heard stories about himself that made him proud of things that people thought he had done, not least in his sexual life. And yes, there were perhaps a lot of times when he lived his life exactly like in those movies that his parents feverishly forbid him to watch when he was a kid, yet practically none of those gossips petty people had been inventing for him were essentially correct. *But, what the hell, let the mob amuse themselves. And anyways, who cares about essence these days?*

And while everyone thought Mojag already had sex with half of the girls in that corporate complex building (the coalition-of-the-willing-girls there was a huge number), he was experiencing the loneliest masturbation period his world had ever known. But, it was not so long that he started catching up with what his male's family tradition prescribed – what his sexual duty implied. It was not so long after he made up for the subjectively postponed, certainly not lost, opportunities.

Mojag just lit his eleventh cigarette, even though he felt no need for it.

Living in an undefined state of mind and surrounding was perhaps not what Mojag had chosen on his own to be his guiding principle. Sitting there on that worn out couch in the insides of what the company called a smoking room, a designated place for smokers, which resembled much more like a waiting room in a concentration camp, he thought of many things.

The only difference from how his brain worked some six months before, was that among the crazy thoughts his brain inflicted on his subconscious was the figure of a girl, which apart from everything else that was happening in his mind, invoked feelings of warmth, peace and security. And those were certainly sensations that should not be confused for freedom, but they were at least emotions of a better origin than any of the other innate compulsions Mojag was guided by. And even though what he was experiencing now didn't seem to fully satisfy his definition of freedom since he felt partially dependent upon someone else's words, the same freedom-concept of his has become somewhat clearer and at the same time, much more free.

What was even more confusing to him was that the girl in his mind, which caused positive and needed disturbance to his thoughts, was a girl that was real, a girl that he had gotten to know in *every* way in the course of the past half a year. He even knew her name, for he remembered that some six months ago in *a usual*, but weird evening in his apartment, she had said her name was Hantaywee. It was way above any explanation he could get of how the girl that was not even a full one night stand, had become his most faithful companion, his *only* companion.

Nevertheless, and even though he wasn't keen on drilling down to finding possible causes of his crackdown to that girl, the distant observer that he ever seemed to be would have probably tried to determine the roots of his emotional walls' breach.

1. Hantaywee probably managed to get to him because she was the most bothering girl Mojag's world had ever known.

But how? In my world, that would not count as a good thing.

2. Hantaywee aroused him as sexually as no other has ever attempted before.

Uh, just ask my neighbors.

3. Hantaywee knew exactly what she wanted, but her insecurity created a basis for potential manipulation.

I could afford behaving like an animal, knowing that she would come back to me no matter what I do.

4. Hantaywee praised music practically the same way Mojag did.

My way of paying tribute to music is certainly not the best, but it is very important that she shares the same musical sentiments.

5. Hantaywee took care of Mojag in all ways possible.

I feel so safe with her, being scared not even by my own thoughts when she is by my side.

6. Hantaywee taught him the sweet meaning of the small details in life.

She makes every second of any experience count.

7. Hantaywee was someone that could sell you the world, and you would accept it with a smile.

She sold me a world, and I never stopped smiling.

8. Hantaywee had a sophisticated sense of humor, similar to Mojag's, only without the annoying irony and sarcasm that he was full of.

When we are not fighting, she never fails to make me enjoy a relaxing smile.

9. Hantaywee gave him memories he didn't have.

Thank you, Hantaywee.

Don't destroy them… please.

10. Hantaywee showed him how to start appreciating life and that embracing life was not a sin.

She introduced me to a novelty I deemed lost forever.

All the coined reasons of that distant observer never worked one against the other, or one without the other. Understanding the whole concept meant that all causes had to be brought together in a certain way to provide Mojag with something that would explain his newest dependency. None of the reasons alone could have possibly added up to what was really occurring at that time.

Hantaywee was indeed THE most bothering girl of them all. He remembered how the first couple of days after they had met, maybe even a week after that, she called for so many times that Mojag's phone was shivering days after in anticipation of her next call. He wasn't such a bastard from the very beginning, for at least ten times he politely told her to fuck off and that he needed nobody. And he did say it with all the arrogance it accompanied.

"Nothing personal", he said at that time. And it was really nothing personal. He had nothing against that girl; he just didn't want her close to him and he simply didn't believe that anyone would be willing to understand him. And how could he have believed otherwise, when not even he himself could understand the life he was unconsciously following.

Apart from that concept, Mojag would have probably agreed to see her at least one more time after the night they had first met, but he was literally afraid to give in. He was frightened because of her way of initial obsession. He had so many thoughts of his own that constrained his behavior and life flow, that he could not afford yet another chain around his inexistent freedom. Concerning the way how she was desperately trying to get accepted and be part of Mojag's world, he would have done anything to prevent that from happening. And it was strange, for he was dying to smell the scent of her smooth skin for at least hundred times more, but his instincts told him, no matter how erroneous they were, and they usually never were, that he must avoid getting close to her under any circumstances. And he wasn't even trying to find any justification to his stupidity, for he always followed his instincts blindly. After all, at one point, his instincts were all he was left with.

That entire period he avoided accepting anyone into his world, he was being as hypocritical to himself as he had never been before, for he had so many concealed emotions, so much to give, but he was as much afraid to let go. And besides, she had said once that she would be leaving any time her parents would decide moving away from the big city, so why the fuck trying to be a hero of yet another failed romance?

She was a beauty that could find anyone else for the comfort she seemed to be seeking, so why should I be the one that she would use to overcome her depression when I couldn't even overcome mine? Perhaps, unnoticeably, in the back of his head, he thought that she might be of help to him as well.

And then, shortly after Mojag thought she had finally understood, if not accepted his determined tone of voice, out of nowhere, she appeared in front of his office door.

At least that much she knew for showing up there instead in front of my apartment building, as she was smart enough to realize that the odds were high that no one would answer even if I were to be at home.

But at work, there was no escape. She knew he had to be there; she could feel that he had no other place to hold on to. Be as it was, the expression on Mojag's face when she appeared at the doorstep, with that phony innocent look in her eyes, clearly and shamelessly portrayed his immediate loss of patience.

What the fuck are you doing here? What are you trying to do? Don't you fucking understand?! And who the fuck let you in this building? He didn't say his tasty words out loud, but she got the message.

As family member of a person working in that insecure company, she had the right to a free passage through the corridors. She nevertheless understood his impatient message, but she was not a girl that would ever seem to quit. It seemed that she had too much at stake, and at the same time she could sense that she could abuse Mojag's potentially naive generosity, no matter how he did not want to admit it.

She pleaded for a company to go for coffee; he immediately turned the option down as he had a lot of work to catch up from all the previous days he had missed out in concentrating on what he had been paid for. But then again, she still seemed as if she would not quit standing at the door without getting at least a comforting answer, so he decided to agree on having a cigarette with her.

"Just for 5 minutes. Then I have to get back", he said. They went out in the courtyard.

The conversation was somewhat formal as he was trying hard to avoid any talk about what had happened among them. In fact, he never even remembered much of what she was trying to say, for he was convinced what she was trying to do; trying to get to him. And that he could not accept for reasons that not even he wanted to be aware of. But there was one thing he did remember, and he was laughing out loud inside of himself when she said what she probably intended the whole time. In the end, when they were parting, Mojag getting impatient to walk away, she said:

"Wait just for one more minute...I wanted to ask you something...I know you think I'm crazy for what I am going to ask, having in mind that you seem reluctant to everything, but...without much obligations, do you want that we have something like a...do you want that we are something like boyfriend and girlfriend?"

What?! What kind of a question is that? Someone might consider it innocently cute, but is she for real?

With all the obsoleteness it encompassed, he knew that whatever he would say, he wouldn't necessarily need to be careful to fulfill it. But then again, for reasons contradictory to his momentary emotions, he simply said "Ok". At least that way he hoped he would probably be spared of questions he didn't want answered; question for which she deserved no answer. And the way he exclaimed the affirmative answer was more indifferent than affirmative; but she didn't seem to mind. She only added with an innocent smile:

"But just to warn you, which I guess you might have already noticed. I can sometimes be very bothering."

"I think I did notice. But I know that you would have to quit on one of the two things you told me last, for bothering is something that I cannot quite cope with. And that I think you have noticed as well."

She did not quit on any of the two things. I coped with every bit of her bothering much more than I thought I could take.

Even now, sitting in the darkness of the winter, he was not able to understand why the hell he had agreed to her gracious offer; for apart from her body, there wasn't anything else that he had initially wanted. He continuously felt a duty to explore her lust and satisfy his libido, which she managed to increase to previously unknown importance.

Apart from all her abilities, it would have been unfair to Mojag to say that she was innocent for he could sense that there were many things about her that she had done in her past, things which he would certainly never wish to know. And besides her entire self-proclaimed depression, "she had a lot of pretty, pretty boys that she called friends"[43], and that was frequently eroding the trust that Mojag had accommodated for her. Mojag in turn had also, perhaps even more pretty, pretty girls by his side, but he could have never referred to them as friends. But that perhaps only increased the wickedness of his fantasies.

Everything that came from her had an annoyingly positive effect on Mojag's spirit. In fact, not only the spirit, but his body and endurance as well, for the sex was something that countered the argument in all its aspects that perfection did not exist. They were having sex every day, not less than five-six times a day, except for Sunday, when they did it only twice. They were usually hanging out at Mojag's apartment, and only sometimes in the spacious apartment of her parents,

---

[43] *Hotel California* – The Eagles, 1977

using every weekend her parents would leave the city. The frequency was not planned, and they had no norm to fulfill, not least because Mojag's work related responsibilities limited his time for dirty things; they just simply had too much passion to do otherwise. And the more they had it, the better it got, no matter how Mojag thought that wasn't possible. Every time he would say to himself" "this one was the best". But then the following time it would be even better. She always knew what to do in bed, on the sofa, in the kitchen, in the bathtub, and the desire was even higher because she would always do things in the best moment. Mojag never needed to ask for anything he would envision, for as soon as he had imagined it, she would already be fulfilling his silent request.

The sex was superb, and that was the only thing in Mojag's life that he didn't need to make plans for. And besides all the healthy prescriptions it accommodated, the sex they were having was something Mojag could fully concentrate in, making sure that it clogged all unnecessary thoughts in his mind.

Most of the time, Hantaywee knew *exactly* what she wanted and she behaved accordingly, making sure her wishes were fulfilled. And for some reasons, which were perhaps not as obvious to Mojag initially, she wanted Mojag so badly that she was prepared to endure anything uncompromising that he would do, just to make sure that he stayed with her. It seemed as if no one before had offered the comfort that she thought she might get.

She was lonely, so she wanted to kill her bore. She had just gotten out of a relationship that would have brought here right out on the street had she continued in the same manner. Mojag always felt good by her side, even though he was initially reluctant to her constant company. And as selfish as he had become, he occasionally felt (ab)used, whenever her requests would not involve sex, for sometimes he felt like an idiot who she desperately needed to overcome her growing insecurity.

"I am not a saint in any way", he often reasoned, *"even though my self-perceived misery might imply all characteristics of one. Regardless, what the fuck she sees in me? What does she want from me? I am not a fucking clown to make sure that she's smiling!"*

In addition, she was dependent upon her parents much more than she should have been. *I mean, she was a bit less than twenty-three, but I suppose by that age one should at least be independent of the parent's dogmas.*

But for what was worse, her parents seemed to be on the verge of getting divorced. It was understandably a difficult period for her, but objectively, the lingering ways of her parents made her reluctant to change her perceptions of life. She needed change, but she was way too insecure to realize the benefits that she might get if she changed certain ways. And besides, she was not a child anymore to feel dependent upon her parents to the extent she was, no matter what their sticky situation turned her into.

There were many girls in Mojag's life, so many of them before, a lot of them asking for explanations they had never had the privilege to obtain, but this one was way out of line and way out of reach. She was trying to contact him at least every one hour a day by any means, trying to get under Mojag's skin as deep as his momentary distractions allowed. That was the explanation why he had behaved like an animal many times, a behavior she arguably didn't deserve. Many times he was treating her in a very bad way, simply to try and make sure that she would stay at a highest distance from him as possible. But her persistence was one of her most amazing qualities. She never quit, no matter how bad a taste he had left in her mouth at many occasions that even Mojag wanted to forget. And she always managed to get him back. And yet again, besides her objective reasons, he could not get a glimpse of why she was so persistent to getting close to someone who couldn't care less about the way of his life and especially for the life of any other being. He wanted nobody else but his family and friends. He was initially way too ungrateful for anything she was doing for him, as he treated her with ambiguity. But she never got confused, and it was amazing how she had chosen to endure such an unfair behavior from his side. He was practically trying to keep her on a leash for whenever his indifference would need a distraction. He almost never called her when she had been initially, and single-handedly convinced that they were together; that they *would* be together.

He would only go back to her when he would feel down and out, left out by the world he had once believed in, with all the pathetic ways his behavior entailed. She was always there for him no matter how bad he had treated her the day before. And even in those times when he would start complaining about his life, he was doing it in such an arrogant way as if he was the only living person that had ever experienced pain and suffering.

Hantaywee was beautiful in all definitions that the word entailed. The perfection of her body he immediately noticed that same night they first met. Six months ahead, he discovered that her inner spirit provided the perfect balance with her appearance of a goddess.

She had vast understanding of music, living all those songs equally emotional to the way Mojag did. Maybe that was a bad thing, but that was certainly what kept him even more attracted to her. Only he wasn't quite sure whether he was getting more attracted to her sexually or in a less meaningful way.

Their record collection was maybe not identical, for his had much more destructive idealism as the ideology behind it, but the way they both lived with music was a perfect harmony. When they were alone, they were getting lost in themselves because of the similar way they responded to music. When they were together, the music they were listening to, made them become like one. The music altogether was one of the most important things that kept that harmony of theirs growing.

Mojag had always been a person with inexistent schedule. He wasn't quite living for the day at stake, for he had some sort of a blurry vision of his future plans. But none of his plans were achievable since he was ever too lazy to commit in doing what he wished for. And that was yet another field in the pool of his vices that Hantaywee helped change. She practically organized his time, virtually sitting every week with him to make a plan for all the things that he wanted done. She would always bring a differently colored paper that would mark the beginning of the schedule for the following week. He felt a bit ignorant, as if she was his mother and he was the helpless child that needed guidance, but that was a good way to make him realize that time was something that he could use, and not something that he should desperately fight against. Even with her scheduling, he was trying to forfeit some of the tasks he was to do, but she was always there to remind him. And whenever she would remind him, his patience exploded, but he had always accepted. And practically always, he was ever grateful that she was pushing him to do things he longed for, things which his laziness and indifferent mind had prevented from happening for such a long period. And whenever fists of fury and anger would consume his brain and he would start falling back into the so much familiar den of agony, she was always ready to bring him back. And she always did. And nobody knew how she managed to achieve that. She found him below *a* bedrock of life and placed him in a pedestal she always levered high.

They were both young, and as much as Mojag was being constantly eaten by his depression at the best times of his life, it seemed that her life was also not as shiny as she appeared to be. But Hantaywee rarely talked about her unhappy moments, and perhaps it was better that way, for he rarely felt like listening, frequently frightened of what she might reveal.

Mojag *never* talked about his moments, but at those times, it was better for people to stay away at a safer distance from him. The details that he knew about her, was that apart from him, Hantaywee had a different life full of style and blazes of momentary glory, and she was not going to be in the big city for all times. At least the latter feature was similar to all the rest that had abandoned him long ago. And in fact, that was perhaps the main reason why Mojag wasn't even slightly keen on getting close to her. He was all too familiar with the procedure of being left behind, and he wanted to avoid it from happening again at any cost. An additional thing that added up to his reluctance to let go was that Hantaywee was way too similar to him. And that was not good. She was a female replica of him, for all the same flirty, deceiving tricks he had brought into perfection, she implemented the best. The efficiency with her was such that she did it in a transparent manner, in a manner that you know you were being cheated, but you could do nothing about it; you would only start dying when you, and if you, would ever hear any of the stories her life had created for her. Such behavior of hers made Mojag's paranoia grow even more in line with his skepticism. And such behavior of hers constantly provoked growing feelings of Mojag's doubt in the sincerity of her words.

She exposed every bit of herself only one hour after I have gotten to know her. How can I possibly not be skeptical? I loved her way that night, but who knows how many of them before had the privilege to taste her in that similar fashion, before she decided to BLOW my mind off? One, two, three, maybe more?! Or maybe even at times when I know she's been mine!

Hantaywee was someone that could sell you the world, and you would accept it with a smile. She sold Mojag a world and that brought his face the happiest smile he had ever put on; that was something he had lost somewhere in his shadowy roam. At the beginning, she was getting offended when he would tell her that he could never believe her because of her ways of exposed sexuality. And perhaps that was partly justified, but it was probably Mojag's paranoia...or was it?

Be as it was, she could have never faked any of the emotions she was giving to him, and even if she was, those were all moments of truth in her lies. And besides, no matter how Mojag denied her truthfulness at times, she knew him for a period of only six months, and she knew much more about him than anyone else that ever got to know him, including himself. She knew all the details of his life he never wanted exposed. Many of the things he had never even told to his best of friends, and with them he had never failed to commit any of the thoughts he was experiencing. Simply, to her, he could say everything he never had the courage to say it to anybody else. At the beginning stages of their romance, he was inefficiently trying to avoid his confessions, but she made them all surface out, and that meant a huge shitload of burden moving away from his chest, and more importantly, far away from his mind.

Hantaywee always taught me how to start appreciating life the same way I have done ever before I got to know my darkest of sides. And she did that not by means of presenting a theoretical concept, but a practical, which she always backed up with flavors that helped me understand the meaning of things.

Regardless how little a thing she would do, she always made it in such a way to caress every detail, in order to make the whole experience unforgettable and meaningful. Even when she would come to visit her father at work, and Mojag had time only for a small kiss, he would meet up with her in the courtyard by the fountain, and every time she would wrap up a chocolate with a beautiful note to make the experience real. Or even at those rare times that they would end up in a fight, she would come back with something that a person could not stay indifferent about. He loved everything coming from her, for all those little things she did were magic.

Mojag, on the contrary, was very dire at making a moment count, for the appearance he was giving out was that he couldn't wait for moments to pass by him. He never did that on purpose, for his purpose he deemed forever lost. And regardless how unintended his inertness was, it was not justified and correct towards the warmth she was giving to him. And many of the moments he would have missed out if she hadn't been there.

Making every second count, fulfilling it to the highest possible levels was something that she was born to do. She had so much emotions, so much love to give, and Mojag was someone that her flirty eyes had chosen, at least for something more than *a blow*. And he couldn't have been any happier, even though he was too scared to admit it out loud. She loved him with most of her heart, trying to spend every second she could only to be with him. And yet again, whenever she said she loved him, he would look at her as if something was wrong. He couldn't recall whether he had said it back at all, but he couldn't hide the emotional book written in his eyes, no matter how hard he *thought* he was trying.

And many times he would sit there in front of the mirror, analyzing himself, and he would start thinking that perhaps he'd be better off not to say those things to her. But why? His concern was way too stupid, for his *philosophy* was that if he wouldn't say it, he would not get even more involved with her. And that was guided by one of his principles that the less you start loving a girl, the less you miss her. But that unfair philosophy of his had never worked and he never learned to discard it. Sometimes he would get impatient and scared because of her obsessions with him, but only to realize that he was too dependent on her love. Hantaywee was his cherry blossom girl.

Not so many people knew about them, because Mojag didn't want anyone mixing with the momentary fulfillment of his life, even though she was usually raising the "mysterious issue" a couple of times. Or maybe very few knew because nobody was asking anything about him. Or perhaps it was because he couldn't stand any people's vicious envy of his happiness, for that was something that infuriated him, the unworthy people of any such surrounding being the cause. For such things, he would send anybody to the firing squads without trial.

But then again, Hantaywee-wise, on one hand it was perhaps understandable that someone was envious, for she was a girl that even Mojag would be envious at anyone that had her by his side. She was the best motivational force to life that he knew about, and there was nothing more he needed in order to succeed. Hantaywee was a beautiful person, one that treated him like the king he never was.

Never before had he any memories in that city that he could emotionally bind them to any girl; she had changed that in all ways possible. She gave him the possibility to have them, and by some miracle, he had accepted, almost unwillingly and certainly unconsciously. She had to put a lot of effort to make him live, for he was ever reluctant to commit in any way.

He was tired the whole time as his ubiquitous loneliness was wearing him out. He wasn't enjoying his loneliness, but he seemed to have forgotten any other way of living, for his loneliness made him forget how it was to be with someone apart from the blue chords of his guitar. But she made it, she made *his life happen,* for her persistence always prevailed. Every bit of that city he had lived in for the past five years before he met her, now started painting itself with the happiest colors ever invented. Many times he would stop and ask her, kiss her lips, just to see if the magic would not pop and go away when he would touch her hair. It never popped. Now even the river, *his* river, the one he thought was exclusively designed for himself only and the company of the wind, reminded him of her touch and her striking scent.

There were few times he needed to go somewhere *abroad,* away from the city for whatever implied reasons. And all those times he was going away, he was going only to come back to her. Mojag felt so secure and safe when he would see her standing there at the airport waiting for his embrace. And nobody had done that for him any time before in the order of the big city. Especially, nobody had done that for him with such passion towards every move he made.

* * * * * * * * * * *

The initial, indefinite curses that Mojag spelled out the day he welcomed her to his endless nightmare, he shortly after replaced with praising that same day as if it marked a change that initiated the beginning of his life. He had placed absolutely no expectations from that girl, but she made sure that he longed for every new moment to be with her. And he did. And she might have not been the type of girl he would marry at any time and at any circumstances, but was certainly his princess of the moment.

Whatever the exact reasons of their story were, he was admittedly way into her. But no matter what those reasons were, their initial spark made way for the beginning of what turned out to be the fieriest romance Mojag had ever experienced, something that he had not even the slightest idea of how it had developed the way it unfurled. And above all, it was unfair to label their relationship as love, for it was much more than that worn out cliché.

By the time he realized she was almost completely under his skin, it appeared as if he had forgotten his struggle with the destructive nature of his own thoughts. But it only appeared that way, for she was his muse; in fact, she was a person that inspired people to write a book about, and at the same time, she was a person capable of getting people to burn and destroy that *same book* they were writing. The Hantaywee experience was the turn on the crossroad he had needed, which made his struggle within meaningful. She gave him a reason to be confident, gave him strength to endure his fight, and gave him something worth fighting for – Life.

Hantaywee, you gave me everything and that's all I got. The only thing I am asking of you, is not to make it all go away.

I will not stop fighting until the night I prevail over myself.

14 HIGHWAY TO THE SKY

It is not a sin to let go your emotions.
It is not a sin to say you love somebody.
It is not a sin to have somebody whom you could
say you love.
It is not a sin to commit.
It is not a sin to have positive thoughts.
It is not a sin to forget the things that kill you.
It is not a sin to be kind to yourself.
It is not a sin to forget.

It is not a sin to enjoy life.

*   *   *   *   *   *   *   *   *   *   *

As a remnant concept from his university days, Mojag never remembered the order of days that were passing by, which implied that he never knew what day of the week it was. With the exception of Friday, which represented life, the rest he didn't even bother noticing whether they were working days or not. All that lost any meaning for him at some undefined point. And that happened again this day as he was waking up his own way to go to work. The only thing that he was not prepared for, although he would be happy about the discovery, was that it was in fact a holiday. But that same idiot was mechanically doing the usual. And he didn't suffer from short-term memory. He finished listening to the one song that he always listened to in the morning while smoking his breakfast (the song had verses that went on like 'I want to wake up in a city that doesn't sleep'), and when he was seemingly ready to go, his phone rang.

'??!!!?!!??!?!?!??!?' were the contents of the bubble over Mojag's head.

What normal person would call at these defining hours of the day?

The short sensation of confusion grew even bigger when he noticed that Hantaywee was the one calling.

"Hey sunshine, good morning! What is it, you cannot sleep?" Mojag answered, thinking he would appear gentle by saying one of his usual lines.

"Oh, please Mojag; stop it with your jokes. I come here to pick you up as if you were a princess, and you still dare to mock me" she said, obviously tired from the inappropriate jokes Mojag had the tradition of making. She never got used to them, even though badly timed jokes were his specialty. That momentary refutable answer didn't anger him; it just confused him, for now he started thinking he ought to know what was in fact happening. She was expecting something he was not aware of, and that was usually a healthy source of a rare fight among them.

"I know, I know, it's just the early morning that makes it difficult to adjust to. So when are you going to be here?"

"Ok, yesterday I told you ten times that I will be there at nine, and you still don't remember it? Do you listen to me at all?"

"Of course I do, but honestly, I thought you were joking" he said it way too confident; there was no doubt in his sincerity.

"Why do you always try to make me loose? I do everything for you, and you never appreciate it. We have been planning this trip for one month now, and that makes me so happy, and now you don't even know about it?"

The moment she mentioned *a trip*, his day finally started defining. He had just remembered that Hantaywee was talking about some trip to a place far away from the city but near the mountains, close by the river's well. And that day was supposed to be a holiday; but that day he was already about to go to work! He didn't even look at the calendar to verify his assumption, for he knew she was too aware of time.

How could I be so stupid, not knowing what day it is?

He knew he had promised Hantaywee that they would go away to find their love a place, at least for a single magical moment. He also desired the idea, but the promise he had made was not a vow of any sort; it was most probably an absent yes when she had asked if they would go to that *picnic* or whatever she had in mind. But with that beautiful girl, all *seven* senses had to be always fully employed for she would have crucified him for anything affirmative he had said that he would eventually failed to commit to.

She was an amazing personification of a goddess, with that irresistible devilish charm. Sinning with her was something similar to Adam & Eve getting expelled from the Garden. Mojag was extremely lucky, although unaware at that time, that she was both his saint and his lust. A saint in whatever definition they might have chosen; she fitted in all of them; a lust in the way her passion was burning and the way she cherished his body. *Oh, yes, the picnic...* And then Mojag responded to his guilt.

"I'm sorry, my love, you know that I'm easily consumed by things that play with my memory. It's really nothing personal. Come upstairs, I'll get changed in a minute and we go, ok?"

"Don't worry silly, although I got a little pissed...You know that I am well aware of your irresponsible behavior. In fact, I was expecting it. But! Don't dare to think that it is justified...! I'll come upstairs, motivate *Woody* with a juicy blowjob and then we are off, ok like that?"

"Uh", he continued something after the "uh", but no one understood the irrelevance. That was all meant to be an affirmative answer full of Mojag's natural excitement.

The journey of their trip got postponed by a short of an hour, but now even Mojag was excited as his morning nausea she had chased away with her lips. They seemed ready as he took his backpack full of things he had forgotten about. He was dressed casually as always. After all, they were going away for a picnic. He had a simple black shirt on, exposing the dark tan of his arms. To mention that he was wearing jeans was redundant, for he was always a follower of the blue *jeans generation*. The shoes he had on were special for him, for they were his black shoes for *all* occasions. He always wore them with a suit, with jeans, with shorts, ma with practically anything.

Her outfit was relaxed as well, but Mojag thought, she looked as glorious as when she would wear those *summerish* dresses he loved. The jeans she had were slightly paler than the ones he had, but that wasn't a difference he cared noticing. The difference that mattered was the way those jeans painted each and every beautiful stroke of her tempting behind. The top was not as revealing as he was used to see it, but it was perfectly in sync with her appearance. It was a color closest to blue, or some variation of it. Mojag had correctly noticed that her sweater was not as revealing, but she had no "helper" shirt underneath. That made way for her sexy stomach to peek out down to where her hips continued her perfect body temperament. *Mmm...her sexy skin...*

They reached the black car that Hantaywee had parked right in front of the apartment building. It was her father's car; he gave it to her so she could show off for a day or two. Mojag had never been that obsessed with cars and all the frenzy they accompanied, but he noticed that the car Hantaywee's father had earned was remarkable. Mojag wanted to drive, but he couldn't find his driving license in the mess of things in his apartment. So that way, Hantaywee had to take over, meaning that she would need to stay focused on the road and on the road only. She started the car and headed off to a place she had in mind, a place Mojag didn't know about. And this time it was not that he didn't remember, but it was only because she had said she knew about a place that was created for them. He always trusted her taste. She only told him that the place was a two-three hour drive from the big city, in southern direction, and of course, it was by the river. The day was already strangely warm considering the time of the year, and as they were approaching the place, it seemed as if they were entering a different weather zone, somewhere around the equator.

Mojag enjoyed every bit of the ride, particularly flavored by her distinguished taste of music, being almost a complete reflection of Mojag's. And he was indeed enjoying the ride, but they were already something short of three hours driving with a single stop in between. It was in his character that his impatience would surface, especially without knowing the estimate of the remaining time. On such occasions, he resembled the annoying kid that bugs his parents every two minutes of what was going on, and of things the kid didn't have knowledge about. "Ay, please, where is this place...?" he would ask, which was more like a rhetorical question, for the only answer he wished for was: "*here* is the *fucking* place!"

And there was a point when she finally said those calming words. In fact, she didn't even need to say them, as Mojag could see the growing congestion of cars, and above all, the innocence of the place's abundant nature.

The place it seemed stood up against the change of the four seasons. It was a completely different setting than what he had gotten used to in the opening and painful moments of the big city's winter. And suddenly, none of the wasteful thoughts that were usually growing in his head mattered. The only thing he was thinking now was that he could not be happier but to be where he now was, and with his beautiful girl by his left side. And that was a new moment in his psyche as he could almost never focus on the things he loved without letting dark thoughts destroy his good mood. But he felt so safe to be with her, and there was nothing in that moment that he couldn't find the courage for, as long as she stayed by his side. *And she always did.*

They had arrived some twenty minutes before they actually stopped and parked the car. The reason was not so much due to the fact that the place seemed overcrowded with people, but because they wanted to find a place where they would listen only to the whisper of the river's stream and the occasional breeze of the wind; neither of them needed nor wanted to be with absolutely anyone else as long as they were together. They parked at the very end of the village's nature, where only lost souls could be found. And the end of the village was much more beautiful than the rest, for the nature there was a wilderness intact. She parked the car on a mild, downward slope, right under the shadow of a huge oak tree. From one side was the road with not so many cars passing by; the other side resembled a savannah with the usual wild flowers and the usual density of green grass. Beneath the *savannah* was the calm course of the river that was the motivation of all.

Hantaywee opened the trunk. There were at least two bags of picnic accessories that she had prepared the night before. She had included even the slightest things in there in order to make the experience as detailed as it could be, and at the same time, even more special than it already was. Mojag took the bags after he had spotted a perfect place for their love. She followed him, gazing at him as firmly and full of love as if he was the last person alive. They kissed very softly, leaving the rest of the passion for a few moments later.

They found their way to their spot, crossing the high grass and a few jealous insects. Mojag dropped the bags on the grass as they started unpacking the picnic setting. It was all happening so fast. Everything that was happening that day was as if taken from the most romantic movie scene. But such movie will never be made, for no one could absolutely portray the warmth and passion this boy and girl were giving out. Even people that were sometimes sitting in their company could feel the lust burning within the air surrounding them.

"It seems it's still too early to open this bottle of wine..." she said, feeding him with a sandwich that she had made, and her food was unforgettable and vital. She always fed him in one way or another.

"Ma, no, my princess, it's never too early for a wine...Let me open it. Did you bring a corkscrew?"

"Ha, I have everything in here. You know that when I plan, there's rarely anything missing" she said rather proud, but very true though.

The bottle of red wine that Mojag had opened a while ago was starting to evaporate. They seemed to be ever thirsty for *their* drink of passion. That was the last thing he remembered observing. The rest he thought of nothing else apart from his happiness that was caused by that girl lying down in his lap facing him, a girl that was the only real princess he seemed to remember.

"My beauty", he said, "since the time I recall things about myself, and from the very first time I started taking responsibilities of my behavior, I was such a sarcastic, annoying human being. Perhaps I still am. Irony was something that described me wherever I went. Everyone thought I cared about nothing that surrounded me. And that was *never* true; I've always cared much more than I should have. But there was a point in my life, which I think is not as far away as I want it to be, a point in which I was going through a period where the elevation of my stupidity went on to unimaginable levels. And during that period, the only thing I remember now, perhaps being an unjustified excuse for my unacceptable behavior is that during that time, I have lost all my beliefs, all things I once stood for. And all of a sudden, nothing had any value to me, certainly not least the well-being of myself, for which corrosion, no one else was responsible for but me. Now when I think about it, probably there were many things valuable to me, things I would have died for, things I would die for now. It's really difficult to stop these philosophies of mine, for I need you to understand what you have brought to me. I really am sorry for all those times I have treated you as a perfect stranger, for at that time, I was even an outcast of my own. What I wanted to say to you is that I once again believe in all the things I once lived for, and I really don't care how pathetic it might sound to these annoying insects and similar other people listening every movement of mine, but you were the only one that made that happen. The only one that made my life *happen*! Thinking back for just as short as I can bear, if I take you out of my life, then I would have to take my whole life away. And many times I would ask myself of the fear of what might have happened had I not met you. Questions like where I would be now hadn't I met you? What would I possibly look like if you hadn't brought the light to me the way you did? As honest as a person can be to himself, I would never want to know the answers to those questions. I am way too grateful to forget treating my princess the way she had always deserved, and above all I love you with all my heart."

Hantaywee had already adjusted to a different angle to see Mojag clearer, looked even more in love with him. She gazed even more with her lovely eyes for it seemed that she needed some extra second to grasp all the things he had just said. She wasn't slow at all, and she was used to Mojag's contemplations about life. The only difference that what she probably wasn't used to, was that this time, his thoughts were cohesive, and at the same time, containing beautiful things directed at her. She finally spoke after gulping repeatedly in sweet anxiety.

"Baby, I think you know me, and you know that I have an answer, at least a comment to everything. But what you just said is something that I want to remember for the rest of my life the way it is right now. And I don't want to ruin it with any other words but with the best kiss I could give, and with love which I would always want to be yours."

"Whatever comes out of you, even at times when you make me lose my patience in an unsustainable, but sweet way, it's effect is always enchanting to my life. You taught me many things I was not aware of; you even gave me confidence for things I never knew I needed it for. And many times, my stupid policy of distancing my heart from your reach made me not say the most beautiful words that I have ever known. And I regret every moment I have not done what I wanted, at least with you. And that is why I want you to always know that I have never had anyone, any fucking body so special to me the way you are. And besides, even with the pain of my reluctance to share my life stories, you know virtually all my past, all my skeletons I thought were always buried in the closets of mine. I was never eager to talk about my past to anyone, not least to you, but now if I had to choose, I would ask for no other living person to say all those things to, but you. All this time, I was ever too afraid to let go, but I never want to do that with you ever again; I have always been trying to find excuses, giving reasons that I myself disliked approving!"

By the time Mojag was revealing the insides of his chambers of usual silence, he noticed that his emotional speech had provoked a few tears rolling down Hantaywee's beautiful face.

"Don't cry", he said, "please don't ever cry", he whispered to her ear as he put his arms around her. She smiled, mildly choking on the tears piled down her throat.

"Ay, don't worry, they are happy tears, and I'm sure you *do* agree with that. I cry because I have never heard you talking in such a way to me, so close, the way I always felt you, the way I know you have always felt about us, and at the same time the way that you have always kept silent. What you've just told me is really a shock as I almost lost any hope that you would ever tell me, even in whispers of what you feel."

"I have really no excuse to fill in and I have decided to cut any bullshit with you. I always knew I needed you, and I was always too scared to say it. And I did all that, or I didn't do that for reasons that even I cannot understand. And I know you are enjoying your happy tears but you deserve only happiness in your life, never tears, no matter what they mean. Just remember, you are the person that made me return to live the way I always did, and perhaps many times better."

He stopped for a little while, gazing up in the sky, as if trying to manage his thoughts coming out directly from his heart, and then he continued. Hantaywee seemed to be excited in anticipation.

"No, wait", he continued, "let me explain it to you a little better, for I really want you to know what you mean to me, and to know of the pedestal in which you will always have the privileged spot, for with you it is never enough. I was learning these foreign languages since I was a kid as my parents had that vision that I might need them one day to be able to experience different points of view. They were correct, but that's a topic for another discussion. I remember that class as if it was yesterday, as it was the class when my steady shyness came out for the first time. We learned many new words that day that I had no idea existed. All were not as difficult as the only word that I loved, which simultaneously was the word that I could never pronounce properly. And I had to say it out loud. And each time I would say it, I would mess it up, and I would start blushing because of the laughter caused by my vocal ignorance. Oh, yes, the word was *kindred spirit*. The inability to articulate it made me forget what it actually meant. And since that class, I never cared to get back to it and try to understand it, for I have never experienced a person that would portray the beautiful meaning of the word. And I don't mind that, for such a long time I have lived not knowing, but when I met you, I immediately got granted the translation I had missed out my whole life. If a soul mate, *a kindred spirit* really exists, then you would always be the one for me."

"I love you Mojag", she said in a silent, but orgasmic delirium.

"I love you too, Hantaywee" he said it bluntly for the first time, "and I really don't want to think what I would do without you; what *could* I possibly do without you."

What followed was something that little children would be forbidden to watch. What followed was something similar to bedroom intimacy, or even kitchen teasing. They were out in the open, free of everybody's dogma's, enjoying the sacred beauty of the surrounding nature. The way their bodies melted into one another caused the occasional flowers to bloom like they had never bloomed before.

Their intimacy could have been only closely compared to their understanding of music. When not in constant battle of changing positions, they were the whole day with whatever song was on the Walkman, each lover's ear holding the transmitting headphone. Perhaps they were no experts in music, but the way a song made them relive a moment was an event ferociously similar. And there was almost no disagreement in their taste of music, as it seemed they had always been taught to grasp the full emotions that a chord gives out. The music and the lust they constantly tamed only to bring it back again, were the things that made them function as a single, complete life. And she even went many steps further to ease his weary head, for he alone seemed to sadistically enjoy the painful moments of the past through the songs he had constantly listened to.

The straightforward concept that Mojag tried to stick to the whole time of his undiagnosed insanity, the one when he would say to the mirror's reflection that he was stronger than his past never worked. And it was not that he was weak for that was rarely the case. The only problem was that he had his past only, and no particular present to hang on to, no present to be stronger for. His present had been nothing else but "just another day to kill". And all that time, he had the music that conceived memories he once had, for he had had no others. But at the present time *she* was the one that became his future, and she introduced him to a music that embedded the confidence she tossed deeply within himself. She had found him in a state of no return from which there were no more walls to cross, but the touch of her lips and the beauty of her heart miraculously managed his salvation.

The day lasted the same time it always did, but they needed so much longer. Like in the song Mojag's rebellious childhood had sung, he wanted the planet to make just another leisure circle around to come back again where it had started off. They both started wishing for that as soon as they realized they were unpacking the leftovers from that beautiful day in the now joyous air of Mojag's apartment. His apartment was their love nest, their lair where they could always hide away from the envy of the outside world. And many times Hantaywee would comment on how she didn't like the setting of his place, the worn out furniture and the little walls of his kitchen. And as many times she would come back and be the happiest girl he had ever met. Mojag perhaps did get pissed in a solemn fury when she would have started bragging as if she was a princess, comfortably used to the way her parents treated her whole life she knew of. *But now, thinking back, I think she was really a princess for she was my Queen.*

After a beautiful dinner that Mojag prepared, they were both amazed of the setting he had arranged for them. He filled the room with all the candles he found in his apartment, and filled the air with delicious scent of good food. He liked to cook on occasions, but his laziness many times told him that his wish would pass if he waited for some moments more. But that day he wished none of those moments to go away for he knew such things were practically impossible to repeat. The day was long gone, but now even the night was trying to go away. They were already happily tired from the emotions *their* day had caused, so they had sex only four times. In fact, they fucked twice and twice they made love, so that way they were both satisfied in the end. *I don't even want to emphasize the love of the sex with her as my whole body is shaking even when I think about it.*

No matter what emotions that day had been invoked in his almost crazy brain, that day Mojag felt *a* warmth he had almost entirely forgotten. It was that compartment of his brain that was covered with dust for such a long time. And that day, after a period of what seemed to be a whole goddamn eternity, his heart revealed what it was made for. *And it feels too good.*

When he looked back at his relationship with that girl lying naked in his lap, he could not stop the amazement of the patience she had for that confusing person she loved so much. *Hantaywee, unlike me, or any fucking other in this world never lost her patience.* She never failed to show the respect in those listening eyes, and she was always taking the highest amount of care that there would ever be.

The new dawn was trying to rise as they remained hugged and asleep in Mojag's little bed. He never liked sleeping with a girl in that claustrophobic bed of his for even when asleep, he needed a space more. But not that day; not that night, for each moment was a magical one bringing about the completion of an enchanting day that nothing could have ruined, not even Mojag himself. And regardless whether history would absolve Mojag as a Don Quixote, there was not a single doubt how *his* history would remember Hantaywee. She was his passionate lover, his sister in arms, his best friend, and the most faithful Sancho Pansa Don Quixote could ever ask for.

I will not stop fighting until the night I prevail over myself.

15 A PRICE IS AN INEVITABLE BASTARD TO PAY

A price is an inevitable bastard to pay. Before you mechanically start thinking of the price tags of the latest fashion apparel, or any other things that are absolutely unnecessary in your life, replace your thoughts with something that is more of a humane origin. The revered price in question that you give away at many points in your life is the price of emotional bits. And many times, there are emotional bits accumulated, which you have to give away, much more then you are realistically able to detach from yourself. And many times you have no choice and there is usually no escape from the price you have to give away. Try never to pay a price for things you are not responsible for; but always be prepared to compensate for what you yourself have enjoyed or learned. And the only true measure of its value is the beauty of the moments you spend with that special person of yours until the end is reached. And the end always comes in the worst moments. But then again, is there possibly a good moment for an end to a beautiful story?

* * * * * * * * * * *

That day was *deep* winter. That's the only usual thing Mojag noticed about it. There was virtually nothing special about it, even though he was perhaps curious to go to that night's event, anticipated by many. That month was the season of the big city's balls, an aristocratic tradition that marked the history of the former imperialists. And that day was the ball he got invited to by the company that earned him his monthly allowance. The whole company was consumed by that event, being the talk of the past months, its organization and its attendees. Mojag could immediately anticipate the fakeness of the upcoming event, but he couldn't care less. And the reasons were not strictly rebellious in origin, but rather emotional. One of the reasons was Hantaywee, who was to be his partner for that organized night, and that was all the completion he needed. Nothing else mattered. Not the setting, not the music, and certainly not the people who waited yet another moment to show off their inexistent pride. Besides, the ball concept was a historical stain of the Royal families, but the only way Mojag could ever feel like a King was because Hantaywee was to be the Queen by his side.

He seemed to have some difficulties dressing up in clothes he had despised in his youth, also because he had finally managed to dig out the only gala suit that would possibly support his slim figure. However, somehow he managed to make everything right. Even the bowtie was in the perfect spot, although he was not so enthusiastic because of its pale color. The timing of readiness was quite decent since the moment he started feeling confident by his firm appearance, Ahote[44] called. He was Mojag's friend from his university's years and they somehow managed to stay close enough even when the puberty of the university's alcoholism was over.

"Hey, are you ready? I'm almost there at your place. I will wait for you on the parking lot in front of your building. Come down as soon as you're ready. I will pick you up and we'll get going", Ahote said, accompanied with swears due to traffic congestion.

"I'm almost ready. Two minutes more. Do you have the roses?"

"Of course! They are red as requested and already blooming!"

"Perfect. Ok then, I'll come down sooner than my usual lateness", Mojag closed the conversation and made a final checkup before leaving.

* * * * * * * * * * *

Mojag greeted his good friend as he was entering Ahote's car. He was Mojag's rare friend from among the coldness of the *Northern* folk, and they had remained friends for a long time, including the period of Ahote's one year absence from the big city.

Ahote was constantly amazed by the mentality of Mojag's *Southern* behavior, full of warmth, compassion, and sharing. That was something Ahote missed out his whole life because it was not his choice to be born in a land of extraordinary riches but emotional sadness, and

---

[44] Native American male name of Hopi origin. Its meaning is *RESTLESS ONE*.

friends whose price was admittedly high, but nevertheless always on sale. And he was virtually brought up in such an unhealthy environment. But no matter his childhood facts and figures, Ahote turned out to be a good person.

Both Mojag and his friend had similar outfits as the ball season implied, Ahote having added more formality to his appearance. Ahote was one of the atypical friends that knew about Mojag's latest love story, and the best that Hantaywee was getting out of Mojag. On that note, it wasn't unusual that he immediately gave Mojag that confused glance and the corresponding question.

"Man, why are you alone? Where is Hantaywee?"

"Ay please, we are not married; we are something much better than that. And that, as you already know, implies that we don't live together", Mojag expressed his honest thoughts wrapped up in his inevitable, usual sarcasm.

"Exactly", Ahote replied with an incomprehensive satisfaction. "So, do we go after her and pick her up?" he continued.

"No, no, she said she got delayed for reasons she wasn't enthusiastic to talk over the phone, so she will be joining us a bit later at the ball." *So much for my grandiose entrance of me as a peasant and the princess by my side*, Mojag thought.

Ahote continued talking, but Mojag's thoughts instantaneously drifted away by thinking what might have gone wrong with Hantaywee.

To be true, I don't mind, but I don't care at all about showing any grandiosity in front of all those fake people at the ceremony; I only care for her happiness. And she didn't say the reasons why, and that sounds awfully strange, for that is not exactly the way she normally is, because for good or for bad, she always tells me everything. Not only that she was reluctant to speak, but she also seemed to choke on some questions that I persisted asking.

Whatever it is, I only hope everything is the way it should be; the way it always was. And I have faith that whatever it might be, we can both overcome it as one.

Mojag spotted a parking place almost by the entrance of the ballroom, which was quite a timely luxury. Especially because the outside temperature was way below the freezing point. Ahote took out two beautiful red roses he had ordered his gardeners to prepare for him. The red roses were a passionate detail on the dull, black colored uniform of the rich world. They pinned them on the right side of their top as the gala's stage was already set. That time, Mojag realized that his frustration was almost kept silent as he had realized that he was officially one of the people he was ever at odds with. *At least for the night.* Hopefully.

* * * * * * * * * * *

Mojag had no concrete expectation of that night's event, just mere curiosity. And he admitted his admiration of the high ceiling and the surrounding walls of the palace's lobby. It was mainly Gothic style, if he had correctly remembered the lines through his absence of the high school classes dealing with history of arts. Like in a gala from a movie scene, the lobby was huge and full of people, most of them being initially stiff and unnatural by the paranoia that everyone else was watching them. Mojag was rigid too, but mainly because the setting was something that was never on the agenda in his world. And while most of them needed a comforting compliment to satisfy their inexistent confidence to act more decisively, Mojag got back to his normal, careless state as soon as he saw the first pair of exposed superiority of a girl's breasts. He was technically not alone there as Hantaywee was joining him shortly after, but that was not a reason enough to deter the laws of chemistry and stop his passionate blood boiling. But even the not so gifted girls and the ugly ones looked astonishing to a corresponding level. Most of them had their dresses picked up with style; some of them should have been banned from the ceremony because of their tasteless outfits. Perhaps there were also men accompanying some of the flirty girls in the palace as well, but Mojag never thought of bothering about it. And besides, the men all looked the same at that event, for some of them being the annual event of a lifetime. That was all that Mojag observed to be the general setting of the night. He bothered no more with details that were of no value to his satisfaction. That of course, did *not* include the many beautiful girls he greeted on his way to the bar on the farthest, southern end of the long corridor, which marked the best strategic location of the place. And besides, the proximity to an inevitable new drink was virtually gone.

Mojag seemed interested in the whole setting of the atmosphere, which was quite new to him; brand new in fact. Ahote in turn, felt like at home on such occasions, as he continued spicing up the whole surrounding of the bar, trying to talk to almost any girl that passed by their side. Standing at the bar, side by side, they both looked like two opposite worlds, not only ideologically, but also physically. Ahote hadn't started losing the promised 30 kilos yet, and that emphasized Mojag's skinny appearance even more. That 'disproportion' was a frequent source of friendly mockery of anyone that knew them.

It all seemed quite relaxed and charming for Mojag, even though there was something in the air that was far away from comforting. One was his obvious disturbance of Hantaywee's momentary absence; the other was more of a philosophical origin in denying the world he seemed to be getting into. And it was a bit weird for him to have any ideological thoughts having all those beautiful women exposing parts of their bodies for the bar's amusement.

He never liked any fakeness in people, in fact he despised it, and there was a ton of it that night. He made an inconceivable analogy in his mind. He absently thought how he felt much more comfortable and close to a human behavior when drinking with his neighbor of his *South*, an older man, sharing that same passion for beer and women. Mojag remembered how they used to sit in his companion's dirty garage on chopped wood, since the neighbor was an old car mechanic. They would sit for couple of hours drinking beer and talking about women and bitches and whores. It was always relaxing and *peoples-like* atmosphere. Subjectively, perhaps it was not even strange that Mojag drifted away mentally to such other extremes than where he was that night, since he always looked for company that he could relate to, and not atmosphere he would feel compelled by. But that was something that most of the attendees of that night's gala would never understand, Mojag thought.

They would probably make a comment like: "Ah, those primitive people, if they could only read my thoughts." Well fuck you, then. What should I say about you and your hypocritical culture then, the one in which even friends avoid greeting themselves for it is considered to be harmful to your status to greet a friend who had just got demoted and earns less than you. Well, that requires not the illusions of your limited mind, but heart, a concept you have been raised to repel. But I don't mind. In fact, I don't give a shit about you. I accept your world the way it is, no matter how conflicting it is to my beliefs. But please, don't dare touching mine, or God forbid, mess around with it.

Mojag seemed to have constant paranoia that all those rich people he disliked, would eventually persist in trying to take his world away. And that was perhaps the reason why he always endorsed to fight a preemptive strike. And that was the same reason why he instructed his mind with aggressive thoughts.

It looked like almost two hours had passed since the time Mojag had started his night. There was still no sign of Hantaywee, but his thoughts were prevented for some short period of time since there were other people that joined his company, good friends he had met at work.

Among them was Numees[45], Mojag's colleague that very quickly became his good friend. She was there with her husband and a whole bunch of friends. Numees was not a close co-worker of Mojag's; they had met randomly somewhere in the company's hallways, and very quickly found a lot of common grounds despite their significant age difference. They both had friendly affection towards each other and she often offered him comforting words at times when he needed

---

[45] Native American female name of Algonquin origin. Its meaning is *SISTER.*

them. And Mojag's reciprocity was equally grateful. He was happy, in some sort of a childish way, that Numees and her group stopped by to have a drink together, as he felt more comfortable to find yet another person he actually felt at ease talking to in the midst of the stiff gala night. Mojag didn't know much of the people she brought with her, but he actively noticed that there were some single and equally tempting girls with her.

The newly created 'ghetto' at the bar was enjoying each others company, if not the rigid atmosphere. They had a fun time, and Mojag reinforced his shattered belief that some of the new people he had met in the big city were worth a lot, and that they could be good friends as well. And as much as the newcomers made his Hantaywee worries briefly go away, Mojag couldn't wait for his girl to come and show her to all the people in the room. He wanted everybody to know that she was his, and perhaps even more, to show that he belonged to her. But the clock was ferociously ticking and there was still no fucking sign of her. That was already much more than Mojag's patience could handle. He excused himself and went out of the bar room in order to call her. He dialed three or four times, but each time nobody answered. He got furious, some of his nerves detaching forever from whatever cells of the brain were responsible for them. Receiving an empty response on the other side of the phone was always a detail that drove him crazy.

He humbly went back to the bar, but the expression in his eyes and his behavior revealed nothing that would expose the drama he never liked being a part of. And it seemed he was always invited to the play.

Talking to his friends as if nothing was wrong, his weary mind realized yet another detail that didn't bother him before. Most of the people looked like happy couples, and if not, most of them were at least not alone. And alone was how he felt that moment. At the beginning of the night, he was filled with positive thoughts in anticipation of Hantaywee's arrival, but such positive thoughts were a luxury for him that lasted not long enough. Immediately he shifted back to his heavy, insecure thoughts and paranoid thinking.

She has abandoned me.

All of a sudden, the whole atmosphere seemed so heavy to him, not a single honesty in the cheering smiles surrounding him. He longed to be homeward bound. He longed to be elsewhere but at such a place where no body would understand anything.

But I don't care, I have myself, I don't need to pay attention to you. I'll be patient. I can do it. She will show up.

And he could have probably done it if it weren't for some new people that joined the whole group at the bar. There were friends of someone Mojag knew, but they were the last people he could have been interested in. For what was worse, one of them was something like the contested son of an influential ambassador of the coalition of the "free world". They all looked as if they had arrived directly from the world of money, and they had regard for nothing meaningful. It didn't even matter to Mojag that the ambassador's son's girlfriend had that sluttish prerequisite in her eyes; such indifference of Mojag's was a weird and rare occurrence.

Mojag never remembered their faces. He only remembered the looks in their eyes, in both of the couples that had arrived. Their expression was giving out the arrogance of the most liberalistic look there existed. They appeared to know nothing besides the large pocket money their mother left them each night they would go to bed. Mojag's patience immediately started fading away, feeling disgusted to be in the presence of people he wanted to disappear. And he said not a single word for a longer while; he enjoyed it better that way. And possibly he would have remained silent, but they stepped on his nerves, and so ignorantly, though vigorously started confronting sensitive things, things that Mojag stood for. All of a sudden, the discussion among them started resembling a political rally. None of them knew anything about Mojag's ideological beliefs; otherwise they would have probably never started. He remained silent for the next five or six seconds, until one of the nameless idiots engaged in an ignorant sermon about freedom of speech and at the same mocking the poor peoples of the world with an utmost disgust Mojag could never accept.

It is a night out, focus. You don't need this, don't lecture on justice now. Enjoy.

"Ma, enjoy what? Should I enjoy being with these lowlifes laughing about people's miseries their guardians have created, or should I enjoy the fact that the one who was supposed to be my side now seems lost?"

Mojag's fury got initiated, but he was trying so hard and so unsuccessfully to hide his rebellion against these folks on the hill. He wasn't sure whether he was shouting out loud, or whether his thoughts were shamelessly teasing his conscience.

Let me sum up for myself. You fucking people dare to give me lectures on freedom of anything!!!!!?

What is so fucking good about the Goddamn freedom of speech your fathers have envisioned for the world, when millions of people are dying because they have no bread to support their basic human needs, those same people you deem are ignorant of your imposed concepts. You think this world is real, that this one represents reality of the democratic world, when it's me and you and a handful of people who are enjoying the benefits of modern capitalism on the back of people who died and are constantly dying in vain so you and I can enjoy?

I am well aware that you are way too ungrateful to even acknowledge the struggle of those heroic people, but at least you could show some respect by not mocking their deprived lives and destroyed dreams. Because your families are taking their bread away doesn't mean that you are better; that makes you the ones who should hang, and not those poor people that are destined to cry a lifetime.

I myself cannot pretend to be fake to say that I've gotten to experience what is everyday life for those people. Thanks to God and to my parents, I have always had a comfortable life, but I was taught to respect the ones that deserve the most credit and create situations to help them, and you are certainly not one of them. I don't even know if you're able to understand my words.

Instead of paying them any tribute, you are praising your father and his office rats as true legends, real Robin Hoods. And they perhaps really are the Robin Hoods of today with the only difference that Robin Hood was stealing from the rich to give to the poor, and not the current, other way around.

The already inappropriate conversation they had initiated for the night got much more intense. No one could have stopped Mojag on occasions as such. They should have been much more thoughtful.

Let me ask you something. Do you really believe in what you are propagating? Is that really your stance? Are you really so devoted to providing for freedom of speech as a basic human right? I am asking because I am a bit confused, and I will you give you a very simple example, which will frustrate me even further and astonish you even more.

When I say I am a socialist, I am ousted as the worst villain of mankind, because I opt for freedom of people and enhancing life expectancy to the poor. Is it so immoral of me that the same freedom you are so enthusiastically promoting at this inappropriate occasion does not apply to my reasoning? I opt for destruction of all the inhumane and unnecessary profits you are making, profits that kill, if not trying to wipe out the planet from people who have never been given the chance to live. And that is not a philosophical statement, and that is not an exaggerated one. It's not my fucking fault that your media perverted the ideology of the poor, admittedly, with the help of the sick men of the iron curtain of the 20th century. And it's not a conspiracy theory, and you know it.

"When I give food to the poor, they call me a saint. When I ask why the poor have no food, they call me a communist."[46] But since communism by default is forced as being the ultimate evil, that means that asking why people die out of starvation is evil and against all principles of the "free world". The only revelation you receive is when you get brain washed by the corporate network news, which have spent giant amounts of money to portray fake compassion for the poor, which is immediately forgotten like the latest block buster movie. But such things are not a movie, they are reality, not yours unfortunately, but a reality of way too many people that deserve so much better. But then again,

---

[46] Helder Camara

you never fail to make a sensation, even from the misery of people you yourself exploit. Even the wars you are waging, what do you think you sick bastards, that if you make a spectacle of the war you wage against innocent people, you think that you are civilized? And furthermore, you mask your intentions to preach for civilized development? And on top of that, you come to me to teach me things that you have no idea what they mean?

"Think, use your brain, they are not smarter than you. They are not even close."

When I say I am struggling for my own thoughts, I am exiled. But let me put it in a different way if this is too much of a load for you to grasp. The first thing that you naively asked me, even before I said my name, was where do I come from and what religion I am. Why was that so fucking important? Less than a second after, you already had your worthless opinions shaped based on misleading attributes, with no respect towards anything else. And then you tell me of fairness? You tell me of freedom? That's indeed so humane and so fucking enlightening. Ma, please, I would politely ask you to fuck off. As soon as I said the name of my country and some views of mine, which are incompatible with what you have been fed, you immediately imposed your limited judgments and stereotypes.

At times like these, Mojag would have loved to tear the whole place down along with the ignorant egoism of the people he didn't like. Now that would be some gala night, wouldn't it?

And after all this anger, you still have the courage to talk about honor as a quality you possess? Your friend left for only five minutes to the toilet, and you immediately started talking shit about him while he was away. And that is not the point, for I don't care about your friend, I don't even like him, but you bastards have no respect even for your closest. But I am sure you wouldn't know what that means; you don't need to waste your vacant expression, for you will still not understand anything that cannot be bought. And your environment always encouraged disposable friends, didn't it?

Fuck you all, and even that is too much for some of you people. But it is my emotional difficulties and your ignorance that make me strong; they make me want to show you otherwise. It brings out the worst in me, but perhaps you deserve to be treated that way. I always expressed my ultimate respect to whatever your vague ideologies are. And you have always discarded mine. And that is why I could never stay indifferent as soon as objects like you start talking about moral and honesty, and freedom of people and freedom of an individual. It is hypocrisy I never liked hearing. It is the hypocrisy I always fought against. And I most certainly didn't want this gala night to turn into a political debate, which I moderated, even though you were the ones that initiated it.

Mojag gave everyone, including the 'innocent' ones, an icy look full of resentment, and walked away without an excuse. He went on to a completely different corner where he ordered a double of whatever he was drinking before, hoping that his thoughts would subside only to be consolidated when the time comes, if it comes, and if he would remain strong enough to make them a way.

The whole time I am devastated because I simply cannot accept being consumed by purposeful ignorance of what some would say "the civilized world". The despair of my own emotional instability and the vanishing ends of the humane, are ever things that I cannot accept. And perhaps Hantaywee is constantly diverting my mind away from the unnecessary thoughts that are only good when fighting for them, not contemplating with them. The weirdest of it all is that she is one of them, acting that same way as if she was a princess her whole life. But perhaps she really was.

Where the fuck is she?

And there, out of nowhere, in the midst of the posh glitters of the detailed scene, his fury of the night and the entire accumulated anger of his world completely vanished. She appeared.

Initially, he could not quite recognize the face in the smoky atmosphere; what he saw was only a dim figure of a beautiful woman's body. That was enough of a hunch for Mojag, for he knew every part and any hidden bit of her mesmerizing body to make a beginners mistake. He didn't give away any emotional sign due to her presence, except for that inconceivable, heart piercing expression in his eyes directed at nothing else but her. But that was their way of communicating as it didn't take more than a fragment of a moment for her to notice his anxious anticipation. Perhaps he even engaged in his justice contemplations because she was not by his side to bring him back. She smiled back at him in the flirty manner she had perfected with someone else, at the same time so innocent.

She was more beautiful than any woman I've seen.

Mojag felt the most sincere butterflies in his stomach when she decisively started walking towards his arms; he felt like those days when he was for the first time in a confusing love as a child. The only one difference from his platonic experiences as a child was that he now got immediately aroused as if they were alone in the elevator of his apartment building. That moment, nothing else mattered. He was a happy boy without the usual uneasiness he was giving out. The revolutionary debate that infuriated his conscience was immediately forgotten and postponed for a more decisive moment.

The redundant noises of the atmosphere seemed to stop the moment Hantaywee came within kissing distance of Mojag. It felt as if there was nobody else in the room, as if the whole atmosphere stopped, for no one else had gotten as far to him as Hantaywee. The kiss marked the beautiful world they have been unconsciously nurturing. It was the most beautiful thing in the world; the soft touch of her shiny lips, her charming breath, and her gentle hands wrapped around his body. Mojag never closed his eyes when he kissed her as he wanted no moment wasted looking at her. And it was needless to say how the whole outer world seemed so little at that special moment compared to their story. Mojag would have perhaps even forgotten that she got delayed for unexplained reasons that were tormenting his occasionally justified paranoia, but then the kiss was over. Hantaywee opened her eyes, which were trying so badly to conceive a smile, but there was something in them that Mojag could not fail noticing; something that was saying more than she was willing to convey. After all, the vivid expression in each others eyes was what had gotten them together in the first place. Her eyes somehow could not hide, not from him at least, the sadness and the pain that she was feeling inside. Mojag tried to prevent himself from asking immediate questions in front of all those other people that were being jealous at the moment because of the beauty by his side. He was never an actor of life, but this time he did it all too well to hide the cold shivers that made shifted his mental balance because of the anticipation of what might have happened. He didn't think of anything in particular, but he immediately thought of the worst.

The show seemed to continue in the way the host had envisaged. Everything was running smoothly whatever that meant. Hantaywee met with most of Mojag's acquaintances, at least those that were still around. He still wanted to reveal her to them all, and to reveal the confidence he had when Hantaywee was by his side. But the bitter melancholy he saw carved in her eyes was everything that his mind was focused on, even though his body behaved much differently. Now it wasn't the atmosphere that made him uncomfortable; it was the unsaid tension that seemed to have spread into his air. He sensed there was something very wrong to anticipate, and he was almost sure that it included him in her equation. It always did, regardless if it was a good or a bad bearing.

Why should there always be something that makes it so fucking difficult?

"But you knew that from the very beginning."

Ma fuck off, you and your beginning, it is all too good. Everything is fine, just some crazy thoughts of mine. Get lost.

"We both know the story. And perhaps she is capable of wrapping up a beautiful lie, but she cannot hide her eyes from you."

Why do you want to destroy us so much? Do you really enjoy it, you sadistic fuck?

"I'm just doing us a favor, and preparing yourself for the objectivity of your own reality."

The night had unfolded many hours ago as it started paving its way to the beginning of the new day. Even Ahote left, who was apparently too tired of the alcohol that he had drunk. Mojag didn't notice who was left from the people he knew. He said goodbye to a couple of them, but he was already way out of everything to remember their faces.

The aftermath of the palace's event seemed as if the event had turned into a post October Revolution scene. Many of the previously proud businessmen and inherited politicians with their polished tuxedos were lying around half dead from their inexperienced lack of alcohol control.

They would have probably found me in the same position as they are had she not appeared by my side. Hantaywee was still by Mojag's side, but the chill in his body observed that he would rather switch places with the drunken of the night only to forget what she inevitably had to say. His princess was there, but it seemed like a lot of things were destined to turn back into empty pumpkins.

* * * * * * * * * * *

"No, you can't tell me that. Please don't, for what am I without you? The life in me is nothing else but magic of your own." Mojag roared in agony, the same agony she so carefully managed to help him defeat.

"Mojag, I can't, please understand me and please don't make it more difficult for both of us. I love you too much and I am willing to quit on my entire way of life just to be with you, you and me escaping together in any place you would desire. And you know it, as I remember all those times I have asked it, those same times you got scared to death by the thought. And each time I sat there crying in my bed by the way you are and the responses you always enlightened me with. But you know and God knows that I never quit; I could never afford doing that for I have never met anyone that makes me look as good as you make me feel. You told me many times, and I know that it is what you stand for, by saying that your family is the first most important thing in the world. 'Something these cold people will never understand', you said."

"I know, and I will always fight for it. It is just that it is so difficult to see you walk away. I never thought it was possible under any circumstances", he almost murmured the end of the sentence with all the honesty there was, being unable to hide his phantomlike posture caused by the drained reserves of his energy for life.

"The reason why I was late this evening was not because I was contemplating whether I should go or not, but whether I could get enough courage to tell you what has happened. But I couldn't hide it from you even a second more. And it doesn't feel better when I say it out loud, for it only gives sound to the wreckage in my heart. I know I am very spoiled and I have to learn to be more independent in the way I perceive life; in the way I perceive mine, but I am the only chance there is to try convincing my parents not to separate. They were fighting for a very long time, but I don't want to even remind myself of the way they behaved today. Divorces are so damn common today, and children suffer so much because of it making their life doomed from the start for most of them. I know I am not a little girl anymore, and I can take care of myself, and my parents separating is perhaps not the end of the world if you look at it objectively, but they are *my* parents, and everything I have is because of them. If they do get apart, the subjectivity in me implies that my entire history and beautiful memories I have will be erased, or forever changed. I am so scared, Mojag. And I cannot possibly ask you to come with me. Please understand me. I know you will."

Will you stay with me, will you be my love.

Family was always the most important; in fact he always pushed her to try and solve the problem of her parents that constantly pressured her, especially in the course of the past month. Perhaps there was nothing much that she could do but he didn't want her regretting for not having tried to make things as warm as they once were.

The rain was viciously pouring down as if it was its first time, Mojag standing out in the open, the clothes he'd rather tear apart soaking wet. He was trying to wake up from this horror he unexpectedly got involved in, but it was far too real to burst. And he was aware of that, but persisted in vain. He stood there, his look directed at her eyes, but his sight passing right through her. He noticed the destroyed look in her eyes, but the only thing his mind focused on was the words she had said.

She is leaving.

Is this a fucking dejavu?

Mojag reminded himself of the indifference towards his world and the world of his surrounding. With a strong voice, and eyes resembling the ones of a furious lion fixed at that special person next to him but so inexplicably distant, he continued out loud the conversation in his head, now meant for her.

"When are you leaving?"

"I don't know yet, but I am afraid it is not going to be more than three days from now. Don't get like this, please", she started choking on her tears, but he seemed way too indifferent even though he couldn't have possibly behaved like that with the thought of having her no more. But his mind persisted in that similar, stubborn way.

"Good. Then leave and never ask about me", he closed up abruptly, turned around and walked away, leaving Hantaywee's painful, weeping sound alone in a strict, sadistic manner. She stood there in the rain, praying for a comforting word of his, but he didn't even make a single turn back at her to see if she was still standing.

I am sorry. I am so fucking sorry, Hantaywee.

Mojag went on walking around the city's corners, noticing nothing else but the voice in his head and the waste in his heart. Whenever he felt that way in the past nine months, he would always knock on Hantaywee's door, asking for selfish comfort, which she always provided him with the care of a mother putting her baby to sleep. But now all that seemed like a dimmed history. What was even worse, in the back of his head, he was still convinced he was on top of things, and that he could go away from her any time he wanted, without the heavy burden a lost leaves on life. But he was so unconsciously wrong, and he knew it all too well to be able to admit it. And that night his illusions of being in control disappeared as if they had never existed. And perhaps there had never been there indeed. He started realizing for a millionth time that Hantaywee was the ongoing link in his chain of happiness that seemed to constantly pass by him.

Hantaywee was the person in his life that didn't only bring him back to a certain state of average normality. No, that would have been too little with regard to all the things she could; all the things she did.

Every little thing she did was of massive, evolutionary importance to me and my will to succeed.

With her, Mojag won his entire world back, along with the beautiful world of hers that she so unselfishly introduced him to. And he had known that almost since the beginning of their encounter, but only now he bluntly realized it with all its cruelty, because she was leaving his world the same way she had entered it. In his mind, and what his emotions always confirmed, ending a relationship of love was never easy. In fact, it was so goddamn difficult. But ending a relationship of friendship was a pain so immense that it could be touched. Mojag's relationship with Hantaywee accompanied both attributes, and he wasn't sure he could cope with what seemed to be the final chapter of a journey so beautiful that even if Romeo's Julia would still be alive, she would have shared her envy that the beautiful world Mojag and Hantaywee had created was something that even the symbol of love herself would be inspired by it.

I will not stop fighting until the night I prevail over myself.

16 JUDGMENT

One evening an old Cherokee told his grandson about a battle that goes on inside people.

He said, "My son, the battle is between two "wolves" inside us all. One is Evil. It is anger, envy, jealousy, sorrow, regret, greed, arrogance, self-pity, guilt, resentment, inferiority, lies, false pride, superiority and ego.

The other is Good. It is joy, peace, love, hope, serenity, humility, kindness, benevolence, empathy, generosity, truth, compassion and faith."

The grandson thought about it for a minute and then asked his grandfather:

"Which wolf wins?" [47]

* * * * * * * * * * *

A moment of judgment is inevitable for each and every one of us. And despite the astonishing work of a Great artist of the Renaissance in a chapel as famous as Mr. Simpson's trial, and much more spiritual then the people being inaugurated in it, designed to spread fear

---

[47] Good Indian (Native American) Story

within the common people, judgment comes very often in each of our lives. What it poetically, but successfully attempts to portray is the direction we choose in life; direction of a way with two ends. One makes you stronger, the other makes you void, as if you have never even walked among the living. The sooner you decide on the verdict you believe it can make you stronger, the sooner you will start living again, standing tall as you always have. A positive outcome of a verdict doesn't necessarily mean that you have to be the strongest person in the world. It simply means that not even at one single point should you stop fighting against the idiocracy of your inner self. A single moment of relaxation in your constant battle with your own self assembles the worst parts in you together, and against you. Fighting for ideologies of terror and oil is unjust no matter how highly paid consultants make it sound necessary. However, fighting against yourself is the most sacred battle you are constantly engaged in, regardless if you are too afraid to admit it or not. And it is sacred because you can hurt no one, but you can only be a better person for yourself and the ones that are dearest in your entire world. There are no collaterals. No media. There is only you and the illusions your brain feeds you with, and the increasing gap between those two war camps. The only one who could lose is you, for doing nothing. The only one who could win is again you, for destroying the obstacles your mind has created for you. And that is the only way to your preservation.

Some would say that religion teaches exactly that, preservation of your own self in a world of temptations and constant change. But what does it actually teach; what religion actually is? Perhaps the definition *I* have cannot be found in a *Western* encyclopedia, for I have never believed in the idea of being manipulated by people who are disrespectfully abusing the Light of God to achieve their goals of terror, corruption and fear. Perhaps not all of them, but the minority of the decent people is historically consumed by the powerful mechanisms to deceive.

However, it is perhaps ungrateful to say that religion is fundamentally bad for its initial concept was possibly essential to give meaning and a steady order to the chaotic herd of people throughout history, to give it some purpose of life.

There is no doubt about it, and the level of my respect towards it borders the respect I have for the epic, historic struggle of the working class and its heroes.

But the respect towards religion stops all those constant moments when it is used for conscious manipulation of the masses and purposeful division of honest traditions of various peoples. And especially in the course of this undefined modernity, it is used as much as possible in that way, even more in the developed world than in the barbaric world of the poor as the riches like to call it. But where do we draw the line? How do we know that we are being manipulated? Apart from an insatiable urge for education, the defense mechanism is very simple. You only need to focus on any priest talking, or to see their robes misplaced in almost any parliament in the world, for they are supposed to be your link to God, and not your link to the president's daughter. Religion is very rarely misunderstood; it is just purposely misinterpreted.

The shameless display of blood diamonds and jewelry on the robes that the Holy Church and the borders of its own state share with the world, inherited from all those bloody conquests in the past in the name of God, could feed the entire black continent for many, many years to come. And on top of that, they still feel they have any moral left in them to preach you to be good and appreciate them so you can enjoy the heavenly afterlife as opposed to the fires of Hades.

Seeking afterlife is a concept that attracts many, and at the same time it is the most ungrateful thing to seek in front of God. God granted us all life, which can be painful or wonderful, or even painful and wonderful at the same time. It is perhaps a constant struggle in order to survive, and for many it is not as easy as entertainment factories frequently portray it. And we are all the same fragile mortals, made from flesh and bones, and some of us with brains. In the basics of us all, there is no difference among any of us, no matter how hard some unworthy scientists persist to ring the division bell between various peoples of the world; there is absolutely no doubt that those very same intellectual people bleed the same way as the races they try to make inferior.

We are all guests in this world, we come, we live, and we are all here to make way for better generations to fix the mistakes their ancestors committed. And then we turn back to dust. But nevertheless, in that beautiful course of a lifetime, we are alive and life deals precisely with that. Nothing before, nothing afterwards. The life we have is at the same time the afterlife some are willing to die for. We have all experienced the concept of afterlife. If we make a good deed, we feel good and satisfied. When the worst in us makes us commit bad things, we are the ones feeling the guilty remorse for the rest of our lives. We create our own heaven and hell, and that is why we need to focus on modest acts and not on ungrateful incentives of another, far easier, and perhaps imaginary opportunity.

And all that is precisely why a religion can tell you only about a judgment of their own device, a judgment that has nothing to do with the human element in most of us. If a person cannot find ways to punish himself, both physically and mentally, no existing and future religions will help him learn his mistakes and guide him on the right track. For religion is the biggest deception in the occurrence of people's history. God is the greatest, God is the only one, and God has nothing to do with religion.

This entire time I have been lost, in fact, I still am, but all that time, I have never quit on God and I have never quit on myself. Belief in God is not a matter of believing in judgment day. Belief in God is not a matter of being afraid to live. Belief in God is not a matter of unconditional obedience to a higher cause. Belief in God is not to be advertised. Belief in God is not to be imposed. Belief in God doesn't mean He has beard. Belief in God doesn't mean He or She is black or white. Belief in God doesn't mean superiority or ignorance. Belief in God simply means superior, abstract, and necessary faith. And that is why I managed to maintain that piece of myself that kept me going. And that is why I am given the opportunity to preserve the emergence of a person, the one compatible with the constant changes of my world. And belief in God is what has been giving me the strength and will to believe in myself. It is now solely up to me to decide whether I can endure the change.

* * * * * * * * * * *

The ghostly figure, almost embedded in that uncomfortable chair of the filthy apartment, was

Mojag's all too familiar posture. He seemed very difficult to recognize; he even seemed unrecognizable to himself, but the crushed expression of the lines on his face and the watery sadness in his eyes implied that it was him, without any doubt. Going back to that state of conscious, that same one he had been so used to, resembled a journey to hell. But the circumstances of his will meant that he had no other choice; it meant that all the comfort he had found in those past months was forever lost. He was not vividly aware that his happiness had lasted for a decent period of time; his mind was all too weary to notice it. And before he knew it, he was back in the combat zone, to the ever failing drawing board of his apartment.

Nothing much had changed in Mojag's apartment since virtually all those times the apartment lived inside of him. And as in those times, there was not a single visible slot on the one table in his apartment, for it was full of empty packs of cigarettes and an elevated amount of empty bottles of alcohol, beer mostly.

Mojag unwillingly engaged in a pictorial excursion as his whole life seemed to be flashing right in front of his eyes. The innocence of his childhood portrayed through the living memories of his dead grandparents; his first childish love, his first high school day when he was standing alone in the midst of the crowd because he was too shy to speak; the day he came to his junior high school class so drunk that his father almost quit on him; his leadership in the violent protests against *Western* bombs in the *Southern* province; the best friends he had left in his *South* and the wonderful memories he had with them; his prom night and the craziness of his prolonged puberty; his first love, now his former girlfriend and the day that he almost got her pregnant; his arrival in the foreign world on that heavy winter's night; his first university class that marked the craziest period of his life; all the girls that he had been with; all the friends he had met; all the friends that he had lost contact with; all the friends that were away; all the rebellious articles he wrote that never saw the uncensored light; all the animosities his nostalgia had provided him with; all the sleepless nights before an exam; the sacred day of his graduation where he was the happiest person in the world; his amazement of the first day at his workplace; the cold end to his long relationship with Aiyana; the warmth of his home in the *South*; the music that both contained and elevated his grief; Hantaywee.

Everything was there and everything was so vivid. He couldn't hear any sounds and he could not feel the coldest breeze coming out of the wide open door of his apartment's balcony. He was trying to find out what the crimes were he had committed, for he was sitting on his own punishment. He thought that if he had perhaps lived his life in a slower and a less noticeable way, many people would have been better off, and many people would have been happier. Perhaps, he would have been different. The way his brain showed him the life he had chosen, and its reflections upon it, it seemed that he had sacrificed and gambled every single thing that kept his life in motion. It seemed as if he had lost all those things that were not only vital pieces of his life, but they were *his* life.

Mojag was sitting in that dirty, worn out chair, face-to-face with his music, virtually obsessed with the entire pastime of his own tasteful experience, along with the recurring paths of his familiar, pathetic agony. What was even more painfully confusing was the unclear goals in front of him, now elevated even more, for it seemed that even the roads that were to be walked upon were unknown. As almost everyone else he had built something with, Hantaywee was leaving too. He had known it from that very first day he tried to maintain his distance towards her, a distance that she overcame as no one else had before. She penetrated the insides of his invincible Chinese wall, and all there was left now were ruins he didn't have the strength to reassemble yet another time. She was Mojag's direct cause of his current state of familiar devastation, even though she was always his savior. It seemed Hantaywee lost the key she had always used to open up the beauties his heart was full of; it seemed as if he was trying to revoke access to all the hidden passages she had to his heart. Apart from all these nasty details, Hantaywee, in his self-proclaimed pursuit of freedom, taught him many things he had initially asked for, no matter how much he wasn't mature enough to contemplate the end. It was his brain that disallowed the synchronicity to form any kind of balance; it seemed as if his brain liked entertaining its cells by grinning at Mojag's misery.

Since the time he left the warmth of his *South* that sacred day of the *old* calendar, Mojag became the person he had always wanted to be. Independent of all the norms that society might have tried to impose to him; he felt strong to oppose. But his entire change meant nothing for he couldn't get out of the norms and obstacles his brain cowardly imposed on him. He was undoubtedly a changed person, more mature and much more determined, but he could not give out any of those characteristics. And he never could because he was ever unwillingly postponing the acceptance of change, regardless what that change meant. When Hantaywee found her way to his life, he thought that she could make all that possible. Perhaps, and with little doubt, she could have done it, for she practically did it. But now she was leaving, and Mojag got himself caught into disobeying one of his principal rule; he felt way too comfortable with her to realize that hope was getting into his brain, devaluing his own ability to belief in himself. He had unconsciously become too dependent on her touch and her ability to influence his progress. But only now he realized the inertness of his behavior. Everything she did for him he was taking for granted, and now everything was slipping out of his reach.

Hantaywee was leaving to a distant place where communication could easily turn into permanent breakdown. Her reasons were perhaps justified, and Mojag never blamed her for that. But none of those analysis and thoughts would prevent her from moving on in a justified, selfish direction.

The night she told him the revelation, he turned his back on her not because of anger. He did it because he couldn't afford exposing his tears to her beautiful eyes; he didn't want to make it even more difficult for her, but he probably did. Especially because since that moment, she had been calling virtually every minute, and all that sleepless time he immovably stared at the phone, and every time his heart would start bursting out, and each time he would not pick up.

Mojag knew that he had to find the courage to kiss her for one more time, regardless if that would be the last. That was the least he could do for Hantaywee had been the only person that helped his subconscious initiate and achieve what Mojag couldn't do for a very long, discouraging period. He needed that one more encounter with her because he could not afford throwing away the track she had directed him on, and all those vital things she had taught him; he could never afford losing all those beautiful moments spent by her side and her warmth; and he could certainly not afford concealing his utmost gratitude towards her. Mojag was thinking about his life and the strategies of his own defeat, but in order to succeed, he needed her, at least that one more time to tell her the importance that she brought to his life.

She brought back that little boy inside of me, which I thought was forever gone. I know I can never be that boy again, but I needed him to reassert my lost basis for life. I know I can never be that boy again, but I need to take that little bastard out in the open and say goodbye to him.

One more encounter with her was possibly the one meaningful thing that gave him strength to defeat the illusions of his mind.

I have to make myself happy of what I have and not sad because my mind feeds me with the entire remorse of the world. And much more vital, I cannot let myself lose my beliefs and everything I stand for, not again. And if not for myself, I have to fight because of her, and that is a motivation I need in order to prevail. I feel the entire anger, remorse, pain, agony and destruction of the world as being my own burden. That I cannot bear anymore, for only now I understand that regardless of the objectivity of the pain I have felt, it was no one else, but my mind that was the source of my self destruction.

* * * * * * * * * * *

Still immovably embedded in the chair, sitting almost in front of the TV, the only light in the room dimmed through the old lamp on his right side. There were many channels of shit on the TV to choose from. He turned on the worst one, even though his vacant expression implied not only that he was uninterested and fed up with the content, but he was inattentive of the moving pictures; he had enough of his own flashing going through his head. Nevertheless, he remained still and fearfully silent; his dry skin giving away strong contrast to his eyes. He could hear a beautiful voice trying to treat him nicely, but he remained unmoved, especially because he didn't like anyone's charity, not even from an imaginary voice. Without even blinking to the distractions in his head, he put both his hands around his forehead as if trying to chase away his thoughts. But he couldn't. They only grew stronger. And as many other times before, he pretended as if everything was all right, even though he was becoming older and all the rest were becoming colder and there was not much fun left anymore. Nothing seemed important, his thoughts the least. But they were persistent. The silence was way too painful, regardless how trained he was to resist. At once, the music portraying his life turned fearfully quiet. He blinked after a long time, his thoughts ultimately unbearable. And then, the releasing crescendo unfolded and it was difficult to distinguish whether it was the music or it was himself that went insane.

All of a sudden, he took all his strength and hit the fucking TV in front of him, at the same time breaking the lamp on his right side. Demolition had begun. Turning on to the table behind him, he took out the things, tearing everything down to pieces. As if not enough, he pierced the center of the table with his right foot. There was a camera of his that got his eye, and it was not spared. He took it restlessly and started hitting it against the remaining pieces of the glass table. He went on to the bedroom, crashing every mirror and each of the expensive art pieces that were on his way. Even the sacred guitar was not spared, for insane destruction was everywhere. Disposing of the silent pieces of the guitar wood, he took the plate full of food from the kitchen and smashed it against the wall. Everything went out of control.

Where are the neighbors? Ma fuck them!

All objects in his way were already upside down. The wine bottle left a horrifying stain on the wall as pieces of glass sprawled down like flies. No, no, it was not over yet; *he* was not over yet. He took out a piece of wood from the broken bed and continued severing the whole assembly of the apartment's structure. The whole furniture was gone, but he wanted even more destruction. He wasn't sure whether he was enjoying the carnage of the material crap, but he was perfectly certain that he was doing it with utmost care and concentration. Nothing else mattered but complete destruction of whatever there was. The TV box was lying dead on the floor but was still fearlessly and miraculously spreading the usual bullshit. He had all the strength in the world as he grabbed the TV with both hands and went on throwing it outside the apartment's unopened balcony window. Glass started cracking everywhere, both on the inside and the outside as the TV finally did shut the fuck up, crashing onto the tarmac few floors underneath. He wasn't planning to jump but started shouting instead to the whole fucking world. He firmly grasped the broken glass of the balcony door to maintain balance as a huge piece of glass went half way inside his palm, stained currents of blood filling the apartment. He couldn't feel a thing, but continued yelling like a madman and shouting words that no one else apart from himself could understand. And than the music stopped and what was left of reality started reappearing. He felt like drowning, losing all the breath he had, but he could not afford quitting on himself. Not now, not ever.

Why are you running away...?

Many times I wondered if I could achieve anything by such destruction, only to show the reflection of the things I have been putting inside my head. Looking now at this educational video of Pink Floyd's 'One of my turns', it seems that the fragility is way too high and requires for a sudden, unconscious crescendo to revert me back to that garden of destructive thoughts and deeds. For a very long time, I have been on the verge of doing that or perhaps something worse than that, but I cannot bear myself longer on the verge of extreme unpredictability. It is my mind that feeds me these dark thoughts, and I don't want them anymore, and those are the real enemies that I am fighting against. And the decisive battle is approaching. And I am not afraid for I cannot live in fear anymore. I was never raised to have disturbing thoughts, and I have never been like that any time before. I might have been strange to people with limited understanding capabilities, but never had I any deranged thoughts passing through my head, and now I am consumed by them. I can't live in fear and I do believe I can prevail. And my arrogant confidence gives me absolutely no doubt that I will prevail. It is a battle of small magnitude, perhaps irrelevant to anyone else, but to me is crucial. If I have no belief in myself, I have nothing left to live for. And now I am intending never to lose again the belief I have always nurtured for myself.

For a moment there, Mojag started contemplating about the inspiring story of the *Barbudo*[48] from the proper Caribbean island who was able to achieve what the *Reds* had never succeeded in any of their attempts. That aging revolutionary was able to defeat his *Uncle* in all the battles he was engaged in.

People have succeeded in battles of a higher cause, and I cannot even cope with myself. In 1874, a prominent writer completed a journey to the center of the earth, and more than a century later, I cannot find a center to the limitation of my own self. How more pathetic can it get? How more pathetic can I get?

The monotony of Mojag's pathetic way had to stop that very moment. Not tomorrow, not five minutes later, but now.

The time is now.

Abruptness and strong character, characteristics that were not his most favorite sacrifices, were absolutely necessary and perhaps the only viable means left to support his victory to his cause of life and utopian freedom. But that was the only way to achieve life, for it was the same as quitting cigarettes. The moment you start debating with yourself, your brain eats you up before it even allows you to realize it, unconsciously reverting you back to a habit that consciously destroys you. Debate is hardly ever good, for the compromise is upfront known by the debate's chief sponsors. Life would run you over if you are waiting for the moment to get the brains and to understand things that your brain purposely misinterprets for you. By the time you become a wise man, you would be good enough only

---

[48] Bearded

for new generations, to teach them how not to make all those mistakes you have made. And what worth is that when you yourself have made nothing right, and the only thing left is regret? Life is not something to gamble with, but to live along. And besides, even if handing out free advices to the cornerstones of eventual new societies were to be an incentive, it would still be wrong for all. For humans can never learn from other people's mistakes by hearing their regretful advices and wise warnings. Humans can only understand it when they have experienced that bitter taste in their own mouth. And many times before, Mojag did make foreseeable mistakes, even though he had been previously warned. But not even that was of concern, for the biggest problem was that he seemed never to learn from them, never to even acknowledge them. No wonder that he kept on repeating them. And that had to stop.

Now, there were only two choices Mojag was left with. The first was to stand back and lay his hands in hope of empty thoughts, or to fight back and embrace the spiritual persona, fundamental in order to stop existing and start living. Fighting back meant that the past had to be buried forever, entailing that some linking bridges needed to be re-destroyed, since some lingering remains were still hanging in an indeterminate state. He didn't want to kill the memories, and that he could never do; that he was never willing to do. He only needed to modify their effect on his present, even if Mojag himself would be the sacrifice for it.

Mojag had always dreamt of being free in all aspects of the philosophy he had believed in, but his approach yielded provisional success only, if at all. He was ever aware that the freedom he lusted for was something only he himself could fight for; only he himself could grant for his own cause. No one else. He had always been a soldier of fortune fighting for personal freedom, but he needed this one more battle to win his war. His night seemed to have arrived.

* * * * * * * * * * *

One evening an old Cherokee told his grandson about a battle that goes on inside people.

He said, "My son, the battle is between two "wolves" inside us all. One is Evil. It is anger, envy, jealousy, sorrow, regret, greed, arrogance, self-pity, guilt, resentment, inferiority, lies, false pride, superiority and ego.

The other is Good. It is joy, peace, love, hope, serenity, humility, kindness, benevolence, empathy, generosity, truth, compassion and faith."

The grandson thought about it for a minute and then asked his grandfather:

"Which wolf wins?"

The old Cherokee simply replied, "The one you feed." [49]

And as the legend says, the winning wolf in you depends on your own will and directives, and remains within you as long as you provide for opportunities to feed it.

And I have fed the evil one that was slowly eating me alive for such a long time, and that I cannot afford doing anymore.

---

[49] Good Indian (Native American) Story

And that I will do no more.

17 EMOTIONAL INDEPENDENCE

Not more than three days later

An emotion might not be our objective, but it is indisputably our driving force. Even in the darkest insides of the worst of us, there is that spark of a sentiment, regardless of its nature, that makes people do things they would never do, if it weren't for that particular mess of chemicals within the guts of every human being. Contradictory to the wise man's posture, a vigorous emotion represents the *moral* in ourselves; we *only* need to make sure its best part comes out.

The way humans are put together, emotions cannot exist without that part of the brain that controls them. But the brain, besides the physical stage it provides us with, has nothing to do with the concept of emotions; it only self-imposes too many questions that persist to make the growing passion void, and to grow illusions that resemble nothing of the initial sentiment. And that frequently happens because the brain is too occupied with control, delegating the incompatibility of its own situation to the emotional machinery. Emotions and reason never get along, and each time they eventually get intermixed on a particular matter, it means you are to be the one in the middle of their radical discussion and it means that you are to suffer because of mixed signals of your own construct. It is a rarity when synchronicity between the two of them can be achieved. And if that does happen, don't stop enjoying your freedom, but at the same time, never forget to be unambiguously prepared to fight back.

* * * * * * * * * * *

Everyone lives his/her own life and everyone is swayed by selfish emotions their life brings to them. And I am no other.

Judging by his life in the course of the past year, Mojag's indifference was about to start gaining on him mercilessly. But an unusually healthy precedent marked that day – there was no sign of his indifference or any of the familiarly destructive thoughts he was into. He was aware that for such, yet another, emotional excursion to hell he was not prepared to engage into; emotional excursion he had already *made sure* was not going to happen again.

Mojag was wandering around the filthiness of his room, but it didn't matter for he had already made a decision. It was so much easier now to wander around in any place when the next decisive step was known upfront and the emotions concerning that step had been settled. He knew what he was supposed to do; he *wanted* to do what he was supposed to do next – his responsibility to admit the end with full dignity. After all, he could pessimistically sense the end from the very beginning of his relationship with Hantaywee. The only thing he was not quite sure of was how their closing stages would unfold. Now he had all that information. And he neither cared about his broken illusions of Hantaywee, nor about the perceived betrayal caused by her departure. No, he simply wanted to spend the night with her, perhaps their last together, and that was all he cared for. Nothing before, nothing beyond that.

He sat on the floor, staring at the adjacent wall. The grimace on his face resembled the one of an ancient thinker ready to spit out the foundation of a new philosophy. His brain, on the contrary, didn't back up his appearance, for while that ancient thinker was supposedly to develop a new philosophy, Mojag was in fact not thinking at all. And he felt too good to be able to breathe normally, without any strain his thoughts usually provided him with.

He started dialing the number that so many times before, if not still, was the only reality he was longing for. The outgoing call was not even given a decent chance to ring properly since it was taken almost instantly after it got initiated.

"Mojag", Hantaywee's fulfilled sound immediately came through the speaker. – "I miss you so much...what else can I say when all I want is you?"

Mojag hadn't called in three days and the sound of her voice exposed nothing of his expected concerns that it would take time to bring back her confidence and good mood. But he obviously didn't want to seek for an explanation why he wasn't receiving the well-deserved treatment.

"Hantaywee...I'm very sorry I behaved like that the other night, I acted a fool and an ingrate. It was just very difficult to finally admit to myself and even worse to feel that the world we have created is beginning to die away." Mojag stopped for a moment, as if waiting for a comforting comment, but in turn received numb silence. – "Be as it is", he continued, "I am sorry I haven't returned any of your calls. Besides having had way too many difficult thoughts, I have no excuse."

"There's no more time for excuses and lengthy debates, Mojag. I don't say it to blame you, in fact I know I can't, but I just say it because I am leaving in the morning and I cannot afford abusing any other moment I am given with you."

"I knew you would understand", he said it immediately only to hide his growing impatience. "I want to stay with you tonight."

"I want to feel your skin so much..." she whispered, almost in hallucination. – "My parents are not going to be home tonight, they are too busy somewhere else, both of them in separate ways. I will be at home by myself, so you can sleep over. And...", her voice turning into a crying whisper. "And in the morning I have to leave."

"I will be there", he replied seemingly firmly, but dying on the inside, his mind instantly consumed by his thoughts that no matter what happens, nothing could be the same among them as it once was; as it had always been.

* * * * * * * * * * *

There was no sign of Mojag's paranoid thoughts while he was lying next to that sinful beauty sleeping by his side. He didn't know where she was going to sleep the next day, but Hantaywee was too special a person to him and he could never afford ruining all those enchanting moments he had lived with her. The only thing that he was perhaps thinking of, but not consumed by it anymore, was that he was fed up with saying goodbyes. Without taking away his gaze at her sleepy, but tensed body, he took her soft dark hair, holding back his tears, and caressing her gently, putting his whispering hands on every part of her face, but trying to make sure she would not wake up before he had left. That day was Tuesday, and Tuesday was always their day of love for reasons that at one point came along. But then again, every day was *a Tuesday* to them. And that day was to be their last. He took out the letter he had written those couple of sleepless nights prior to meeting her that same, farewell night; he read it out loud to himself only to make sure that he had not missed a single thing.

My Hantaywee,

These days it is hitting me real strong. It is that bitter feeling when yet another beautiful chapter is finishing. But this is much more than yet another chapter, for a whole lot of a wonderful experience ends perhaps right here.

'Tonight I could write the saddest verses', Neruda wrote. I perhaps never understood those Nobel lines as well as I do now. But I am sure that some things are better left unsaid for their revelation could kill everything that has been achieved.

The very first day I saw you created distractions to my blood pressure, but that day I could have never thought that we were going to get as close as we did. Especially at that time, it was extremely difficult for me, my private life, my work, everything seemed to be suffocating me, with the help of my illusionary mind, and I never learned how to handle it. I know I would have never succeeded without you. And I sincerely ask myself what would have been left of me had you not entered my life. I have so many things to thank you for; you really helped me much more than I thought I needed! I am just now realizing how your small things were giving me strength and faith in myself. I owe you a lot and that is why I sometimes preach to you how to live your life; you probably know better for yourself, but I am just asking you as a very good, and as a very special friend/boyfriend/lover, to consider some of the things that I have been always telling you. For it seems now that we are parting our ways, which makes it very difficult for us to be there for each other.

Our relationship is truthfully one of a kind. It is perhaps even too technical a term to simply call it love, for it is something much greater than that, a single irreplaceable experience.

I never meant to show you the insides of me, and now you are the one who is my inside. And I can never be as grateful as to say that I was very happy that you were the person to whom I have exposed every bit of myself. In times when no one seemed to want me to be understood, you did understand me. And you went all the way along to bring me out of the bedrock I had hit at the time I made you mine.

This big city before was very grey because I had no memories with someone like you. Now, all these places remind me of all those beautiful moments we had together. The river, the restaurant, the bed…Ah, the bed, or any other part of our apartments, starting from the kiss and on to the sex; it is something that could be compared to nothing even close to that. It is something that we have created and we are the ones who will always remember it.

I already miss your small nerving questions that I never liked; I miss the stupid music on my phone inspired by your wake up call in the morning! I miss your beautiful smile and sensible jokes; I miss your comfort; I miss every single part of your being. And I miss you so much that it takes all my oxygen away.

The past three days I could not sleep. The only thing why I was maybe trying to fall asleep was to wake up believing that losing you is only a bad dream. But it never worked that way. You have been a wonderful experience that brought me back the life that I have always tried pursuing. You brought all of that back to me along with the charms of that long lost little boy inside of me. But without having you by my side, I realized that I had to let go of him, for he always managed to get hurt by being constantly and cowardly dependent upon someone else's world.

And when someone asks me how I would describe our story, I would simply turn on the verses that we always longed for.

'You and I just have a dream
To find our love a place, where we can hide away'[50]

Take this red rose as an everlasting symbol of our world. And whenever you need me and wherever you are, its scent will always bring you back the passion that I have always felt for you.

With all the pieces of my heart,
Mojag.

Holding back his tears started becoming unbearable, but he successfully managed to resist. He was silently putting his clothes on when he got distracted by a photo of Hantaywee's parents, hugging each other, and having their most sincere smile on their faces. – "What a happy family, right?" he sarcastically commented in a silent reproach as Hantaywee's father was banging his friends' wife perhaps at that very same moment Mojag was looking at his happy face on the photo with his life's companion – the woman he had two children with.

Mojag was ready. He folded the letter in its chosen form, already full of sweat from the anxiety of his hands, and put its containing envelope on top of Hantaywee's already prepared suitcases. On top of the

---

[50] *You and I* – The Scorpions, "Pure Instinct", 1996

envelope, he left the most beautiful red rose that had ever grown. He kissed her cheek, perhaps the last one in the same setting of their story, making all the effort to keep her sleeping. Without turning back to gaze at her beauty yet another time, he opened the door and left.

* * * * * * * * * * *

By the time Mojag reached his apartment, it was already 4 in the morning. And he went straight back home, without the usual *walk of contemplation* when he would always reevaluate recent decisions or significant changes in his life. This time, and perhaps for the first time ever, he had concluded his contemplations *before* he had made his envisioned change a reality.

Mojag's apartment was the all too familiar place; dirt, cigarettes, smoke, alcohol, broken glass, food leftovers, a guitar. The apartment obviously needed serious redesign of the interior, but nevertheless it was a lovely place that usually offered partial safeness when being in it. However, it was perhaps way too much time Mojag was wasting inside his apartment's confined walls. But this time, he actually *knew* why he needed to be there, for there was one other thing he had to take care of.

Other times he would have surely said: – "Ok, let me listen to this painful record just one more time." But now, listening to it for one last time meant a possibility to going back to a state of conscious he never wanted to be in, in the first place. Mojag had an enormous collection of music records that he always tortured his heart with, records whose chords were probably created by the saddest musicians the world had ever gotten to know. And he always felt emphatic towards those musicians reliving their chords as if they were reflecting his own notes. And each time he would go deeper and deeper in a state of amplified depression. Fuck those concepts.

Without a single sign of preemptive remorse, he completed packing virtually his entire collection of songs that reminded him of many things his past life had remembered. And he was uninterested in dividing the records that provoked good memories from the ones that embedded a sick mood in his emotional spirit. He packed them *all* in. And yet, it still didn't seem enough to convince him of his determination. And so, he continued.

He started opening up each and every storage place in the apartment and all of a sudden, all letters, and all *historical* items of his past were carefully making company to the records in the bag that he was holding firmly. All those items were much too valuable for him to treat them the way he did, but those were memorabilia of a period once lived and now dim, period he would like remembering only on his own will, and not due to sentiments caused by a weeping sound of a familiar guitar riff, or a letter full of beautiful words of dear people that were no longer part of his present. By the time he made sure he had included everything, Mojag realized that he was meddling with his past for more than three hours as it was already some minutes past 7 A.M.

I hope I'm not going to miss them today, for this thing cannot wait even an hour longer.

Mojag managed to come down at the exact moment when they were about to leave.

"Wait, wait", he shouted at the garbage collector, having that huge, black plastic bag over his shoulder, which was heavier than his own weight. – "Sorry, I'm a little late, but I guess it wouldn't be a problem if I contribute now."

One of the garbage collectors reacted in a professional manner as he seemed used to customers that had last-minute-of-the-day, disposable package deliveries. He went out of the vehicle and came up to Mojag to help him load his burden onto the truck.

"Wow, that thing looks massive, my friend. What do you have in there?" the garbage collector rhetorically asked, with a healthy dose of curiosity.

"My past", Mojag replied without a single grain of hesitation, and threw the damn bag onto the machine.

18 A CLASSLESS MIND

Three days later

"The crime of good men who can't wrestle with change,
Or are too afraid to face this life's misjudged unknowns
You're not hurting anybody else's chances,
But you're disfiguring your own."[51]

* * * * * * * * * * *

A mind is a beautiful blessing as long as its control is not corrupted. Its corruption frequently comes silently and it is difficult to notice, but its corruption comes from no other source but from the instructions of your own device. And it is only you who can consciously prevent implanting thoughts in your mind that are going to be haunting your days. You don't need to relive thoughts on purpose just for sake of remembering the bitter feeling they invoke. For one day you will wake up in a city that never sleeps or in any other, and you will realize how all those thoughts that were eating you up, were in fact an unnecessary illusion that have ignited the senseless fear in you,

---

[51] *The worst joke ever* – R.E.M., "Around the Sun", 2004

which inevitably prevented you to face life at any and all given moments of your life's circumstances.

Most of the time, the emotional surge you carry, turns negative because of the way you are loading your head with things that are either way too paranoid to be true, or way too real but way too heavy to persist remembering them. Never persist in instructing your brain with thoughts that kill your chances, for the difficulty of taking them out of your head can easily reach unmanageable proportions. Don't let illusions consume your world, for as one of the biggest peaceful revolutionaries said: "Man is the product of his thoughts. What he thinks, he becomes."[52] And what you must never allow to become, is a slave of your own illusions.

And that was when I decided to break free.

* * * * * * * * * * * *

Hi, I am Mojag, and I can finally speak for myself.

It is over. The long and bitter experience was not an illusion, for the magnitude of its realness was far too big to be considered delusional.

I can see my breath freezing as I confidently pace through the white cover of the street. I'm trying to find the name of the street at any of the address plates of the buildings I leave behind. But I cannot find any, as if the street has no fucking name. I could ask somebody as there seem to be various people that might know the name of the street. But I don't ask them. In fact, I know exactly where I am; I simply wanted to know the name

---

[52] Mahatma Gandhi

out of mere curiosity. It seems so much easier now, almost natural, to think of details that I hadn't bothered noticing, since I was too occupied with my thoughts whenever I passed through this same street.

Now, I am not trying to find any metaphysical gaps of the footprints embedded in the snow; I am not looking for a way to follow them so they can take me to a comforting place. I am human and I understand the essence of my fragility, but it makes it so much different when I am stomping with my arms assertively around the future.

* * * * * * * * * * *

To be honest, reality is that in the course of the past year, I didn't enjoy suffering. It just somehow came along. The truth is that I was too afraid to let go and to accept the natural changes to the status quo of my own projection. And the status quo changed very frequently. But nevertheless, change counts only when you accept it and start living it; otherwise it only anchors your further opportunities. The change of my circumstances always lied within me, and with no one else, and yet I was always trying to find signs elsewhere, only to realize that it is much more just to my own self to believe in a wrong ideology of my own intellect and selfish emotions, than to follow a correct one as prescribed by someone else and the illusions it creates.

I've always been trying to be a Bohemian, and I have learned what the ways of a roamer and a wanderer are. Their philosophy, as any other in life, implies that reluctance to change allows time to run you over. And everything around me was and is mercilessly changing, so how could it have possibly been so difficult for me to change myself? And many times before I had cowardly felt that it was so much better not to know many of the things I am now aware of, because that way I would live a more ignorant and a more peaceful life. And as many times now, I pose that same question to myself. What is life worth for if you cannot allow yourself to change and experience pleasure 'n pain in order to succeed the way you have envisioned it to be?

"Champions take chances, and pressure is a privilege."[53] I wouldn't categorize myself as champion, but I did take a lot of chances, and I was even more privileged to feel the heat of the pressure. Many times I was afraid, and many times I was not, but the experience grew each time. And now, when I think about my father's words, each time I would experience that particular, vomiting urge in my stomach caused by the pressure of new horizons, I realize how real his words were, at times when they were meant to give me comfort. He said: "What is life worth if your lifeline remains static? Life is to live, and not to struggle for ignorance." And his words are always so damn true.

* * * * * * * * * * *

I am still walking on that same street, even though I have no particular direction in mind. And it feels good, for each path appears to be satisfying.

In fact, I have been walking quite a bit already, but I don't mind. I don't even feel signs of fatigue. I stop for a moment, only to briefly reflect on the possibilities of

---

[53] Billy Jean King

the new turns. The street opens up in three directions but I still choose to go straight. The snow is everywhere. Nothing can replace the sun that is nowhere to be seen, but the snow makes me feel good as well.

* * * * * * * * * * *

It is perhaps contradictory, but I have always believed in any decision I have made and at the same time I have perceived most of them as a complete disappointment from which I would never be able to recover. But then again, the ideology of either failure or success is the biggest illusion that one allows for the mind to create for oneself. The reason for the skepticism is that your mind always thinks of the consequences of an action, which in turn provides the healthiest basis for negative result. Failure can teach you many things that you can apply at any point, and in any aspect of your life. Failure can teach you how to succeed in a manner that would be real. The success that your previous failures have brought you, will become yet another illusion if you start feeling comfortable and forget about the constant fight with yourself and the unjust that you let your mind absorb. There is no such thing like too many tries, for nothing else matters but a battle won, and the things you do to make sure the triumph remains. Until this very beautiful moment of clarity, I have never achieved to hold on to any triumph I have accomplished. And all that because of pathetic reasons, in which I always looked for and found inexistent excuses for everything that was happening in my surrounding and in the surrounding of my insides. And in that way, I have always been short of acknowledging my present and dealing with it accordingly. As one of the best sportsmen ever, once said, putting this whole philosophy in a beautiful statement, 'I have missed more than 9000 shots in my career. I have lost almost 300 games. On 26 occasions I have been entrusted to take the game winning shot . . . and missed. And I have failed over and over and over again in my life. And that is why . . . I succeed.'[54]

Many times before I have failed to apologize to myself because of the inhumane way I was treating my own being, revoking the well-deserved credit for many of the fine things I would do. And it was not a matter of actually saying the words "I'm sorry". That was the easiest part. I could have easily done that. But I didn't, up until this moment. The reasons are simple, for saying sorry means not only that you are sorry for the things you did, but it also means that you will not repeat those same things you were once sorry for. Only then the apology is worth listening. And only now I can deliver myself such an admission of guilt. And it feels so damn good.

Some would say that if you want to change the world, you have to do it but one random kindness at a time. But in order to tailor the world to the needs of your touch, you need to know your own world first. And only then you would be able to do *any* kindness, for you need to start being kind to yourself first and then to others.

Many people in my nostalgic *South* often conclude that the days before had been better, when streets were

---

[54] Michael Jordan

willingly ruled by the earthly concept of brotherhood and unity, in times of aspiring equality under the banner of socialism. But were the actual days really better? Or were *we* the ones who were better human beings? The categorization of *we* is what is fundamentally wrong with their statement, or rhetorical question for that matter, because nobody, apart from a few, ever thinks if *I*, the inherently selfish person himself/herself, as an individual was better. It is when each of us would try to understand ourselves and put *us* as individuals in the front lines, only then *we* could possibly emerge in becoming better than we were yesterday. One random act of kindness cannot begin with someone else, but it is you who need to initiate it, for how can you possibly be kind to your surrounding when you are initially not kind to yourself?

There can rarely be a justified excuse for pathetic attitude towards life. But one thing is certain, that relying too much on other people can submerge the strength and the courage you carry within. And we make it so distant to realize how potent the strength of an individual can be, when it is in fact so close – inside of us.

* * * * * * * * * * *

"Another crossroad? This never ends. What street is this? It all seems completely different than when I initiated my journey."

This junction seems to be a huge one. It resembles nothing like any of the previous ones I have traveled across. And there are a lot more people who seem lost, panicking their way to their indecisiveness.

I spot a familiar face in the middle of the junction, who seemed like an official directing the way of the people. I have no idea where his familiarity comes from, but I don't even try recalling.

"Where can I turn?" I ask.

"To the right, my friend, for sure. Everyone's going in that direction. It can't be wrong", the man replied in a gentle tone, but obviously he was only gathering statistics.

"Thanks", I say, and continue straight on. I don't take the suggested turn for a simple reason – I feel much more confident this way.

* * * * * * * * * * *

I have never liked the exclusionary nature of any kind of arranged people's associations, in which conformity is mandatory and fake pride is guaranteed. The price that you have to pay to be in any of those clubs is your own identity. And it was not that I was never tempted to aspire to such concepts, for there were many occasions. The only deterrent I had was the membership to my own little world. My membership to my little world is the best acknowledgement I have ever received. And that little world of mine is the club of my family and friends. To be in there, you need no registration fee, or any kind of application form. The things you do need are respect, love, modesty and utmost honesty.

When I was a child, there was an entertaining show on the then, state TV, and it was a show for grown-ups. It was a super lame show, and its core pattern was hosts asking people who they would choose, had they the opportunity to live the life of a celebrity for one day. Everyone asked had an answer, already well prepared before their actual turn to speak back. At that time, I didn't have a particular motivation to choose who I would want to be had I the chance. I wasn't a celebrity child back then, and I am neither a child nor a celebrity now, but in the course of the past year, I have longed to live at least one day of the life of Mojag, the life of myself, for it seemed I had lost touch with it somewhere on the way. I was longing for that every single day of the pain I was experiencing. And today, I made way for that day to arrive. And from this day on, and wherever I will be, I will fight for its persistence until the very end.

* * * * * * * * * * *

I confidently continue pursuing the road I choose, leaving the past footprints deep in the snow, with my back up against the opportunity cost of the crossroads left behind. I am not even curious to find out whether each new turn on the street has a name; I am only getting to know new experiences that cross my way. With every other time I choose my own way, I pull the trigger, which makes sure that I keep on going straight, making the best of my journey.

To be honest, I lost track of time since I started walking. The more turns I confide to, the more they appear. It makes me realize that the street is in effect without an end. Because wherever it ends, there is another one, and then another, and another one after that. But I don't care, for every other turn I take, I make sure that the purpose of my journey remains clear.

...and I continue walking.

19 GOODBYE 20TH CENTURY MAN

Three days earlier. Present day.

There used to be a place that contained all the beauties of nature. It was perhaps Mojag's top of the list of his most favorite places. There might have been so many other places of the world that offered so much more to see, but this particular place always invoked special sentiments in him. And besides, it always provided him with the entire freshness of the air and cold water from the mountains where the *Village* was based. It always enabled him the opportunity of having a clear mind. And he never failed to use that chance, for regardless whether it was a drinking marathon that he was attending, barbecue lunch with his friends, or a weekend to escape from the world; he always had a peaceful mind. There, in the midst of nowhere, he was always alert about everything he would do, not counting of course, the objective misbalances that a heavy beer night had left him with, in a lot of different occurrences.

That same *Village*, which inspired and healed Mojag, was exactly one hundred kilometers away from the city where he was born. The road to the *Village* involved a highway in large part of the trip. However, in the last twenty minutes of driving towards the beautiful destination, one had to pass through equally beautiful surroundings of a mixture of highlands, lakes and mountains. It was nature in all its untamed beauty, as it had been uncorrupted by people for many centuries before, although the opportunities for that had been many.

Those twenty minutes of driving were always extended due to many of the sheep that clogged the road, along with their accompanying shepherd dogs that were barking around the passing cars like wild beasts. The dogs always looked fearful, but they always got lost out of sight at the sound of the car's horn. When untamed horses would start appearing on both sides of the rigid road, somewhere distant in the highlands, it signified change of altitude. From that sight on, the altitude was only increasing, for the destination of the *Village* was placed approximately 2000 meters above sea level. The outside toilet of Mojag's grandparent's house was exactly at that level, right there at the edge of the cliff. It was always scary to do the natural body requests in such an atmosphere. But one gets used to that.

The *Village* was a place of historical heritage of Mojag's *South*, and at the same time, it was a historical heritage of Mojag's childhood's summer times. It was in fact, a very famous attraction to many foreign tourists as it was well known for its traditional weddings from the past. The tradition was preserved up until present days, but unlike the fifty weddings the ancient inhabitants cheered for at that same, summer's day of the calendar year, many years after, there remained a single wedding that made sure the tradition lived on. That day was not the day of the all so familiar wedding. And that day Mojag never made it to the

Village. That day it seemed he had a different agenda, but nevertheless, he made sure he had preserved the clarity of his mind that the surrounding always offered him.

In fact, Mojag had no idea how he managed to end up there in the first place. He found himself past the twenty minute drive even though he had no car, or even a bicycle. What was even more unusual to witness, was that he didn't even bother questioning his mind how the hell he had managed to have ended up there. He just kept on walking, his face blurred, but the determination in his eyes firm.

Mojag had past the road of the twenty minute drive, but he had at least twenty minutes more walking to reach the *Village*. That was orientation-wise, but as suggested, he seemed to have the least of intentions to get to the *Village*; it seemed he only wanted to initiate the nature that surrounded him. He was carrying something on his back that looked like a huge rucksack. It was undoubtedly heavy as his pace was slower than usual. It was slow, but it had to be painful as well, because the bag looked like a huge shadow that was consuming his weight. But not even for a single moment he stopped.

He walked past the football fields of his childhood's unsuccessful football career. That was where he made a different turn to the one he would normally take. The road to the *Village* was only one; the rest was the wilderness of the mountains where he used to chop wood with his grandfather when he was a disobedient kid. Mojag chose the wilderness, which only increased the altitude, making sure that his burden grew heavier. He didn't even give out a blink of complaint, but he faithfully continued pursuing his responsibilities.

His whole expedition should have lasted much longer since he almost reached the top of the mountain. It was not the highest one of the mountain group, but Mojag didn't mind. It was only that the dark was slowly starting to swallow the beauty of the nature, or maybe making it even more beautiful, but Mojag didn't even notice. Reaching the mountain's peak didn't make him look like the passionate alpinists that couldn't conceal their pride of conquering yet another height. No, reaching the mountain's peak was unquestionably not his objective.

Mojag stood there in the surroundings of the naked rocks that intermixed with the greenness of the innocent, untouched grass. Still standing, he gazed around in all four sides of the world without putting it any thought. He seemed to be fulfilled with the familiar view from above. He made a movement to take the backpack off him, but he appeared to have changed his mind. Instead, still having that massive thing over his head, he sat down on the grass, facing West, and closed his eyes. Usually he did that to clear his mind from thoughts, but now he did it because he wanted to enjoy the freedom of his mind, nothing coming in or out. He did seem like he was enjoying the freedom but at the same time, he seemed he was patiently waiting for his *night* to arrive.

It was not such a long period that Mojag found himself in a delirious state having his eyes wide shut, but it was a period long enough to make sure that when he opened his eyes, it was pitch dark. Nothing could be seen in the nearby surrounding, except for the distant, lively blueprint of the neighboring town where Mojag's eyes were now facing, that same neighboring town Mojag never figured out whether it had the shape of a frog or a scorpion. But it didn't matter. Shortly after, his eyes got used to the darkness, and he could feel the confidence coming back. There was no sign of a living soul, but the deep howling of the mountain wolfs across the nature. Mojag was surprised that he didn't even blink on hearing the creepy conversation of the wolfs, for he didn't get scared even for one fraction of a second. And why would he; he had a clear mind and an even clearer conscious. And besides, that same nature helped him overcome his deadly fear of darkness when he was a kid; there was no reason not to overcome any of the meaningless fears any time after that.

The cigarette in his hand started igniting its filter. He could have smoked one more, but his determination meant otherwise. Having previously taken a deep breath, he slowly exhaled. To the surprise of the sleeping observer, Mojag's heavy burden of the rucksack over his head was mysteriously gone. It seemed he had somehow managed to loosen the chains he carried all the way to the top. Mojag did notice the *lightness* of his sudden circumstances, but there was no particular emotion on his face. He placed his right hand inside the back of his jeans, and took out what appeared to be the gun his father taught him how to shoot with when he was growing up. His father also advised him never to take out a gun unless he had the intention of using it. Mojag always abided to that concept, including that beautiful night under the sky full of stars.

The howl of the wolfs stopped. It seemed like they were announcing that the time had come. And the time *had* in fact arrived. Mojag checked the barrel of the gun; it had a single bullet and as many chances. It was ready. He gazed upon at the sky, praising the wonders of the abundance of stars above, which navigated people's ways. Never before had he seen things clearer than he did on *his* night. He wasn't pondering anymore on that dangerous, but irresistible pastime. He simply took a heavenly ride through the silence as he knew the moment had arrived, for killing the past and coming back to life.[55]

He fired only once, and only that single shot he was able to take, for after the echo of the fired bullet had subsided, there was nothing left but a *dead* silence in the most beautiful place in the world.

* * * * * * * * * * *

A single gunshot woke him up from his deep sleep. He had no recollection of the events. He could feel the calmness in his palms, the clarity of his thoughts, and ultimately, he could feel the victory in his fight for *freedom*, in his fight for the moment, in his struggle for himself. He went on to the mirror to provide physical sense to the mental image he felt embedded in him.

Standing in front of his own reflection, naked and vulnerable, but self-confident and unafraid, Mojag recognized, maybe for the first time ever, that he was perhaps everything he wanted to be.

---

[55] *Coming back to Life* – Pink Floyd, "The Division Bell", 1994

ABOUT THE AUTHOR

Branko Jovanovski leads a self-imposed lifestyle for as long as it is written. Like a proper dreamer, he lives in his own world and occasionally lets people in. He creates his own values, constantly challenging himself, and he sometimes tries to find a meaning. The form of literary fiction best describes his work, without hiding his sentimental convictions of pure existentialism.

Until today, he has made one mistake in his life that stands out much more than the rest: he had said he knew himself before having realized how wrong and doubtful that statement was, and how complex one's awareness of his own realization could be.

If by coincidence this book evolves into an immediate inspiration to you as reader, and more so as an active participant in it, you could share your personal observations and ideas at

TheIndifferentConcept.com